Kidnap
The
Pope

JACK DUARTE

To: Dick
As always, thank you!

Jack

For information, address Cloud 9 Press,
634 Central Ave, Lexington, KY 40502.
ISBN: 978-0-9894367-9-3

Cover by Chris Inman, Visual Riot
Interior Design by Chip Holtzhauer
E-pub Design by Mark Vorenkamp

Also by Jack DuArte

Dedication

To Lisa Sins Hart

A voice of happiness is silenced.
She is sorely missed.

Acknowledgements

In the United States:
Barbara Antle, Herb Miller, Brother William Dardis, S.J.,

And, Mark O. Rodi, Dr. Michael Rooney, Roy Schully, the late Adrian Colon, Paul Revere, Ray Rizzo, Billy Vosberg, Ricky Sins, the late Kenneth Adolph, George Reitmeyer, Jack Saux, Wayne Kempff, Eddie Bosworth, Rich Scelfo, Tony Rabasca, the late Bobby Boasberg, the late Albert Dittman, Jack Dardis and Vincent Liuzza.

To My Editors:

Sharon Ryan Rodi and Robin Ryan Popiolek for their expertise.
Richard Francis for his time and effort.
To Susan DuArte for her exactness and complete attention to detail.
To John Duarte for his always exceptional
insight into the flow and substance of this novel.

Foreword

Thursday, March 10, 1938,
Jesuit High School,
Carrollton Ave and Banks Street,
New Orleans, Louisiana

Constructed in 1926, the multi-story, red brick building dominated the landscape on prominent Carrolton Avenue in the Mid-City Section of New Orleans. The building was the pride of the New Orleans Province of the Society of Jesus, more commonly known as the Jesuit Order. It was also the home of New Orleans' finest boys' high school. Originally situated in the city's business district at the corner of Baronne and Common Streets, the new edifice attested to the Crescent City's steady outward growth and the school's need for improved facilities and more space to hold its growing student body.

The stately school and buildings was the end product of a group of Jesuits that had come from Paris in 1837 to establish a college some 150 miles west of New Orleans near the modern day city of Opelousas. The location was Grand Coteau, Louisiana, and was still used as a spirituality center for members of the order and Catholic lay people.

On Jesuit High School's second floor, a singular priest was slumped into his favorite couch. He was deeply involved in a book he had recently started reading. The work was a slightly worn copy of the *Catholic Historical Review* by Fr. Peter Guilday, the Professor of Church History at the Catholic University of America in Washington. Published in 1915, the copy had seen plenty of use at the upscale Jesuit school by both the faculty and staff during its tenure. It was about 10:25 in the morning and well into Father Michael Sins Rodi's daily two-hour break from his normal class schedule.

He looked up when the door opened as another black-robed priest entered and looked around.

"I knew this is where I would find you, Father," the newcomer offered. "You always spend your free time reading on that couch."

"It's the most comfortable place I know," Father Rodi returned. "It even beats reading in my room at night."

"So you say," the second priest replied. "So you say..."

"And what might you want with me, Father Rizzo? What brings the assistant principal out this fine morning?"

i

"Our beloved principal has a job for you, Michael," he smiled while using the priest's first name. "It seems that Monsignor Reitmeyer over at the Archbishop's office has a visitor in tow, a Jesuit priest from Rome. The archbishop is quite proud of our school and wants this fellow to have a complete tour of our campus. Since you are the only one available right now, you have been designated as the guide. "Father Revere," he smiled again referring to the principal, "said for you to take the rest of the day off and give this guy a real tour. I will cover your later classes for you."

"What about lunch?" Rodi asked, looking at his watch. "There's really no place to eat around here to bring a guest. Our meals at the rectory are nourishing but not the type to offer a guest."

"Father Revere thought of that, too. I've already made a reservation downtown at Arnaud's for the both of you. You can take the school car. I've already checked and no one is using it today."

Excellent, Rodi thought. *This could be more fun that I first imagined. I have heard that the food at Arnaud's is quite excellent and that the owner, Count Arnaud, is quite a character. It is also an unexpected break from my daily routine, not that I'm griping or anything.*

"They should be here in a few minutes," Father Rizzo motioned with his hand. "Should I bring them here to meet you?"

"I'll come with you, Father," Rodi replied good-naturedly. "We wouldn't want them to get the idea we just sat around all day, now would we?"

Father Rizzo didn't reply but opened the door into the school's long hallway. It was clear to him that his message had gotten through to the young priest.

Exactly ten minutes later, two priests knocked and then entered the principal's outer office. Father Kenneth Colon, the school's prefect of discipline opened the door and pointed to Rodi.

Father Rodi rose and extended his hand. "I'm Father Mike Rodi and I have been appointed your guide for the day."

"I'm Monsignor Reitmeyer, Father, and this is Father Robert Leiber of Rome. He is interested in Jesuit High School and what has been accomplished here."

The visitor extended his hand and shook his younger counterpart"s hand firmly. Father Robert Leiber was middle aged, around 50, Rodi guessed. He was of medium height and balding on both sides of his head. His smile seemed genuine to the young priest who had immediately recognized his name.

"It is an honor to welcome a distingushed scholar at Gregorian University to New Orleans and to Jesuit," offered Rodi. "It is seldom we have the opportunity to meet such an important person during our daily duties."

Leiber was impressed with the young priest's candor, but responded casually. "Actually, I'm only on a bit of a holiday. "I've been to Mobile on Curia (the Catholic Church's governing body) business and decided to come to New Orleans at the last minute. Monsignor Reitmeyer has been so kind as to show me some of the city and it's all been quite beautiful. He mentioned the high school here and I wanted to take a look. Education is so vitally important to the Vatican and you people seem to be working wonders here."

Father Rodi studied the man and was instantly charmed with his charisma and calm demeanor. Here was someone he could easily identify with, someone with whom he felt an instant rapport.

"Are you ready for your tour, Father?" Rodi asked.

"Oh yes, by all means. I'll just leave these bags here and pick them up when we leave."

The tour took more than an hour to complete during which Father Leiber asked numerous questions. He was impressed with the structure and the classrooms. The pair walked into several classrooms and stood in the rear, observing the teaching. Leiber said nothing but seemed to absorb the entire experience.

Around one o'clock Father Rodi consulted his watch and mentioned lunch to his guest.

"You are in for a real treat," he remarked after Father Leiber concurred. "Something special is in order."

The pair left the school and walked to the rear. A semi-new 1934 Ford Coupe was parked behind the school, painted black except for thin white lettering that identified the vehicle as part of Jesuit High School.

"It sort of resembles a Mercedes, doesn't it?" questioned Leiber. "With the front grill angled back it takes on that look. The bumpers are not as prominent, and maybe the angle is not as great. It looks to be a fine automobile."

"I really haven't had the chance to see many Mercedes, Father," confessed Rodi. "At least not in New Orleans or here in Louisiana. The last time I saw one was when I visited Chicago."

"You will in time my boy," Leiber answered. "All in good time."

Rodi unlocked the doors and started the engine. It was less than a ten minute drive to Arnaud's Restaurant in the 800 block of Bienville Street in the city's famous French Quarter.

At the restaurant's entrance on Bienville Street, a tuxedoed Maître D' greeted their arrival. "My name is Schully and I'll take you to your table," he announced warmly. "Always glad to have members of the clergy here with us. The oysters are fresh and really tasty. They just came in from the near the mouth of the river."

The meal lasted the better part of two hours and by its end Fathers Leiber and Rodi both realized they could easily become friends for a long time. Their faith and outlook on life seemed somehow similar.

Near the end of their meal, the proprietor, Count Arnaud Cazenave, made his way to the table and regaled the pair with several stories about Arnaud's and its rise to fame. He joined them and ordered a bottle of Bollinger 1928 for their enjoyment.

When it arrived, he pronounced the vintage as marvelous and not to be forgotten.

Leiber tasted the bubbly and concurred. "Excellent, my dear Count. You have *bon goût*."

"*Je vous remercie, Père*," Cazenave responded.

"And what about your title, Count Arnaud. Most certainly French, I presume."

Cazenave looked around the other tables and leaned forward. He spoke in a low voice so that only the two priests could hear. "I cannot fabricate my title to representatives of the Holy Church. My title is of my own design and I am afraid that my holdings are limited to the confines of Arnaud's.

When I opened up this place and sought to raise the level of cuisine, some of my friends suggested I have a title to accompany my lofty ambitions. It started as a sort of dare but my customers seemed to enjoy it and started calling me 'Count' on a regular basis. Now, whenever the place is mentioned, I am Count Arnaud from France and everyone is happy."

Leiber laughed and patted the owner on the back. "Your secret is safe with us, I promise you that. I have not had a happier meal in some time, and I will never forget the Shrimp

Arnaud or the wonderful redfish and oysters you served. Nor will I ever forget Arnaud's noble proprietor."

The three laughed again, and Father Rodi signaled their waiter for the check. Count Arnaud stood and bid his guests good bye. He quickly moved away so that the priests could pay the check. He had also included the cost of the bottle of champagne on the bill. After all, he wasn't in the restaurant business to lose money, was he?

Chapter One

"This is the epitaph I want on my tomb:
'Here lies one of the most intelligent animals
who ever appeared on the face of the Earth.'"

— *Benito Mussolini*
in a remark to Count Galeazzo Ciano
19 December 1937

Thursday, March 10, 1938,
Palazzo della Farnesina,
Via della Lungara,
Rome, Italy

More than 5,400 miles to the east, a uniformed German officer was allowed entry to the Library Spezioli of Fermo, just off the Palazzo Venezia that formerly served as a convent for Dominican nuns. He was directed to the Sala del Mappomondo, so named for an incredible map of the world created by Ambrogio Lorenzetti in 1345 and shown in that location for several centuries. The Sala del Mappomondo currently served as the official offices of the head of the National Facist Party (Partito Nazionale Fascista, PNF), Benito Mussolini.

The German officer was none other than royally-bred Prince Philip of Hesse who was the grandson of a German emperor and great-grandson of Britain's Queen Victoria. In the early 1930's, he had become an influential Nazi proponent and party member for several years. Nattily attired in his Luftwaffe uniform, Prince Philip was shown into the walnut-framed offices where a diminutive figure in uniform stood to greet him.

Benito Mussolini, 5 foot 7 and the possessor of a deeply receding hairline was the de facto dictator of Italy since 1922 and was known to the world as 'Il Duce'.

1

Mussolini extended his hand to the German and exclaimed, "Nice to see you again, Prince Philip."

"Most certainly, Duce. Unfortunately I am here on business. I would much prefer to be here and enjoy the wonderments of your magnificent city."

"These are troublesome times, Prince Philip, for everyone involved. I know you are aware to what I am referring."

Aware that the formalities were concluded, the prince nodded stiffly and handed a letter to Il Duce. He then stepped back.

Mussolini immediately recognized Hitler's handwriting and opened the letter. It read:

Mussolini crumpled up the paper and looked directly at Prince Philip. "Are you aware of what's included in the letter?"

"No, Duce. The Fuhrer does not inform me of the contents of his correspondence. I am merely the courier."

Using nobility to deliver his messages is certainly clever, mused Mussolini. *And, on this occasion, the son-in-law of the King of Italy. I wonder how many others within the German nobility have joined Hitler in his cause. I would think there might be more than one would imagine...*

"Thank you for your time, Prince Philip. It was nice to see you again."

"Of course, Duce. As you said, these are important times for all of us."

Prince Philip bowed and turned toward the door, leaving a perplexed Mussolini's behind.

This course of action on Germany's part will not set well with a number of people, and the pope in particular. Hitler promised to consult with me before taking any action against Austria. The tone of his letter tells me he has already given the order. I must carefully consider my next move for the future of my country. I have already come out in favor of Austrian independence and everyone knows that. The Catholic Church has been adamant on the subject and I don't know just how the pope will react. This could be a big mess if Italy does not do the right thing. I must think about the consequences...

Friday, March 11, 1938,
Offices of the Fuhrer,
Wilhelmstraße 77,
Berlin-Mitte, Germany

The tempo inside the Fuhrer's offices was at a pitched level. A few hours earlier, an order had gone out from the German leader to his top military leaders to convert *Unternehmen Otto,* a war gaming scenario for a war against Austria, into a military operation that would be ready by the next day. The move allowed Germany's Wehrmacht to strike quickly if Austrian Chancellor Kurt Schuschnigg refused to hand over the reins of its government to pro-Nazis in his cabinet.

Additionally, most of the German High Command had hastily assembled at Hitler's lavish offices on Wilhemstrasse. Commander-in-Chief of the German Army Field Marshal Walter von Brauchitsch stood near Hitler along with Luftwaffe chief Hermann Goering and SS head Heinrich Himmler.

"I believe Schuschnigg will concede in a matter of hours," offered Goering. "He really doesn't have any choice. The radio broadcasts of our troops massing at his border have surely reached him by now."

"I'm not so confident," chimed Himmler from behind his wire spectacles. "Our reports say he was willing to wait until the vote on Sunday. He seems quite determined."

"When I met with him in February," Hitler advised, "he did not seem to me the type of leader that would take a chance. I yelled at him a couple of times and he just stood there like a wounded animal."

"I agree with the Fuhrer," Goering added. "He has little backbone."

"What might you do with the potency of the German Army standing at your border?" Field Marshal von Brauchitsch questioned Goering.

"I would capitulate, Field Marshal, and so will Schuschnigg."

"He has no right to keep 10 million Germans from fulfilling their destiny," spoke an agitated Hitler. "No right whatsoever."

The inner circle of the Nazi high command all shook their heads in agreement. Several lower ranking officers came and went with various updates from Austria and from the Wehrmacht, which seemed to be having some problems with its mobilization.

Hitler noted the urgency on von Brauchitsch's face and asked. "Any problems, Field Marshal?"

"Just some minor ones associated with our first full mobilization, Fuhrer. I expect them to be solved within a few hours."

"They had better be," Hitler warned. "I want no foul ups when we cross the border. The entire world will be watching. You are keenly aware of the consequences. Tomorrow will be a historic day for the Third Reich."

"Do not worry, Fuhrer. Everything is under control. We could even cross now if we wanted."

"You will wait for my order," Hitler commanded. "Everything must be in place. The world must know we acted correctly."

"Jawohl, Fuhrer. I understand perfectly."

Hitler then walked over to an enlarged map of the Austria-Germany border that had been set up on an easel. The small group followed him over. He pointed to a small dot on the map, just into the Austrian side. "This is where I will enter Austria," he said softly. "The town of Brannau am Inn is where I was born. It is my destiny as well as the destiny of Germany. The world will never forget it."

"Wouldn't it be wiser to cross the border at a more advantageous spot, Fuhrer?" said a voice just outside the group.

Hitler turned to see who had uttered the suggestion. A suddenly worried Wehrmacht oberst looked at the Nazi leader and explained, "I only meant that there might be more opportune crossing points for our troops, my Fuhrer. I meant no disrespect."

Hitler immediately turned to von Brauchitsch and ordered, "Send this man in with the initial units, field marshal. And make sure he is in the front lines and not in command."

Field Marshal von Brauchitsch nodded and turned to his aide. "See it is done immediately."

Friday, March 11, 1938,
Mussolini's offices,
Palazzo della Farnesina,
Via della Lungara,
Rome, Italy

Benito Mussolini hurriedly summoned Count Galeazzo Ciano to his office to discuss Hitler's letter. In addition to being the Italian Foreign minister, Ciano was also Mussolini's son-in-law.

Upon his arrival, Ciano noted that Field Marshal Pietro Badoglio, the Chief of Staff of the Italian Army was already seated in front of Mussolini's large desk. He nodded to the Duce and took a seat next to the army officer.

Something important has happened to have the field marshal here too. I wonder what it is.

Mussolini spoke to Ciano in a concerned tone. "Hitler has sent me a letter that he intends to annex Austria within 48 hours. He asks for my agreement, but we both know what that means."

"Did he consult with you before taking action?" Ciano asked. "I thought you told me he would discuss any matter concerning Austria before he took action."

"That is also what I understood, but you see what he has done. I'm sure the orders to invade have already been issued."

"The Holy Church will not be happy, Duce. You know what their emissaries have been saying to us for months. And the pope, he will be the unhappiest of all."

The field marshal sat silently, absolving himself of the political issue.

Il Duce spoke again. "I have thought about this through most of last night, and I can't see any choice we have other than to agree. To concur with him would go against my stated position, but Hitler seems intent on some sort of mission and we certainly don't want to offend him.

Field Marshal Badoglio raised his head and strongly agreed.

"We are not equipped to handle the German problem, Duce. Maybe in time if we continue building our forces."

"We have no recourse," said the 36-year old Ciano. "It would be better for us to agree with the move. He will probably be most grateful for our support. It could turn out to be a plus for our country. The pope and the church will just have to understand..."

"You must go to the Vatican as soon as you can gain an audience," Mussolini directed. "I don't want the pope hearing about this from any other source. Call them right now and tell them it is of vital importance. And keep me informed."

"I will see to it, Duce." He rose and gave an informal salute in the Facist manner.

"I will remain here with the field marshal. Be on your way."

Ciano hurriedly left the room. His car would take him to the Vatican in a matter of minutes.

Friday, March 11, 1938,
Mussolini's offices,
Palazzo della Farnesina,
Via della Lungara,
Rome, Italy

After a long series of deliberations with members of his party and office staff, Benito Mussolini had finally made the decision concerning Hitler's notification the day before. He picked up his telephone and ordered his secretary to call Adolf Hitler. He quickly combed his mind and reassessed the many scenarios that he had considered on the issue. Satisfied he was making the correct choice, he sat back and waited for the call.

It took almost fifteen minutes, but his secretary finally announced that Hitler was on the line. He picked up the receiver and spoke with a calm demeanor in near perfect German. "Fuhrer, it is good to be able to talk to you again."

"Yes, Duce. Things are hectic around here, but I felt I must take your call at once."

"Thank you, Fuhrer. I am pleased you did."

"So, Duce. Do you have something you wish to say to me?"

"Yes, Fuhrer. I wanted to address your letter concerning Austria."

Hitler did not respond and waited for the Italian leader to continue.

"I have consulted with my staff and party leaders and I want you to know that I have no problem whatsoever with your actions concerning Austria. We consider the matter to be immaterial to Italy and fully support you efforts."

"I am pleased to hear it, Duce. Very, very pleased," Hitler said emphatically.

Mussolini felt his heart pounding and his pulse rise as Hitler continued.

"I will get back to you, Duce, once the steps have been completed. I must go now."

"Go with God, Fuhrer."

Friday, March 11, 1938,
Offices of the Secretariat of State,
Palazzo del Governatorato,
The Vatican,
Rome, Italy

A monsignor who served as an assistant to Cardinal Eugenio Pacelli, secretary of state for the Vatican, moved quickly to the desk of his superior, causing the prelate to look up from his reading.

"Yes, Monsignor Dardis. What is it? You look worried."

"Your Eminence, there is an important call for you from Vienna. The archbishop says it is most urgent. I know you left orders not to be disturbed, but…"

"Put the call through, monsignor. You have acted correctly."

The phone on his desk rang once and Pacelli picked up the receiver.

The familiar voice of Archbishop Theodor Innitzer almost shouted through the receiver.

"Eminence, the Nazis are about to enter Austria. My priests along the border say the entire Nazi army is gathering and the local radios have been saying an attack is imminent. What are we to do? I need your help and guidance," he pleaded.

"Calm down, Theodor," Pacelli said calmly. "I thought you were a big backer of the Nazis. Didn't you fly Nazi flags and endorse some of their actions. I thought you would be happy if the Germans were in power."

"They made certain promises, Eminence. And, they agreed to let Austria manage her own affairs. I have no idea what will happen if they actually cross the border. Our chancellor has called for a vote but the Germans seem intent on moving before the vote is actually taken. There is panic here in Vienna and elsewhere. I'm not sure what to do about the church and our members," Innitzer sighed.

"I don't think you will be in immediate danger if the Germans enter, but the future is another matter. Even though Hitler is a Catholic, I don't believe he places much value in that fact. The Holy See has something of a standstill right now regarding the Nazis and the German Catholic Church, but the relationship is tenuous at best."

"That's not encouraging, Eminence. It would be the same here, wouldn't it?"

"Our role is to see that the Holy See perseveres, no matter the circumstances, Theodor. It might not be the easiest path to follow. But, we must do it everywhere there are enemies of the Holy Church. Is that clear?"

"Perfectly, Eminence. I will do my part."

"Go in peace in the name of our Lord."

"Thank you, Eminence. God bless you."

Saturday, March 12, 1938
Offices of the Fuhrer,
Wilhelmstraße 77,
Berlin-Mitte,
Germany

Hitler's temperament turned from edgy to almost euphoric after receiving the phone call from Benito Mussolini. He had admired Mussolini for almost a decade and felt he was one of a few people in the entire world with whom he could identify. Their visits and time spent together were pleasant memories and he honestly felt that Mussolini's goals and those of the Third Reich were somehow linked together.

He quickly dispatched a short, hand-written note to Il Duce stating that he would never forget him for taking this action. He added the salutation, "Never, never, never, no matter what happens!"

His attention soon returned to the large map in his office. Various units of the German Wehrmacht were positioned across the Austrian border with arrows pointing the direction which they were moving. He nodded his head in approval to the delight of his staff.

"Yes, it has finally happened. Germany will be whole once again. You may all take pride in this incredible event. We are all Germans and we must take delight in our actions."

A chorus of "Heil Hitler!" resounded throughout the offices.

Chapter Two

"Go forth and set the world on fire."

— *St. Ignatius Loyola,*
founder of the Society of Jesus

Tuesday, May 24, 1938,
Jesuit High School Faculty Lounge,
Carrollton Avenue and Banks Street,
New Orleans, Louisiana

It was the rare time at a high school when the faculty had a chance to rest after a full year of classes. Summer heat and accompanying humidity made it unpleasant to venture outdoors in New Orleans, so most of the religious faculty who remained on the campus chose the comfort of the school's sizable faculty lounge.

Father Michael S. Rodi was among the dozen members of the Society of Jesus that filled the room on this particularly humid afternoon.

He was immersed in a historical journal when the school's amiable principal, Reverend Sidney Revere approached. The older priest sunk into a brown leather chair next to Rodi and addressed the captivated priest.

"Just who do you know in high places, Michael?" the school's leader posed in a caring manner. "It seems to me that whoever it is must certainly be important in our society."

"I'm not sure..." Rodi answered hesitantly. "I certainly don't..."

"Here. Take a look at this. It was delivered to me a few minutes ago. Tell me what you make of it."

11

Rodi took the folded letter. The Society of Jesus logo was prominent on the stationary. He looked at the typed communication and read out loud.

It is hereby directed that Father Michael S. Rodi, S.J., take the necessary steps to relocate to Rome to begin work at the Pontificia Universita Gregoriana.

Father Rodi must report to Piazza della Pilotta, 4, by 1 June to begin his duties. It is suggested a brief vacation be afforded Father Rodi prior to hs journey.

For the Superior General,

Scelfo, R., S.J., Adjunct

The young priest stared at the document without speaking. He finally looked over at Father Revere and exclaimed, "I'm sorry Father. I have no idea what this means. I'm as flabbergasted as you are..."

"Surely there is some reason behind this. After all, it comes from the head of our society."

"For the life of me, Father Revere, the only contact I have had with Rome was..." Rodi suddenly stopped in mid-sentence.

"You realize something, Michael. Go on. Out with it."

"Father, do you remember the Jesuit from Rome who visited us this past Spring?"

"Yes, barely. He was German wasn't he?"

"Yes, you are correct. His name was Robert Leiber and he taught Church History at Gregorian University. I gave him a tour of our school and we went to lunch at Arnaud's. That was about it."

"And you have had no contact with him since that time?"

"He sent me a thank you note about two weeks later. That was all."

"You must have made a considerable impression on the man. At least it certainly seems so."

"Father, I'm not sure I want to go to Rome. I love it here at Jesuit and enjoy my teaching duties."

"You have no choice, Michael. You know our society's precepts. Our vow of obedience is paramount and you have been directed to Rome by the head of our order." He paused a moment and reflected. Then he continued, "I will hate to see you go. You are well on your way to becoming a fine teacher."

Rodi acknowledged the compliment but remained silent.

"Gather your belongings and make plans to visit your family. They will be happy to see you. Spend as much time as you like. We will make your reservations for you and will get word to you when they are finalized. We will have a special dinner for you tomorrow evening so you can say your good byes to everyone here. It will be a good time."

"Whatever you wish, Father. It will be hard to say farewell. I have some close friends here."

The school principal rose and patted the young priest on the shoulder. He smiled as he departed the lounge. "See you tomorrow night, Michael."

"Yes, Father," returned Rodi. His mind was already filled with the wonderment of the situation. He was already aware that his entire world would change and that he had little to say about his future. He wondered what would be expected of him in this new venue and, more importantly, if he were up to the task.

Wednesday, September 27, 1938,
Mussolini's offices,
Palazzo della Farnesina,
Via della Lungara,
Rome, Italy

An excited Count Galeazzo Ciano, Italy's foreign minister and son-in-law of Benito Mussolini burst into the Duce's inner office practically sprinting. He took a deep breath and addressed the leader of Italy.

"Duce, I have a most important matter to discuss."

"I can see that, Galeazzo. You didn't bother knocking or announcing yourself."

"Sorry, but this is too important. You will see."

"Get on with it," Mussolini returned tartly.

"I have a telegram from Lord Perth, Britain's ambassador. He had just talked to Prime Minister Chamberlain who has requested that you come to Munich. He feels that your presence will influence Hitler to delay the ultimatum on the Sudetenland. He wants me to return his call as soon as possible."

I'm sure he does, mused Mussolini. Since Hitler's deadline to Czechoslovakia to surrender the Sudetenland is but hours off, things are quickly coming to a head. The rest of Europe is in quite a panic over Herr Hitler's antics. It is interesting that the British come to me to act as a mediator. They must think me closer to Hitler than I actually am. I am beginning to think that Hitler is a bit mad. His manners and crudeness condemn him to be the person he is. But he certainly has balls, really big ones...

Mussolini's gaze returned to Count Ciano. He paused for another instant, and then replied. "Go back and tell the ambassador I agree and he is to inform Chamberlain. I will travel to Munich tomorrow and settle the matter. "

The Duce nodded his head and Ciano turned and departed. He pushed a button on his desk and his secretary, Luigi Gatti, immediately appeared. He approached his leader's desk.

"Yes, Duce. What is it?"

"I want you to get our ambassador to Germany to approach the Fuhrer at once with this message. Tell him, "Whatever happens, I will be at his side, but that I request a 24-hour delay before hostilities begin. In the meantime, I will study what can be done to solve the problem.""

Mussolini again deliberated. *The other nations are naïve about the possible results of this meeting in Munich. Even if I can convince all involved to act prudently, I can't see any agreement having much permanency or real bearing. If I am reading Hitler correctly, his course doesn't stop with the Sudetenland. He believes his Third Reich is divinely inspired and cannot be compromised. If he is right, Italy will fare better if we are his ally. If he fails, only God knows what will happen then.*

Thursday, September 28, 1938,
Offices of the Fuhrer,
Wilhelmstraße 77,
Berlin-Mitte, Germany

André François-Poncet, France's Ambassador to the Weimar Republic since 1931 was involved in an animated tête-à-tête with Nazi leader Adolf Hitler. The sometimes heated discussion in German involved Germany's plans to take over the Sudetenland region of Czechoslovakia that was mostly inhabited by ethnic Germans. The Czech government had diplomatically asked both France and Great Britain to intervene of its behalf and attempt to pacify the situation. Mustachioed Ambassador François-Poncet had been around for most of Adolf Hitler's rise to power and knew he faced a daunting task when dealing with the German leader. He was attempting to make a point when one of Hitler's aides interrupted the discussion. The aide handed Hitler a piece of paper with a message on it.

Hitler read the message and turned to François-Poncet and said triumphantly, "My good friend, Benito Mussolini, has asked me to delay for 24 hours the marching orders of the German Army, and I will agree. Of course, this was is no real concession, as the invasion date was already set for 1 October."

François-Poncet sighed but chose to remain silent. He had been briefed by his country's leadership that France would not entertain any military conflict with

Germany unless Britain was also involved. He knew this discussion would prove fruitless as had many past meetings with Adolf Hitler.

The career diplomat wondered what was in store for his country in the upcoming months and years. He felt that this new Third Reich of the National Socialist Party was comparable to a wild animal with a progressively unsatisfied hungriness. He wondered if this craving could ever be satisfied.

"It is the last territorial claim which I have to make in Europe, but it is the claim from which I will not recede and which, God-willing, I will make good."

— *Adolf Hitler*
Sudetenland speech at Berlin Sportpalast
September 1938

Thursday, September 29, 1938,
Main meeting room,
Führerbau, Arcisstrasse 12,
Maxvorstadt,
Munich, Germany

Late night lights burned brightly throughout the splendid, recently completed, four-story building that served as the Nazi Party's Munich administrative headquarters. Adolf Hitler, chancellor of Germany, had called a conference to decide the fate of the Sudetenland, the German-inhabited part of Czechoslovakia. The Nazi leader had pressured the Czech government in recent months to cede the Sudetenland to Germany or suffer the consequences of military intervention by the powerful German army. While Czechoslovakia maintained a modern army of its own and was prepared to defend its borders, it had appealed to Great Britain and France to act on its behalf to avert a war.

The Prime Ministers of Britain and France, Neville Chamberlain and Édouard Daladier, attended to represent their countries' interests. Italy's Benito Mussolini had arrived the day before to join the meeting. He had been invited by Chamberlain in an attempt to influence Adolf Hitler.

At 69, Neville Chamberlain was viewed in Germany as an appeaser; something Hitler believed to be a profound weakness of the career civil servant. He had entertained Chamberlain at his home, The Berghof, a few weeks earlier. In subsequent meetings, he related to a group of supporters, "Well, he [Chamberlain] seemed such a nice old gentleman, I thought I would give him my autograph as a souvenir." Daladier was a proven diplomat whose country, along with Britain, presently had a common defense treaty with Czechoslovakia. He had been recently informed by Paris that France wanted no part of a war with Germany.

The meeting began and Mussolini offered his peace plan to the table. In reality, the paper had been given to the Facist leader by Nazi officials and included the same proposals extracted from Hitler's current ultimatum to the Checks. When representatives of Czechoslovakia attempted to join the conference, Hitler refused them entrance. They waited outside the meeting room while the fate of their homeland was decided.

In effect, the hands of the western powers were tied and the fate of Czechoslovakia was already settled. The two sides went back and forth for several hours, but Hitler remained firm in his demands. Either the "poor mistreated Germans" within the Sudetenland are allowed to become Germans by his prescribed deadline or he was prepared to send his Wehrmacht into battle.

Just after midnight, the weary diplomats gave in to German demands and signed an agreement whereby Germany agreed to occupy the Sudetenland on October 1. The Munich Agreement also promised no further intrusion on Check territory. Hitler's dream of *Lebensraum* was now on decidedly firmer footing.

Hitler was also amazed that he was able to get what he wanted without a single military action. He seemed exasperated when he told a meeting of his Army officers the following day, "I did not think it possible that Czechoslovakia would be virtually served up to me on a plate by her friends."

Friday, October 7, 1938
Pontificia Gregorian Universita,
Piazza della Pilotta, 4
Rome, Italy

The past months since his arrival in Rome had literally flown by for Father Michael. S. Rodi. Upon his arrival, he was quickly able to confirm that his appointment to the Pontifical University was indeed the work of Father Robert Leiber, S.J., the worldly priest he had entertained some months earlier in New Orleans.

They met about an hour after his arrival at the school when he answered a knock at the door to his Spartan quarters.

"I see you made it over in good fashion," the senior prelate smiled and greeted Rodi warmly. "I am delighted that you are here. I hope you had a good crossing."

"Yes, Father. It was my first time on an ocean liner and I was only sick for one day."

"That happens to almost everyone, Michael. By the way, do you mind if I use your first name? I prefer simplicity and formal titles tend to sometimes get in the way."

"I would be honored, Father. By all means."

"And, I am Robert when we are alone. I hope that isn't uncomfortable for you."

"Not if you wish, Father, er, Robert."

"Good, then the matter is settled."

Father Leiber looked at his younger counterpart and detected a hesitation.

"Is there something else?" he questioned amiably.

"Yes, Robert. I have been wondering about it since your letter of appointment arrived."

"Go on."

Rodi took a short breath and began. "Why me, Robert? I'm sure I'm no different from many young priests. I have no great skills that I know of and can't for the life of me guess why you selected me. I'm still in a sort of daze about it all and have no one else to ask."

"Humility is good for the soul," Leiber returned. "I expected as much." He considered his words for a moment and continued. "I must admit I was impressed with you on our first meeting. You were calm, collected and a marvelous host. You reminded me of myself when I was a young priest in Germany with the entire world ahead of me.

I also felt we had a number of common interests and some similar viewpoints on the Holy Catholic Church and its provocative history."

Rodi smiled knowingly at Leiber's witty insinuation.

18

"I see," Rodi replied. "I guess I wasn't too clever in concealing my attraction to your career and accomplishments."

"Good thing you didn't," Leiber countered with a laugh. "I wouldn't have taken such notice if you were dull and uninteresting."

"Good point. I'll keep that in mind in the future."

"And, Michael, there's one more important fact. My duties at Gregorian aren't my only responsibilities. In fact, they occupy only a small portion of my time."

Rodi gazed intently as Leiber continued. "This is for your ears only. The rest of what I will tell you is completely confidential."

Rodi nodded.

"I also work directly with Cardinal Eugenio Pacelli, the head of Vatican Secretariat of State. You will find that his office runs the Vatican in many instances. Our pope is always the last word, but Cardinal Pacelli is the second most powerful person in the Holy Church.

You will also become quickly aware of the problems facing Europe at the present time. Adolf Hitler has become a main force and seems hell-bent on reuniting all the Germans in Europe. What else he is planning is open to speculation.

Here in Italy, we have our own little dictator, the Duce. The church has supported him so far in order to keep Catholic schools open and for most of the Catholic Action groups to continue their work. So far it seems to be working out but the pope seems to be getting tired of the little blacksmith's son. He was unhappy over the entire Austrian debacle, and that's just the start."

Questions began to form in Rodi's mind, but he dared not interrupt his erudite benefactor.

Cardinal Pacelli sees some really dark clouds ahead for Europe and possibly the rest of the world. I first met him when he was working in Germany, in various positions for the church. He impressed me as an incredibly intelligent and feeling person and possibly the finest diplomat in the entire Holy See. We have remained close for a number of years and he has respected my opinions on many matters that come up.

If his assertions are correct and Europe is thrown into war, the Vatican will play an important part in whatever happens. Cardinal Pacelli will be in the middle of everything and that means I will be also.

19

Looking ahead, I believe I will need an able young assistant to help with various situations that might arise. He must be fluent in both German and Italian and your excellence in Latin will help you develop the necessary language skills for the job. You will study those languages and become skilled in their usage as soon as possible.

You must apply yourself resolutely, for the timetable for all these possibilities is completely unknown to anyone. Have I said enough?"

"Yes, Father, I mean Robert. It's a lot to digest for someone who has only been in Rome for a matter of hours."

"Your classes begin on Monday, Michael. Take the weekend off and see some of the sights of Rome. It's a most enchanting city."

"You bet I will," Rodi prated, immediately realizing his enthusiasm had gotten the best of him."

"Here's some *lira* to help you on your way." Leiber handed the young priest a stack of bills.

"This is way too much, I don't need…"

"It takes a lot of *lira* to just take the bus," warned Leiber. "This isn't as much as it might seem."

"Thank you anyway."

"I'm off to a meeting right now. I'll check in on you next week."

"Thank you again for everything, Robert. I can never repay you for your kindness."

The senior priest had already turned and walked toward the door.

"Just learn German and Italian and I will be happy," he voiced as he opened the door.

Father Michael S. Rodi, S.J., paused as the door clicked shut. His life as he knew it before seemed now to be something of a blur, a slow cadence of events and places that were at the moment only warm memories. He realized his future could be unbelievably different.

Monday, January 31, 1939
Private Chambers of Pope Pius XI,
The Vatican,
Rome, Italy

The past few weeks had turned into a proverbial imbroglio for Pope Pius XI and the entire hierarchy of the Holy Catholic Church. The pontiff's failing health, he had already been given the last rites but had recovered, along with a pending political crisis that seemed to be coming to a boil, put everyone involved in a crucial dilemma.

Pius XI had become increasing intolerant of Benito Mussolini and his party's racial outlook and his views on marriage. The old pope wanted to make a final statement before his papacy came to an end. Many of his subordinates in the Roman Curia had tried to convince him that the move to alienate the leader of Italy was perilous at best, but the pope stuck to his guns and continued to prepare the damning encyclical. He knew that his message would influence all Italian bishops and hence all Italian Catholics. His nature was to be skeptical of everything, and he thus continued to ignore the pleas and recommendations of everyone involved. Rooted deeply in his mind was the hope that this last encyclical would somehow keep his treasured Italy from becoming even more united with Germany and its increasingly diabolical ambitions.

The tenth anniversary of the Lateran Accords (agreements between Italy and the Vatican) was to be celebrated shortly and the pope decided this event was the perfect platform on which to read the encyclical. All of Italy's bishops would attend and the fact that Pius XI had named almost two-thirds of them during his reign made the event a homecoming of sorts in his mind. St. Peter's was the perfect setting for the occurrence and the pope directed his staff to prepare the necessary documentation to create the encyclical.

Then the question arose as to whether Mussolini would attend the event. Cardinal Pacelli informed the pope he thought it unlikely Mussolini would appear. The pope promptly replied, "If he does not want to celebrate the tenth anniversary, I will do it by myself." Pacelli stared blankly at the Holy Father and was powerless to voice a response.

The wheels were set in motion and the first drafts of the encyclical were given to Pius XI.

In his position as Vatican Secretary of State, Cardinal Pacelli was particularly exasperated with his dear old friend and tried talking to him one more time. The weakened pope replied negatively once more and Pacelli saw it was useless to try and persuade him anymore. Only Divine intervention could postpone the event that Pacelli believed to be potentially harmful to the Holy Catholic Church.

It was now Thursday, February 9, and the now failing pope was assured that the printed copies of his message were ready for distribution. He retired for the night with a low pulse and shallow breathing.

Later that night, the last rites were again applied. He was kept alive with the use of an oxygen mask but by four a.m. it was evident he was dying. Pacelli and a group of others gathered by his bedside and asked for his blessing with tears running down their faces. Pius XI opened his eyes and barely muttered, "God bless you, my children" and also a faint, "Let there be peace."

He died at 5:31. As the chamberlain, Pacelli was tasked with verifying the death. He tapped the prone pontiff softly on the head with a silver mallet and called him by his baptismal name, Achille. Receiving no response, Pacelli voiced the ritual assertion. "The pope is truly dead." He reached down and pulled the Fisherman's Ring from the pope's already cold finger.

Chapter Three

"Hitler distrusted the Holy See because it hid Jews.
The Germans considered the Pope as an enemy."

— *Jewish historian Richard Breitman,
professor, American University in Washington, D.C.*

Thursday, March 2, 1939
Offices of the Secretariat of State,
Palazzo del Governatorato,
The Vatican,
Rome, Italy

Father Robert Leiber, S.J.'s, elevated state of anxiety definitely befitted the occasion. The Catholic Church's conclave to elect a new pope after the death of Pope Pius XI nearly a month before had finally convened behind closed doors, not far from the offices in which Leiber waited.

The highly intellectual and historically-oriented German priest had wrestled with a number of possibilities prior to the closing the day before of the doors of the Sistine Chapel by the Swiss Guards.

He had been handed a copy of the *New York Times* that had steadfastly predicted the election of Cardinal Giovanni Piazza, patriarch of Venice, as the favorite among the Sacred College of Cardinals. Another American newspaper, the *Boston Globe*, picked Cardinal Alfredo Ildefonso Schuster, archbishop of Milan, as its choice for the honor. Other insiders around the Vatican made note that Cardinal Jean Villeneuve, archbishop of Quebec, was the outstanding non-Italian with a good chance of becoming pope.

Numerous scenarios had crossed the mind of the middle-aged prelate during the seemingly endless hours of waiting. His close association with Cardinal Eugenio Pacelli, the Secretary of State for the Vatican, Carmelengo of the Holy Roman Church, and member of the Roman Curia, made him favor his close friend in the secret balloting. This favoritism was also shared by a number of others within the Vatican and was even dictated by a dying Pope Pius XI when he all but endorsed Pacelli as his replacement.

But, Leiber also reasoned, *there are many historical precedents that would act against Pacelli's election. No one holding the secretary of state office had been elected pope since Clement IX in 1667; no one serving as Carmelengo had been elected since Leo XIII in 1878; and no member of the Roman Curia was elevated since Gregory XVI in 1831. There is also the fact that Pacelli is a Roman by birth. He would be the first Roman elected pope since Clement X, way back in the 17th Century.*

Also, Europe is on the brink of war, and Pacelli is undoubtedly the best diplomat in the Catholic Church; hardly anyone disputes that fact. He has also served the Holy Mother Church in a number of different roles in Germany. He loves the German people and has always wanted what was best for them. He would make a wonderful pope, and I pray to Almighty God that the 62 cardinals gathered over in the Sistine see it my way.

There is always a chance they will choose a spiritual leader as pope, but I think the circumstances surrounding this election favor a diplomatic approach. I guess I must just bide my time. Some of these elections take days to complete.

Around 5:30 in the evening, a great roar filled the square around St. Peter's Basilica as a stream of white smoke suddenly bellowed forth, signifying a new pope had been elected. It suddenly turned black and the cheering stopped. Within minutes Vatican Radio broadcast that a new pope had been elected and the black smoke was a mistake. The new pope's name was Eugenio Pacelli and he had chosen the name of Pope Pius XII.

Leiber had been listening to Vatican Radio's broadcast and sat back when he heard the incredible news. He walked out into the halls where a number of Vatican employees were cheering wildly. He shook hands with several people he knew along with a number of exultant strangers. In his mind, the day was a brilliant day for both the Catholic Church and the world in general. He knew his beloved Holy Catholic Church was again in good hands.

Thursday, March 2, 1939
Offices of the Secretariat of State,
Palazzo del Governatorato,
The Vatican,
Rome, Italy

Father Robert Leiber, S.J. was in transit at the sprawling Palazzo del Governatorato when he happened to see Father Michael S. Rodi, S. J. walking off to his side. He hailed the priest with a wave of his hand.

"Isn't the news wonderful, Michael?" Leiber began. "Our cardinal is the new pope. Everyone I have talked to is ecstatic about the election."

"I must offer both of you my most sincere wishes, Robert. I know this means a great deal to you both."

"And to the Holy Catholic Church, Michael. The flock is the real beneficiary of this historic happening."

"Most surely, Robert. Does this mean a change for you?"

"I haven't spoken to the Holy Father since the election. He has been way too busy to see me. He has so many official duties to perform now that he is pope."

"I know it will all work out for the two of you. You have been together for some time."

"Yes. That's true. I have no idea what he has in mind for me. Of course, we all serve at the pope's wishes."

"I will wait until the dust clears. That's an old saying that's popular in our American South."

"I understand the meaning. Your American idioms are quite colorful. I will summon you as soon as anything is decided."

"Why me, Robert? I can't see the new pope needing my services."

"It is I who will need your services, Michael. With the prevailing winds of war we are facing, I have hopes that you will be of great value to me and the Church. Why do you think I insisted you become fluent in both German *and* Italian? Did the reason for my action ever cross your mind?

He's got me; I should have guessed this before. Germany and Italy...Leiber foresaw all that would happen and prepared me for it. I am dumb to have not guessed before this... the fact is that Jesuits take to language like fish to water...

"I'm beginning to see that it wasn't pure chance, was it? You knew what would happen."

"I *guessed* at what might happen and I just proved to be correct in my assumptions," Leiber chided. "It's always better to be lucky than always right about things."

"True, Robert. Absolutely true."

"I must run now, Michael. I am a bit late for a meeting. I might even find out what's going to happen next. One never knows."

"You will call me when you need me?" Rodi questioned.

"As soon as the dust clears, correct."

"Yes," Rodi laughed. "That's about it."

Sunday, May 21, 1939
Il Duce's Study Car,
Aboard the Palazzo Venezia,
Between Rome and Berlin

The fully-armored six-car special train that served as Benito Mussolini's office on trips was a special gift to Italy's leader from the Italian State Railway in 1933. Designed for efficiency and governmental usage, the *Palazzo Venezia* accommodated Mussolini and his staff comfortably but lacked the ostentatious luxuries of other similar trains utilized by current world leaders.

The occasion of Il Duce's visit to Berlin was originally planned to endorse a tripartite military alliance between Japan, Italy and Germany. However, problems developed when the Japanese insisted the focus of the pact be aimed at the Soviet Union. Both Italy and Germany believed the pact should be aimed at Great Britain and France. As a result, Japan withdrew its support for the measure.

Germany insisted the pact be signed at the Reichskanzlei in Berlin and Mussolini agreed. He boarded his private train in Rome for the more than 800 mile trip into Germany.

Some two hours into the trip, Mussolini's son-in-law and Italy's Foreign Minister Count Galeazzo Ciano appeared at the door of Il Duce's study car.

"Yes, Galeazzo, come on in. I have a nice bottle of *barbera d'Asti* opened. Will you join me?" Mussolini offered cordially.
"Thank you, Duce. I haven't had much time to drink lately." *The only wine I enjoy these days is at a formal dinner or when I call on one of my lady friends, which is becoming less and less frequent.*

"You must take the time. Wine relaxes you if you drink in moderation. Some doctors even say it is good for the heart."

Ciano acknowledged the advice and poured a medium sized glass of the red wine. He held it up to the light and sniffed before he took a sip."

"You can't rid yourself of old habits," Mussolini chided. "I never bother with all that fancy stuff. I just drink it down. If I don't like it, I throw it away and open another bottle."

"I was taught to appreciate wine in a certain manner, that's all. I'll drink it the way I enjoy it."

Mussolini noted Ciano's remark and ruminated. *A nobleman will always stick to his roots no matter the circumstances. I guess it's all inbred or something the gentry can't help. I know my daughter Edda loves this fellow, but sometimes he is difficult to take. When I think of the 4,000 people who attended their wedding, and of what it actually cost, my God, was it really worth it?*

A few minutes later, Ciano again spoke. "Duce, there are matters I want to discuss before the signing of the pact."

"Of course, Galeazzo. I am always willing to listen."

"First of all, you know my feeling about the Germans. I don't trust them for one minute. I know that you enjoy Hitler's flatters, and I know he respects you a great deal, but this pact is better for him than for us."

"Why do you think that, Galeazzo?" I have considered it carefully, and it seems to me mostly that it is mutually beneficial to both countries."

"Only if both countries adhere to its provisions," the younger man replied. "We have no guarantee Herr Hitler will wait the three years we have agreed to before initiating a war."

Mussolini considered the words and spoke again. "I don't think he will instigate any action in the near future. The consequences could be quite troublesome. If any country actually stands up to him, he could lose everything."

"You know him better than I, Duce. Do you think he fears any country right now?"

"You have a point. But I still don't believe he will act until we are ready to join him in battle."

"But, Duce, you are aware of Italy's economic circumstances better than anyone. The war in Spain has depleted our funds and our own expert, Carlo Favagrossa, has told us it will take at least three years for our country to be ready for any major military operation. And that's if the Spanish Civil War ends tomorrow."

"You are a pragmatist, Galeazzo. "I don't believe Favagrossa and his economists are all that correct with their calculations. Our country has always risen to whatever heights necessary for Italy to survive a real crisis. Plus, we have some nearby nations we could easily exploit if the situation warrants it."

"You mean Albania and Greece? I'm not sure that victory there would be so easy for our military. Our forces are pretty thin right now and our hands are full."

"You worry too much, Galeazzo. Haven't I been able to figure out all this before?"

"Yes you have, Duce. I am not arguing as to what you have achieved," Ciano conceded.

"And, are we not still confined by our Mediterranean prison? Unless we do something that changes our country's partially landlocked position, we will always be subject to the British control of the seas. You might throw in Egypt, if you wish. If we gained control of the Sudan, we would link Italian North Africa and Italian East Africa and have an actual presence in the Mediterranean."

"I am aware of all the possibilities, you need not remind me. I just want what is best for Italy. You know where my loyalties lie."

"I will give the matter more thought, that I promise you. I'm not sure that we have much choice anymore; events seem to be heading in a certain direction. I am hopeful that this pact satisfies Hitler's desperate need for closeness between our countries, as the Germans assure us it will. We must wait and see. I believe it creates an axis between Italy and Germany, a very strong axis of power."

Ciano mulled over Mussolini's words and finally spoke. "And, Duce. One more thing. I know you want to call the agreement the Pact of Blood, but I have reports from back home that many aren't in favor of that title. Perhaps you might think of something that conveys strength and determination as opposed to bloodshed. There are political aspects to think of."

Mussolini regarded his subordinate and thought. *He might well be right about some of this. Pact of Blood does carry some negativity. I really don't care a hoot about the people in Rome or their opinions. But, I don't want anyone to think of Italy as a country of savages. I should probably consider something else. I am also afraid that Galeazzo is becoming something of a dove, even if I have groomed him to be my successor. I must watch him carefully during the coming month, that's for sure.*

Friday, May 19, 1939
Pontificia Gregorian Universita,
Piazza della Pilotta, 4
Rome, Italy

Seven and a half months had passed since Father Michael S. Rodi, S.J. had begun his linguistic studies at Gregorian University. He was immersed in his lessons of German and Italian and was thankful that his firm knowledge of Latin had allowed him to learn both languages at the same time.

He was particularly proud of his German, thanks to a German Jesuit priest who taught at the university. Father Günter Kempff was only ten years older than Rodi, but the two had bonded on the first day of class. Kempff was also a Berliner and sought to teach his willing pupil the German language he so dearly loved.

In addition to his duties at the university, Kempff was also an assistant at the German Church of Rome and its Bishop Alois Hudal. The church was properly named the Santa Maria dell'Anima, a medieval building that was started in 1380 and completed in 1542. It was the home for Germans in the eternal city and served the everyday needs of Rome's sizeable German community.

A third priest, Italian Father Anthony Rabasca was also a student at Gregorian University. He was also studying German and became close friends with Rodi. They practiced speaking with each other and correcting obvious slips that occurred.

Kempff was keenly aware of Rodi's prowess with his native language. Early in Rodi's studies he had counseled his American friend about his approach toward the German language.

"When speaking German, you must think like a German," he encouraged. "Germans are almost always exact or precise. They also speak fast. To speak German simply for the sake of speaking will do you no good. There must be a purpose to what you are saying. You cannot think in English and attempt to translate it into German and vice versa. By the time you are finished here, you will be able to speak German as if you were born in Berlin."

Rodi considered what his teacher had offered and realized he was already well on his way to achieving his goal. On visits to Kempff's church in Central Rome, he was already at ease with the priests and members of the congregation. He would think in German as soon as he passed through the ancient doors of the old church.

"This is such a delightful place," he remarked one Sunday morning after Kempff had celebrated mass. "It is so warm and inviting. When you consider that people have been coming here for centuries, it's almost irresistible."

"I know, Michael," Kempff replied. "I love this church. I feel the Lord had something special in mind for me when I was appointed here. Plus, I always get invited for dinner when I say mass. There's nothing like a hearty German meal to make your day."

Rodi nodded but chose to remain silent. He almost started to tell his friend about the incredible food that emanated from his home town of New Orleans and its tremendous reputation that had spread worldwide. He chose instead to remember to invite Kempff to a meal at the university where he would prepare a special file gumbo. His mother had recently sent him a special package of ingredients that included filé powder, a main ingredient of a true gumbo.

He promised himself to remember to also invite Father Rabasca to the meal.

Monday, May 22, 1939
Reichskanzlei,
Wilhelmstraße 77,
Berlin-Mitte, Germany

The elongated table that served as the signing place for the formally-phrased Pact of Friendship and Alliance between Germany and Italy was packed with mostly high-ranking German military and diplomatic figures. Seated were Italy's Foreign Minister Count Galeazzo Ciano, Adolf Hitler, chancellor of Germany, and Joachim von Ribbentrop, the German foreign minister.

Directly behind Ciano stood Benito Mussolini, leader of Italy's Facist Party and the unequivocal dictator of that country. Hitler's number two and Luftwaffe head Hermann Göring stood directly behind Hitler as the two signatories affixed their names to the double documents.

Ciano had reservations about the agreement up until the final moment he took his seat at the table.

"Duce, I really wish we could avoid this. I still have deep reservations."

"I have studied it again, Galeazzo. I find no real fault. Did von Ribbentrop confirm the three years wait we supported?"

"He would have agreed to anything to get Italy to sign, Duce. I don't trust his word one bit," warned Ciano. "His record on matters of honor is highly questionable."

"We must take him at his word. It is too late for us to back out."

"As you wish, Duce. I will sign the agreement," Ciano answered reluctantly.

"Good. That is for the best." Mussolini paused and continued. "And, Galeazzo, I have considered what you have said about the name I should use. I've decided that Pact of Steel is better that Pact of Blood. By changing the name we are appeasing some in our government that wish an inspirational war. You should refer to Pact of Steel in your remarks. I believe Hitler will enjoy the phrase."

"Hitler already likes the word axis that you used in referring to the arrangement. Von Ribbentrop mentioned that to me when we talked."

"Good. I enjoy making everyone happy. Too bad I can't do it all the time."

A German oberstrumbannfuhrer appeared and motioned for Ciano and Mussolini to follow him. It was time for the signing. The two Italians straightened their freshly pressed uniforms as they pushed forward through the sea of military figures.

As the formalities ended, the pair was invited to a special reception that Hitler hosted for his inner circle. One of the women, a stunning blonde in her early twenties, caught Ciano's eye.

Von Ribbentrop noticed the Italian's interest and confided to his Italian counterpart, "That's Sigrid von Lappus, the Fuhrer's newest mistress. They just met and he is quite smitten with her."

"I would say the Fuhrer has exceptional taste in women," Ciano noted. "Exceptional taste."

"Yes, Count Ciano. In many things…"

The two parted as Ciano took note of the other dignitaries gathered in the room. He secretly wished to go and talk with Sigrid but knew better. Besides, there were plenty of other women around that wouldn't get him hung.

Tuesday, May 23, 1939
The Oval Office,
The White House,
1800 Pennsylvania Ave,
Washington, District of Columbia

Secretary of State Cordell Hull held a copy of the *Washington Post* and reread the Berlin story for the third time. President Franklin Delano Roosevelt held copies of both the *New York Times* and the *New York Herald Tribune* so as to be able to compare both papers' treatment of the story of the German-Italian alliance.

"Cordell, I think both papers just followed what the Nazis gave them. There's no real difference in the coverage that I can see. Probably have to wait until tomorrow to get any editorial slant on the signing," Roosevelt casually remarked.

"Yes, Mr. President. Same thing with the *Post*. There are only two aspects that bother me at first glance."

"Go on, Cordell. You have good insight into these matters."

"Thank you, Mr. President. First, the three-year waiting period is out of character for the Germans. I don't believe they can wait more than three or four months. Our intelligence backs that up. I believe they are already making plans to gather up more land and more countries. Our intelligence points to Poland, but we have little to back up that assertion."

"I saw the same report you are mentioning. I felt there were too many guesses involved."

"Right, Mr. President. We need more facts before we can be certain."

"You said two aspects bothered you. What's the second?"

"The word 'axis' that was attributed to Mussolini. If he did coin the phrase, he is something of a genius. The word seems razor-sharp to me and certainly is memorable. I went back to it several times while reading the article."

Roosevelt peered again at the papers and finally replied. "Yes, I believe you are correct Cordell. The term reeks of mystery and intrigue. I fear it might easily become their calling card."

"Yes, Mr. President, I believe so."

"It will be interesting to see what the Soviets say about all this. I wonder how such a pact fits into their scheme of things. Too early to tell, but I would guess they would have strong opinions on it. Keep our intelligence people on this, Cordell. I want to know what everyone is thinking before it comes out in the papers.'

"Certainly, Mr. President. I'll attend to it right away."

The Secretary of State placed the paper on Roosevelt's desk and walked toward the door. He was already deep in thought.

Thursday, June 1, 1939
Offices of the General Secretary of the Central Committee,
Communist Party of the Soviet Union,
The Kremlin,
Moscow, Russia

A casual wave of his hand by Iosif Vissarionovich Djugashvili motioned for his top advisors to begin the meeting he had called. While in his thirties, the diminutive Soviet leader had changed his name to Joseph Stalin which meant 'man of steel' in Russian. After the death of the founder of the Communist Party, Vladimir Lenin, in 1924, Stalin had ruthlessly assumed control of Russia and had directed the country in a manner that lived up to his last name. Since 1936, he had instituted an incredible purge within the country that eliminated most of his enemies including a host of Red Army generals. The purge was now ended and Joseph Stalin was now prepared to tackle the international problems facing his country.

It had been more than a week since Germany and Italy had banded together and formed the Pact of Steel between the two countries. The agreement was still the most talked about event in Russia, and indeed, on the entire planet.

Joseph Stalin was worried, and rightly so. Kremlin insiders correctly believed that practically all the Western powers actively disliked the Soviet Union and openly feared its military potential should there be any upcoming wartime scenario. Stalin was fearful of Germany and its Nazi leader, Adolf Hitler. He frequently reminded himself that Hitler spoke in his early career that he "aimed from the first to become the destroyer of Marxism," and that "the army we are building grows more from day to day, from hour to hour."

"Comrades," Stalin began forcefully, "we have some important decisions to make on behalf of Mother Russia. You are all aware of the Pact of Steel and how it might affect us. Hitler is an amoral leader who will stop at nothing to see his country triumphant. Our spies in Germany tell us there are already secret plans for his military, but we cannot tell against whom these plans will be directed."

Sounds of general agreement from those around the table followed his words.

"Minister Molotov and I have talked a great deal the past few days and we believe a similar pact could be struck between us and France and Britain. Their aims have mostly been peaceful and certainly not as aggressive as Germany and Italy. It makes sense to us that these countries' interests would best be served in allying themselves with us."

All of the seated ministers and staff shook their heads in agreement.

Stalin continued, "I want you to concur that we should go forward with this path and also agree to let me promise to send a large number of Russian troops should any war break out."

Stalin pointed toward War Minister Marshall Klementi Voroshilov and spoke, "General, what are those numbers?"

"Comrades," began Marshall Voroshilov, "we are in a position to promise 120 infantry divisions, 16 cavalry divisions, 5,000 heavy artillery pieces, more than 9,500 tanks and over 5,500 fighter aircraft and bombers."

"That's a little more than one million men," added the Chief of Staff of the Red Army, Boris Shaposhnikov. "It's a sizeable force and it is ready for action."

"Comrades, it is time to act." Stalin again returned in a voice much larger than his 5 foot 4 inch frame. "We cannot wait a moment longer. If we do, the world might pass us by."

"Yes, yes," came a chorus from around the table. "It must be done now."

"Minister Molotov, please see to this as soon as possible. You realize the importance of such a pact."

"I do," replied Molotov. "I'll start immediately."

Saturday, June 3, 1939
Kitchen at Pontificia Gregorian Universita,
Piazza della Pilotta, 4
Rome, Italy

It had taken father Michael S. Rodi, S.J. almost a month to arrange the dinner for his friends for which he was now deep in preparation. He had gathered the ingredients from local vendors and was sure he had what it took to make a *bona fide* New Orleans creole gumbo.

In addition to his friends, Father Gunter Kempff and Father Anthony Rabasca, he had taken the liberty of inviting Father Robert Leiber, S.J., his benefactor in the Vatican Secretariat, to the dinner. A generous head cook had made a section of the university's large kitchen area available to the young priest.

Rodi dove deep into his memory to resurrect the recipe he had watched his mother prepare on numerous occasions during his youth. He had searched for a written recipe but had found none that seemed accurate in his memory.

He knew he was correct in starting the cooking process by making a roux. The roux involved mixing flour with bacon drippings over a low flame until the mixture became smooth. Then he whisked the roux while still over the fire until it turned an almost mahogany brown color.

Next, he added all the ingredients he had remembered: celery, garlic, onion and green bell peppers that had been chopped into small pieces. He also added small pieces of sausage (he wasn't surprised that there was no *andouille* available in Rome) and cooked over a medium flame.

Then he used a large soup pot borrowed from the cook and added water and bouillon cubes that had been boiled into the mixture. The roux was then added and stirred. Finally, the now aspiring and perspiring priest/chef added salt, some sugar, and the hot pepper sauce and seasonings his mother had sent him. As an afterthought, he also added tomato sauce and some file powder after the mixture had cooked for almost an hour.

He had chosen shrimp as the main ingredient since he had found a vendor and was assured of the crustaceans' freshness. He now added the shrimp and sliced okra that had first been cooked in vinegar. A large bowl of long grain rice had also been prepared.

Rodi intended to add additional filé powder if his taste test warranted it before serving. He looked at his creation and thought At least it smells like the gumbo my mother used to make. *As long as my friends find it tasty, I'll be quite happy.*

His guests arrived singularly and Rodi indicated a small table just outside the kitchen area he was using. He moved to the table, shook hands with his guests and offered them a glass of freshly chilled *frascati* he had found in a little wine shop. Another bottle of *gavi di gavi* had been set aside to accompany the meal.

The group was seated when Rodi began serving the gumbo. The smell alone was enough to whet the appetites but the sight of the shrimp and other ingredients brought comments from each guest. Rodi took his place and served himself a large helping. He tasted the concoction and developed a huge smile across his face.

"This is what I remember it tasting like," he offered.

The others at the table were too busy gulping the flavorsome morsels to answer. The only question in their minds was would there be enough left for seconds.

They are all eating as if they haven't been fed in a week. I guess this all turned out for the better. I might have to try something else in the future.

Sunday, June 4, 1939
Berghof,
Berchtesgaden, Germany

It was a glorious early Sunday evening for the Third Reich in Berchtesgaden, located in Southern Bavaria near the former Germany-Austria border. Adolf Hitler had invited some of his inner circle of the Nazi Party to his home, The Berghof, for a private celebration following the signing of the German-Italian Pact.

The Fuhrer and his lover, Eva Braun, were at a heightened level of enjoyment as Minister Heinrich Himmler raised his glass to toast the event. "To the Third Reich. May she live for a thousand years," he proposed. A series of clinking glasses followed in short order.

"And, to our Fuhrer," added Minister Hermann Goering in a loud voice. More clinks followed along with a chorus of, "To our Fuhrer!"

"Thank you, gentlemen," Hitler replied. "I have not accomplished all this alone. Our great country stands on the precipice of a wonderful achievement that will shape the entire world for generations to come.

The events of the past few days are just the beginning. Germany is on its way to becoming invincible and the countries of the world will soon see it for themselves. We have charted a prodigious course for our country; and history will bear witness to our accomplishments.

We each have important tasks to accomplish, and not all will be easy. But, if the destiny of the fatherland is to be fulfilled, then sacrifices must be made by everyone involved. I see each of you as witnesses to this historical event, and workers in the fight towards National Socialism.

This glass of fine *moselle* is testament to our efforts," he paused, raising his glass. "It is pure and reflects the greatness that comes from our soil. The same goes for the German people and the purity that issues from their loins. If all factors remain united, then no one can possibly stand in our way."

"Heil Hitler!" Goering shouted. "Heil Hitler!" An even louder chorus resounded throughout the house.

A few minutes later, Foreign Minister Joachim von Ribbentrop approached Hitler and Eva Braun who were standing next to a window. He smiled, nodded to Braun and said. "Fuhrer, our plans have worked perfectly. The Italians agreed to everything without much hesitation. I got the feeling that Ciano wasn't too happy, but he signed the document anyway."

"I'm sure Mussolini told him to do so. Nothing happens in Italy without the Duce's approval."

"He did insist on my promising that Germany would wait a minimum of three years before declaring war, Fuhrer. Of course, I promised whatever he demanded. If I would have hesitated, I'm not sure what would have happened."

"It was the appropriate response von Ribbentrop. I've always used promises to secure a means to an end."

"And what do we do next, Fuhrer?"

"Our next venture is with Poland, and I'm not sure taking it will be as easy as the Sudetenland. The Poles have always been a scrappy lot and willing to fight over even small matters."

"How much time will be involved? Will it take years for us to achieve success with the Poles?

"Oh, no Minister. I do not foresee it taking too much time at all. I have already given some orders to put events in motion as we speak. If I am correct, it will only be a matter of months."

"But, what about our promise of three years wait, Fuhrer?"

"The Italians will have to accept the fact that inevitability comes before honor, minister. It is our country's fate to deal with situations as they occur, and not wait for the most opportune time in the minds of our allies. They will get over the fact that we broke our promise, I assure you of that."

"Most certainly, Fuhrer. I did not mean to imply..."

"No matter, minister. You did what was necessary." Hitler raised his glass and sipped his wine in a most deliberate manner.

Von Ribbentrop was keenly aware that the conversation was over.

Sunday, June 4, 1939
Mussolini's private residence Villa Torlonia,
Via Nomentana, 70,
Rome, Italy

Benito Mussolini sipped a glass of *vernaccia di san gimignano* under an improvised canopy on the grounds of his magnificent Villa Torlonia. He and his family had lived there since 1925 under an agreement with the Torlonia Family for the worldly sum of one lira a year.

Mussolini's second wife, Rachele, appeared with a platter of antipasto. She was a striking woman and totally devoted to her husband. Mussolini's pet lion cub, Ras, lay next to the Italian leader and barely raised his head as Rachele approached.

"He will soon be too large for you to keep unchained," she stated, pointing toward Ras. "The servants are already fearful of him. We must consider giving him to a zoo or somewhere else where he can be allowed to roam and enjoy his life."

"Not at this time, he is still my pet. I enjoy taking him for rides with me. The people love and fear him at the same time. Something like their feelings for me, don't you think?"

"Whatever you say. You will do what you want anyway..."

"Not true, my love. I always listen to what others say." The Duce picked up a black olive and a piece of *pepperoncini* and swallowed them with delight. He also selected two pieces of *provolone* that he also quickly downed."

"The *provolone* is quite nice, Rachele. I always prefer the aged to the regular."

"You haven't eaten regular provolone for fifteen years. We are quite spoiled in our appetites."

"Italy's first family should eat well. It's the least the country can do for us. After all, we receive no salary, so some of the side benefits should be of such nature as to make us comfortable."

"I'm not complaining. It's just if anything ever happened to you, I'm not sure how we would survive. We are not wealthy people, or need I remind you?"

"You do that frequently, Rachele." Mussolini's tone had become irritated.

"Can you make do with this *antipasto*? Dinner isn't for several hours."

"I am fine. You needn't worry."

"Very well," she concluded. "I will leave you to your reading."

"One more thing, Rachele. I almost forgot."

"What is it?"

"What do you think about the Catholic Church in the hands of the new pope? Have you heard anything?"

"The people I meet seem to be happy about things. Not that I'm out all that much. Without the old pope's constant ranting about you and the treatment of Catholics in general, it seems like everything has cooled off. Not that our newspapers are objective, but there hasn't been much mention of bad relations since he took office."

"He is a godsend, take my word for it. He understands the big picture and what part Italy will play in the future. He seems quite tolerant of Hitler and his actions and that factor is good for our country. I hope he remains so, because of what I know lies ahead."

"What do you mean, Benito? What lies ahead? You make it sound dire…"

"Nothing to bother yourself over, Rachele. Just matters of state…"

Mussolini dropped his head and returned to his reading.

Chapter Four

> "I agree he was an adventurer
> but I can't agree he was mad.
> Hitler was a gifted man. Only a gifted
> man could unite the German people."
>
> — *Joseph Stalin*

Tuesday, August 15, 1939
Offices of the General Secretary of the Central Committee,
Communist Party of the Soviet Union,
The Kremlin,
Moscow, Russia

Joseph Stalin and Soviet Foreign Minister Vyacheslav Molotov were involved in a serious conversation at the general secretary's cluttered desk.

Stalin was becoming more unsettled as the conversation continued.

"So they have not given us an answer to our offer, Vyacheslay Mikhailocvich. Do you think they ever will?" he remarked, referring to Britain and France.

"Admiral Drax has told us he has been authorized to talk, but not make deals," Molotov replied. "I believe he himself wants to make something happen, but the British government seems much too conservative to act."

"It's Czechoslovakia all over, that's what it is. The British are willing to hand over to Herr Hitler whatever he wants to appease him. It's obvious that Poland is next. We know that the Germans are already beginning preparations to invade Poland."

"Drax also said that Britain has only sixteen divisions that are combat ready at this time. I am amazed at that small number."

"They are unprepared for war, Vyacheslay Mikhailocvich. What have they been thinking about what's been going on? If they don't stop Hitler now, it may soon be too late. Surely they realize just how serious we are about the pledge of troops and equipment."

"I tried to make it clear, Iosif Vissarionovich, that we were *very* serious in our offer. I think Drax believes me but I can't account for London's interpretation."

"What about France? Have they said anything?"

"Nothing. They seem to be waiting for something to happen, and I can't imagine what. Time is running out but neither country seems aware of it."

"If Britain and France won't act, then we must act ourselves. I hate to say it, but we might be better off if we can contrive something to work *with* Germany rather than against them."

"I see what you mean, Iosif Vissarionovich. Even if Germany hates and fears us, it is better to have an agreement between our countries than a war."

"Precisely. If you have not heard back from Britain and France by tomorrow, please contact von Ribbentrop and see that he comes here for a meeting. Better to meet in the Kremlin than in Berlin. Our advisors will all be here."

"Consider it done, Iosif Vissarionovich. Consider it done."

The Russian minister of foreign affairs rose and exited the room. Stalin gazed at a nearby map of Europe and thought. *If Britain and France would stand up to Hitler right now, we might very well avert a war. The way things are headed tells me that war is for certain. All I can do is try to protect my country from her enemies. This isn't going to be an easy task and now I'm not so sure about purging all my army generals over the past year. They might have come in handy if things get out of control. Oh, well, what has happened is in the past and I have no control over past actions. I must be sure that what I am doing is best for Russia. Of that I must be very, very sure.*

August 23, 1939
Cabinet Room, West Wing,
The White House,
1800 Pennsylvania Ave,
Washington, District of Columbia

The Cabinet Room of the White House adjoins the President's Oval Office and permits an excellent view of the Rose Garden. It is Georgian in style and was completed five years earlier. It contains French doors, a fireplace, and busts of George Washington and Benjamin Franklin by noted French sculptor Jean-Antione Houdon. An incredible painting of the Declaration of Independence by Armand-Dumaresque hangs above the mantle.

The large room seemed empty as the president addressed the hastily called meeting of certain members of his cabinet. Seated was Secretary of State Cordell Hull alongside Secretary of War Harry H. Woodring. Across the table sat Secretary of the Navy Claude A. Swanson and several members of his staff in naval dress.

Franklin Delano Roosevelt sat at the head of the table. His private secretary, Marguerite LeHand, better known as 'Missy', occupied a chair just behind the president that was equipped with an armrest that supported her notebook. A black waiter had just poured water for the group around the table.

"I know you are anxious to get started," began the President. "And, I must thank you for responding so quickly to my call for this meeting. Our sources in Russia, highly-placed sources I might add, have just informed us that the Russians and Germans have signed a non-aggression pact to prevent an attack on each other for a period of ten years. If our sources are correct, there was a good deal of territory exchanged between the two.

The Soviets gave up their Baltic States of Estonia, Latvia and Lithuania and the two decided to divide up Poland using the Narew, San and Vistula Rivers as markers.

We believe the second part of the pact is to be held secret, since Poland is still a sovereign nation. But the reality of the meaning seems clear to our intelligence experts. Germany will attack Poland in the near future and Russia will do nothing to stop her from taking this action."

"Mr. President," Secretary of State Hull posed, "We were under the impression that the Soviets were attempting a pact with Britain and France. What happened to that?"

"It is my guess that our friends in those two countries were either too slow in developing an agreement or that the governments were too afraid of the Soviet Union to get it done. There are Communist movements in those two countries as well as here in the United States; I need not remind you of that unpleasant fact. Thing is, these movements are somewhat popular with our intellectuals, are they not?"

"There is something of a following in certain factions of our country," Secretary Woodring inserted. "But I have been led to believe they are mostly concentrated in

43

small, splinter groups and nothing to be worried about. I don't believe they pose a real problem."

"Probably not, Mr. Secretary. But I always want to keep an eye on anyone who opposes our form of government, no matter how insignificant they might be."

"Certainly, Mr. President. I believe the FBI has a master file on these organizations. Mr. Hoover and his men keep a tight rein on these types of organizations and their members."

"That's all good, Mr. Secretary, but I believe we are getting away from the matter at hand."

"Yes, Mr. President."

"It kinda makes sense from Stalin's standpoint," Secretary Hull observed, his Tennessee accent prominent in his speech. "He wants to protect himself from Germany and he thinks this is the best way to do it."

"If everything we have learned about Herr Hitler is correct, Hitler's promise not to attack isn't worth the paper it's written on," chimed in Navy Secretary Swanson. "He is a proven liar who is willing to promise anything to get what he wants."

"Precisely my thoughts, Mr. Secretary, the president answered. "I think this pact has major implications of a war in the near future. If I were Poland, I would mobilize my military at once."

"What about *our* people in Poland, Mr. President?" Secretary Hull asked. "Should we remove them?"

"They will be all right. They have diplomatic immunity and we will not be at war. I'm not sure how long we will keep them there, but they should be all right for the time being."

"All right, Mr. President."

"What I want from you two," he pointed at both Wooding and Swanson, "is to have your staffs start working on what we need to beef up our navy and merchant marine. One way or another we are going to play an important part in whatever happens. If Germany invades Poland, then Britain and France are duty bound to come to the aid of the Poles. That means that Britain will in turn ask us for help and we are obligated to assist wherever we can.

I want some quick work on this and some definitive recommendations. We don't have a lot of time to waste."

Both secretaries nodded their assent.

"I have spread out most of the intelligence information we have received from all the parties involved. It is all classified Top Secret, but your staffs all possess the necessary clearances. I want this information verified wherever possible with your own sources and a scenario put together of the possible consequences. And, I need it sooner than later. Am I understood?"

Again the secretaries nodded their agreement. They rose from their respective chairs and began perusing the large amount of material spread out on the table.

Friday, September 1, 1939
The Polish-German Border

It was a little more than a week after Germany and the Soviet Union surprised the entire world by signing a non-aggression pact on August 23 that supposedly would keep the two world powers from attacking each other for the next ten years.

Now feeling secure from Soviet intervention, Germany began heavy bombing of major Polish cities. Under the Nazi guise of *Lebensraum,* or "living space," the first of more than 1.5 million German soldiers crossed the Polish border with only limited resistance from Poland's outdated and ill-equipped army of only 600,000. A number of brave Polish cavalry units attacked armed mechanized German units and were slaughtered in the process. The Germans introduced a new term to modern warfare, the *Blitzkrieg,* whereby masses of German military units attacked simultaneously and created disorganization on its foe.

The attack violated Germany's 1934 non-aggression pact with Poland and made its Pact of Steel agreement with Italy fall short of its proposed implementation date by about two years and slightly less than eight months.

Some two thousand tanks and upwards of one thousand aircraft took part in the attack and easily broke through Polish defenses to advance on the Polish capital of Warsaw. Three weeks later, after constant shelling and bombing, the city surrendered on September 27.

By then, all hell had broken loose and the world was at war. Both Britain and France had stood by their guarantee of Poland's border and had declared war on Germany on September 3, just two days after the initial Nazi invasion. True to form, the Soviet Union invaded eastern Poland on September 17 in order to claim their split of the besieged country. The demarcation line for the partition of the country between the two powers was set along the Bug River. Scattered resistance continued until October 6, when the country was completely occupied.

Even with the declaration of war, neither Britain nor France actually attacked Germany. France went into a full military mobilization but their troops stopped short of German defensive positions and French forces settled back into their barracks along the Maginot Line.

On September 4, a Franco-British meeting determined that no major ground or air operations would be undertaken against Germany. Great Britain did indeed send bombers over Germany to drop propaganda leaflets and make reconnaissance of the areas, but no direct contact with the Germany military was ordered.

Adolf Hitler had reached out to Mussolini when he originally planned the assault for August 26, but cancelled the attack when the Italian dictator told him that Italy was not prepared to go to war at that time. Mussolini later assured the German leader of his political backing and the order to attack was rescheduled for September 1st.

Adolf Hitler knew he was taking a big chance when Germany attacked Poland. Many of his generals were not in favor of the move and asked for more time to get the Wehrmacht better equipped for battle. On several occasions prior to the beginning of hostilities, France had insisted that the Poles not mobilize and that factor helped the Germans easily overrun the poorly equipped nation.

The Second World War had officially begun with the appeasement governments of both Britain and France afraid to take more than token steps to prevent Hitler from seizing additional territory. The United States was quick to condemn Germany's action but President Roosevelt was determined to keep his country out of the conflict.

The world settled back to see what came next to the world stage and in what form.

Friday, January 12, 1940,
Private Offices of Pope Pius XII,
The Vatican,
Rome, Italy

Joseph Müller was born a Roman Catholic in Steinwiesen, Upper Franconia, in Northern Bavaria. During the period of the Weimar Republic, he worked as an attorney and became politically active as a member of the Bavarian People's Party. From the beginning, Müller was also strictly anti-Nazi. When the Nazis gained power, he defended many opponents of the Nazi regime.

Eventually he became a central figure in the German Resistance's attempt to replace Hitler with a coup led by several German generals and high ranking officials. As early as mid-1939, he began a series of trips to the Vatican to secure the pope's cooperation on what was planned by the secretive group.

Müller's identity was simply referred to as "X" on all his trips. His intermediary was Pope Pius XII's Private Secretary, Robert Leiber, S.J. In addition to correspondence between the German Resistance and British Intelligence, some documentation even contained a list of individuals that would assume major roles in a post-Hitler environment.

Leiber held that Müller was the representative of Colonel-General Ludwig Beck, former Chief of the German General Staff and other high Nazi officials and passed along the information to Pius XII himself. The pope reviewed the material and made decisions for the Church based on the contents of the documents.

Leiber stood as Müller entered his office. The two had become friends during the course of Müller's repeated visits.

"It is good to see you again, Joseph," Leiber began in German. "What is it that you have for me on this visit?"

"Right to the point, my dear Father. You are a typical German in your approach."

"I am a typical *priest,* Joseph. And a busy one, I might add."

"Thank you for seeing me so quickly. I don't want to stay any longer than necessary."

"There are no spies here, Joseph. This is the Vatican for God's sake. We do the work of the Holy See here, and little else."

"I have important news this time for His Holiness. The coup against Hitler has been planned for next month or even early March. Because there are a number of people involved, the planning is at all times quite difficult.

The leadership of the Resistance in Germany is encouraged by the talks with British Intelligence and is thankful that the pope has acted as he has. We even believe that both Generals Halder and Brauchitsch will come over to our plan. It is all in the works."

"I will pass this on to His Holiness. Will you be able to wait for his reply?"

"I have taken a room at the Hotel Sole al Pantheon on the Piazza della Rotunda. It has an excellent view of the Pantheon from my second floor window.

"I am sorry Joseph, but the view from your room is of little interest to me. Please do not take offense."

"None taken. I am registered under the name Wilhelm Vosberg."

"I will send a young priest with the pope's reply. I cannot be seen outside the Vatican. I know you understand."

"Thank you, my friend. Your reward will come."

"My reward will be in heaven, Joseph. Yours will also."

Leiber smiled and shook Müller's hand. He watched as the emissary put on his fedora and exited the office.

Monday, March 11, 1940,
Private Offices of Pope Pius XII,
Vatican City,
Rome, Italy

Pope Pius XII signaled to Father Robert Leiber, S.J. to close the door to his private offices. His staff knew that once the door was closed, the new pope was not to be disturbed.

"Have you been able to settle in, Father? I'm sorry this is the first real chance we have had to be alone. I never realized how busy I would be as pope."

"It is a great office to hold, Holiness. But thank you for asking. I am fine and almost settled in. You need not worry about me."

"Good, Father. I wanted to discuss just how we would handle certain sensitive matters that will most certainly arise."

"Of course, Holiness. What can I do?"

"Well, most importantly there is the matter of Italy and Germany. The Holy See's position on certain matters affecting these countries will be somewhat different than those of my predecessor. While I loved the man, Pius XI was quite blunt and felt the necessity of stating the church's positions in a most dogged manner. I supported his actions but I believe there are more refined methods of dealing with them.

I am opening dialogues with both countries that will attempt to improve the Holy See's relations along with those of Catholics in both countries. This will not be an easy path for us to follow and will not be popular with many other countries around the world. It is clear to me that our faithful have much to lose if the entire world goes to war and I hope to be able to do what I can to make all this as bearable as possible." He paused and then continued.

"And then there's the question of the Jews. Pius XI was quite clear as to what he wanted to do but I think it is much more complex an issue than we first realized. My private sources in Berlin tell me that Herr Hitler intends to eradicate the world of all Jews. The entire world! Do you realize what that means, Father?"

Leiber paused to contemplate the pope's words. Finally he spoke, "There are millions of Jews throughout the world Holiness. Surely he couldn't mean *all* the Jews."

"That is what my sources tell me, Father. Remember, the population of German is mostly Catholic and so is the German military. I believe that more than forty percent of the German armed forces are Catholic, certainly more than any other religion."

"And you feel these people would not support such actions against the Jews?"

"I have no way of knowing. I don't think the Nazis will announce the fact that they intend to exterminate all Jews. That would be foolish on their part. Remember, I have seen Hitler's rise in popularity first hand. He is shrewd and ruthless. So far, no one has really stood up to him and that has provided him with some successes. But, he will eventually make a mistake and fight a country that has more to lose than he thinks."

"Do you have any country in mind, Holiness?"

"Two that come to mind are Russia and the United States. Both have significant Jewish populations and ideologies far removed from those of the Nazis."

49

Leiber pondered the pontiff's words as Pius XII spoke again. "And, dear Father Leiber, if the British government changes for the better, I believe Great Britain will provide more of a fight than they have thus far. That could be quite difficult for Herr Hitler, something like waking up a hive of bees."

"I see what you mean, Holiness. The British have always been great fighters."

"Now, about our own matters. What measures have you taken to protect our, --- I dislike using the word--- *clandestine* dealings with others?"

Leiber paused again. He chose his words carefully. "Holiness, I have tried to establish a means of handling everything. We will not use the phone lines for any communications, but only documents delivered by courier. For really sensitive matters, I have a special person in mind that I trust completely. He is an American priest that is actually assigned to the Gregorian University. He is fluent in both German and Italian and I feel able to interpret inflections in tone and words. He will commit your answers to memory and relate them word for word. Should he be interrogated, his cover with the Gregorian University should stand scrutiny. He has been here for several years and knows his way around Rome. And, as I mentioned, I trust him completely."

The pope thought for a minute and spoke. "I knew you would come up with something like that, Father. For our sake, I hope it all works. There is a great deal at stake for everyone involved."

"I have taken that into consideration, Holiness. I feel comfortable with the way my plan has evolved."

"One more thing, Father. I want you to go and see Cardinal Maglione and Monsignor Tardini as they will play an important role in the Vatican's undertakings during the coming months."

"As you wish, Holiness," agreed Leiber, unsure of the pontiff's motives

"Just mention passports," the pope noted, sensing Leiber's uncertainty. "I have already talked to them but I want you brought into the network."

Leiber nodded his agreement.

"And lastly, Father. I have already had two sessions with our brother cardinals from Germany. I have taken some of their advice and established clear communications through the German nunciature. I believe this will allow us to keep a clear head about our church's positions in Germany. I have also told them that it is entirely possible that you, or someone you designate, might visit them sometime in the future. They are aware that your presence would be on a most secretive basis."

Again Leiber nodded to the pontiff.

"That's all for now, Father. I'll let you know more later."

Leiber bowed slightly and turned and left. Pius XII was already absorbed in reading a document on his desk.

Thursday, May 9, 1940
Private Room, 1st Floor,
10 Downing Street,
Westminster,
London, England

England's Prime Minister Neville Chamberlin ushered two figures into a small room off the main corridor of the hundred-room number 10 Downing Street. It was late afternoon and Chamberlin's guests were Foreign Secretary E.F.L. Wood, Earl of Halifax and Winston Churchill, First Lord of the Admiralty. The three sat in comfortable Queen Anne high back chairs and were served an afternoon tea by a member of the prime minister's staff.

The meeting was an embarrassing gathering for Chamberlin who had just witnessed more than 100 Conservative members of Parliament (his own party) vote against his government—a clear indication that he could no longer serve as the island nation's leader.

It was Chamberlain's notion that this meeting would determine who would be the next prime minister of Great Britain.

No stenographers were present as the three principals discussed the future of their country.

"Gentlemen," Chamberlin began, "I'm quite sure you both realize just why we are here. Today's events show me that my policies are no longer in keeping with the will of our elected representatives. I see that something must be done to change the direction of our country's course of action. You two are the principals if we are to form a new government. This must be done quickly for the sake of everyone involved.

After this meeting I intend to go to Buckingham Palace and offer the King my resignation. I'm sure he will accept and it is up to us to offer him a suitable replacement. You are both aware of my policies and the manner in which I have conducted the duties of this office. I need not say more on the matter."

Neither Churchill nor Lord Fairfax said anything and remained seated. In due course, and after sipping his tea, Chamberlain continued.

"After considering our options, I feel it would be best if Lord Halifax head a new government for Great Britain. He has the support of a great majority of our Conservatives and that party has dominated the House of Commons for the past half-decade.

But my offer is based on the condition that, as head of the Conservative Party, I would remain in government and retain leadership of the House of Commons. Mr. Churchill here would fully run the war while Lord Halifax would take over the government and manage it in the House of Lords. I realize this is a bit unorthodox, but our country is in a most difficult position. I have had calls from the Labor Party with some suggestions but I feel this is the best possible course.

Since you are the potential leader of our country, what are your feelings Lord Halifax?"

The Earl thought for a minute and finally replied. "If I understand what you are proposing, Britain is to have a three-headed government that would be expected to agree on all important matters put before it. This does not seem workable to me at all. Were I not in charge of the war nor the House of Commons, I fear I would be nothing more than a titular head of our country. I would be nothing more than a cipher." He paused again. "This scenario is not suitable for me nor would it be for any leader. Our country needs a singular leader that can unite all facets of our country for the upcoming struggle. Our enemies are ruthless and will stop at nothing to get what they want. Britain must also be ruthless, lest our way of life fall into the surrounding seas and become nothing more than a footnote to history.

I am sorry to refuse your offer, Prime Minister, but I must do so. I think it would be unwise for me and our country to do otherwise. I trust you understand my position, Sir."

Chamberlain remained passive and contemplated his next words.

"Thank you, Lord Halifax. I see your point. I feel it is important that we agree on a person who commands the support of all three major parties in the House of Commons. We need a tireless leader who will be as ruthless as our enemies as they are to Britain." He paused again.

Both leaders looked over at Churchill. The pudgy 65-year-old statesman looked down and lit a cigar, his favorite brand from Cuba, a wide-ringed Romeo y Julieta. It caught immediately and Churchill took a deep draw.

"Prime minister," Churchill began slowly, "It seems we are at an impasse. I agree that something need be done and quickly. I anticipate our enemies will act rapidly as they will perceive our government as weak and indecisive. The recent vote against you will fuel their resolve even more. They will act quickly and that means additional problems for us and our allies.

I believe I am the man for the job, period. I have fought against appeasement for many years and our enemies are well aware of my record. I have no intention whatsoever of bowing to Herr Hitler's demands for anything. I foresee an expansion of German military forces in the near future and the real possibility that Germany will attack the British mainland without recourse in the near future. We must be prepared for any eventuality and that means taking decisive actions.

Any delay could prove disastrous for our nation and our people. I just hope it's not too late. I hope you both see the importance of what I am saying."

Lord Halifax waited a moment then spoke first. "Given the dire circumstances we are facing would Mr. Churchill as head of Britain be acceptable to you prime minister? I feel you have the deciding hand in all this."

Chamberlain sighed and slumped against the back of his chair. He continued to ponder the question and slowly replied, "While I have not agreed with Mr. Churchill's policies in the past, I must say that I see no other course of action, Lord Halifax. I'm not sure my proposal could not have worked out, but Mr. Churchill is quite correct in his assessment that something must be done with great immediacy." He paused again and correlated his thoughts. "What I want is whatever action is best for the British people. Then so be it. I agree with Mr. Churchill and I will ask King George to appoint him as soon as possible. My best wishes go with him in this most perilous undertaking."

Chamberlain stood and extended his hand. "Thank you, Winston, for coming to the aid of our country at this dangerous time. I will give you all the help I can muster, of that you can be sure."

Lord Halifax also stood and extended his hand. "Good luck, old chap. I think you will need all the luck in the world."

"*We* will need more than luck, My Lord," Churchill replied in an even manner. "Our country faces a truly hazardous path if we are to survive. I will need *everyone's* help if we are going to come out of this mess as a whole country."

Chamberlain was the first to leave the room. He was on his way to tender King George VI his resignation as Britain's prime minister along with the news of the new agreement that would guide Great Britain for the foreseeable future.

Chapter Five

"So long as the Duce lives,
one can rest assured that
Italy will seize every opportunity
to achieve its imperialistic aims."

— *Adolf Hitler, 1939*

Sunday, January 14, 1940
Hotel Sole al Pantheon,
Piazza della Rotunda, 63
Rome, Italy

Father Michael S. Rodi S.J. knocked softly on the door to Room 234 of the extensive Hotel Sole al Parthenon. A full-faced man in his early 40's opened the door and smiled at the young priest.

"Good afternoon , Father," he exclaimed, "I have been expecting you." He offered his hand and shook Rodi's with a firm grip.

"I'm Father Rodi," the visitor explained in German. "Father Leiber sent me."

"He told me as much. Sorry to interfere with your Sunday afternoon."

"We work every day at the Vatican, Mr. Müller. It comes with the job."

"Have you any news for me from the pope?"

"Yes, but I'm afraid not much news."

Müller's face sagged slightly as Rodi continued. "The pope has been made aware of your situation but doesn't feel there is anything he can do until after the action is completed. He feels he cannot interfere in the actions of sovereign nations even though he is sympathetic with your goals. He hopes you understand his position.

In the event you are successful, he will be happy to act in any capacity you see fit to bring this horrible war to an end."

Müller considered Rodi's words and smiled again. "Please thank the Holy Father and my friend Father Leiber for their time and consideration. I understand the position of the pope and the Holy See. I will report back to my associates."

"I hope you have a safe trip home, Mr. Müller."

"Thank you, Father Rodi."

Rodi offered his hand and turned to leave. Müller walked him to the door and patted him on the shoulder.

"My thanks again, Father. I hope to see you again under better circumstances."

"Me too, Mr. Müller. Me too.

Monday, June 17, 1940
Mussolini's Offices, Partito Nationale Fascita,
Palazzo della Farnesina,
Via della Lungara,
Rome, Italy

It was officially one week since Italy had declared itself at war with Britain and France. It had become apparent to Benito Mussolini that Germany's decisive victories over several European countries and excellent results in two Scandinavian countries meant the war he was now fighting would have an extremely short life.

He had ordered Italian troops into Southern France and, after some initial progress, the Italian troops had become stalled at the fortified Alpine Line. Il Duce had also ordered the beginning of his Western Desert Campaign, a move aimed at expanding Italian colonization in North Africa by taking land from both France and Britain.

When his Chief of Staff Marshal Badoglio had opposed the move on the basis that the army was ill-equipped for such a mission, Mussolini stated simply, "I only need a few thousand dead so that I can sit at the peace conference as a man who has fought."

He now sat at a table with Badoglio and several of the marshal's staff officers.

"So we have stopped in Southern France, have we?" Mussolini questioned.

"We did capture the town of Menton, Duce. But little else. The French have excellent defenses along the *Ligne Alpine*. Our commanders are asking what to do next..."

Mussolini looked over at Badoglio and was about to speak when a note was handed to him by one of his secretaries. The Italian dictator read the note and threw it on the table.

"The pitiful French have just announced that they will seek an armistice with Germany," he said disgustedly. I knew this would happen. This war will be over before we can claim enough territory to make it all worthwhile."

He thought for a moment and spoke again. "What about North Africa, Badoglio? Can we capture these places without much trouble?"

Badoglio hesitated and eventually answered. "Duce, I fear there will be more problems in North Africa than in France. Both the British and Free French forces are well equipped. We have some supply problems already. I have not yet received word from the on scene commanders as to our exact progress. Our initial reports indicate we have not met any main enemy units but have stopped our advance to await resupplying."

Il Duce slammed his fist on the desk and shouted, "Are we capable of doing anything right?"

Badoglio remained silent, unwilling to provoke his leader any further.

Mussolini stepped away from the table and again ranted. "Do not call me again until you have better news. I want results, not excuses. I have personally guaranteed the Council of Ministers that our military's actions are necessary and our wonderful country will prevail. I do not intend to have those promises go unfulfilled. I want results and will accept nothing short of victory. Does everyone here understand?" He looked around but the officers stood almost rigid in their postures.

Mussolini shook his head in revulsion and quickly walked out of the room. The officers stared at the receding figure as he disappeared behind the door.

An hour later, Italy's Foreign Minister Galeazzo Ciano received a call from Mussolini's secretary to be ready for a quick rail trip to meet with Hitler at Munich. The secretary said that Hitler expressed desire to meet with the Duce to clarify the terms of the armistice with France. Ciano was to meet with von Ribbentrop while Hitler and Mussolini met privately.

To Count Galeazzo Ciano, the war seemed nearly over. For some reason, however, he found this prospect somewhat unnerving.

Friday, July 5, 1940
Luftwaffe Command Headquarters,
Reich Air Ministry Building,
Leipziger Straße,
Berlin, Germany

"I have given the Fuhrer my word that our bombings will start tomorrow," bellowed Reichsmarschall Herman Göring to a room full of Luftwaffe subordinates. "I want no explanations, just results. After all, we are only bombing shipping in the English Channel, and the protection the British put there should only be minimal. Am I correct?"

"Yes, Herr Reichsmarschall," answered Wilhelm Keitel, Oberkommando der Luftwaffe and second in command of Germany's air resources. "We are in a position to begin the bombings tomorrow morning. I would prefer that we wait for additional fighter aircraft to be moved closer to the shore to be able to protect the Stukas and Junkers. Another few days and this will be accomplished. Remember, we have only occupied Paris since June 14. Give us the additional days and then the RAF should not have such an easy time with our bombers."

"I have promised the Fuhrer, Keitel. You know what that entails."

"Jawohl, Herr Reichsmarschall. I understand fully."

"We must take our chances. After all, our bombers are the most feared and our pilots are the most well-trained aviators in the entire world. Just look at our results in Spain."

Certainly we did well in Spain. We had no air opposition whatsoever. But, I must admit, it was a good training exercise. Our men are really excellent fliers. No need to say anything further, he won't listen anyway.

"I will give the necessary orders, Herr Reichsmarschall. You can assure the Fuhrer that the deadline will be met."

"Good. Then our meeting is over. I have another appointment on the Wilhelmstraße that I must attend to. Gentlemen, thank you for your attention."

The room came to an abrupt silence as heels clicked to attention. Göring raised his hand in a half-hearted Nazi salute and uttered a methodical "Heil Hitler" to the officers. A chorus of "Heil Hitler's" followed his departure from the room.

Sunday, August 25, 1940
Royal Air Force Fighter Command,
RAF Bentley Priory,
Near Stanmore,
Middlesex, England

Air Chief Marshal Hugh Dowding concluded his daily morning walk from the home he shared with his sister Hilda in nearby Stanmore to his offices at RAF Bentley Priory. The antiquated military site consisted of some 40 acres and was the home of the Royal Air Force's Fighter Command and the Royal Observer Corps. It was also the site that controlled Great Britain's fate as the island country's war with Germany intensified.

Dowding's companion on the walk was British General Frederick A. Pile, head of Anti-Aircraft Command and his close friend. This morning's conversation involved the German Wehrmacht's stepped up actions and the start of the "Battle of Britain."

"They are throwing everything they have at us," Dowding conceded. "Yesterday Jerry hit London for the first time and our reports were heavy civilian casualties. Our boys in the 11 Group really had their hands full. It's a good thing that Park is in command there, he will give the Hun his money's worth."

"Thanks for letting me know, Hugh. We heard rumors and I dropped by the control room. There was so much going on I didn't dare get in anyone's way," Pile responded. "I haven't yet seen the reports from yesterday."

"Good of you, old man," Dowding responded, referring to the control room. "Each person in the CR has a job to do and you might have been trampled in the process."

Pile grinned and spoke again. "Seriously though, Hugh. Isn't it about time you received credit for refusing to commit to Churchill all our fighters to the action in France? Lord knows what we would do if we didn't have all the Hurricanes you saved along with the new Spitfires. We would be up shit's creek without the proverbial paddle."

"The jury is out on that, Freddie. The Hurricanes are able enough but the new German fighters make them somewhat obsolete. The new Spits are another thing entirely. They are more maneuverable than anything the bastards have and our pilots really love them. If we can get enough of them built as quickly as possible, I think we have a fighting chance. If Lord Beaverbrook's Air Production Ministry can rev it up a bit, we will give Jerry a real run."

"I hear through the grapevine that Beaverbrook has taken over the production facility at Castle Bromwich from Lord Nuffield. That's a positive step, isn't it?"

Dowding grinned and replied, "Grapevine huh? That's supposed to be hush-hush."

"I'm certainly not telling anyone, Hugh. I only thought you..."

"I sat in on a briefing a little over two months ago. Nuffield was a top man but his experience was mostly in motor cars. Lord Beaverbrook understands what is needed and will provide a steady hand. I have reports that the newer Spitfire MK IIa's are already being stepped up. We have about 30 already deployed and expect another 30 or 40 this month. They will be a godsend to squadrons at Biggin Hill, Hornchurch and elsewhere. The first went to 611 Squadron and I can't wait to see their operational results. The new Merlin engines are what really make a difference..."

"Thank God for our morning walk," chided Pile. "If it weren't for you, I'd never be in the know."

"Your Anti-Aircraft Command put on quite a show around London if my reports are accurate."

"We do what we can, Hugh. After all, we are all in this together."

Dowding nodded his assent and stopped. "This is where I say goodbye, Freddie. Hope your day is better than mine will be."

"We will both be up to our arses in it, Hugh. And we both know it..."

"See you, Freddie." He waved to his friend as he took a path towards the offices of Fighter Command. He knew he would be in for a long day.

Saturday, September 7, 1940
Nazi Party Headquarters, Braunes Haus
Brienner Straße, 45
Munich, Germany

The Nazi party's national headquarters in Munich was a renovated three-story stone structure that had been named the *Braunes Haus* after the color of the party's uniforms. It had been used for almost a decade by the Nazi elite and was a symbol of the party's rise to power in Germany.

Adolf Hitler maintained an office there that included a life-sized portrait of Henry Ford, a person he greatly admired. The *Braunes Haus* was also the resting place of the Blutfahne or "blood flag", the Nazi flag that was carried at the head of the party's famous Munich beer hall demonstration, the Beer Hall Putsch, in 1923. Gunfire by Munich police spattered the blood of a number of Nazis on the banner and the flag became the symbol of the National Socialist Party.

Hitler enjoyed returning to Munich, the city he considered as mostly associated with his party's rise to power. He had just left the Reich Chancellery in Berlin where the plans were finalized for the all-out bombing of Great Britain.

The office of Rudolph Hess, deputy fuhrer under Hitler, was the German leader's destination on this early Saturday afternoon. Hess was Hitler's close confidant and was extremely devoted to both Adolf Hitler and the Nazi Party.

Hitler entered the office without knocking and strode directly toward Hess. Forty-six-year old Rudolf Hess rose and smiled warmly at his visitor. "Welcome back to Munich, Fuhrer. It is good to see you. You should come here more often."

"Yes, I probably should, Rudolph. Something about Munich gives me strength and vision. I've always felt very welcome here."

"Even when we were in jail at Landsberg, Fuhrer? I don't recall your being happy there?"

"That wasn't a bad time for me, Rudolph. I was allowed many visitors and was given time to dictate my books to the Jesuit. I am of a mind that the time was well used."

"I agree. It could have been much worse for everyone. Actually, it was cozy in a weird sort of way."

"I did not come here to reminisce," Hitler suddenly became serious. "I wanted to let you know what is happening with the military and also find out what strides have been made with our Jewish problem. I would talk to Himmler about this, but he seems to be elsewhere."

"I am unaware of his movements, Fuhrer. He was here a day or so ago. We talked at that time."

"First, about our war plans. You should know what is happening in case anything ever happens to me. After Göring, you are the head of the Third Reich."

"Nothing is going to happen to you, Fuhrer. I'll see to that myself."

"There are always people who oppose my wishes," Hitler returned. "I am resigned to the fact that there will always be plots against the Third Reich and me personally."

"When one aspires to greatness, there will always be obstacles, Fuhrer."

"True enough, Rudolph."

"Now, about the war. I know that everything is going as I planned. I've see the latest reports."

"Yes, we have been most fortunate. No one has dared stand up to our military. But, that might change in the near future…"

"I don't understand…"

"I have given orders for the concentrated bombing of most British cities. I have also begun to finalize Operation Sea Lion. When that time comes, we will invade Britain and bring that godless country to its knees. Much of the equipment is already in place to invade, but I still don't believe the time is right. We will wait until this bombing blitz has run its course. I believe the British will give in once their situation is hopeless. That might very well end this war."

"I believe you are right, Fuhrer. They will soon run out of supplies."

"Yes, if everything goes as we planned."

"You mentioned something about change…"

"Yes. Our strategy could easily backfire. The new premier seems to be able to rally the British. We knew what Chamberlain was all about---appeasement. Churchill will have none of that and seems determined to strengthen his military. If our bombing doesn't devastate Britain, I fear we might have awakened the sleeping lion."

"You will figure out a solution, Fuhrer. You have so far."

"And, there are also the Russians. I fear them more than the British. I see them waiting to pounce if we make any mistakes. I think we will have to deal with them sooner than later."

"But we have an agreement with the Soviets."

"Agreements are exactly what you want them to be, Rudolph. Each side uses the agreement to its own advantage. When there's no more advantage remaining, then the agreement is broken. It's been that way throughout history."

Tuesday, October 15, 1940
Offices of the Foreign Ministry,
Palazzo della Farnesina,
Via della Lungara,
Rome, Italy

As Italy's foreign minister, Count Galeazzo Ciano recognized it was his place in history to increase Italy's territory in Europe no matter the cost. He also conveniently considered recently-conquered Albania as his personal grand duchy and looked southeastward for his next victim. Greece, in his undaunted opinion, would offer little resistance to the combination of Italian air power and Italian Army troops should a war commence.

He had called together Francesco Jacomoni, Italy's Albanian minister as well as Chief of Staff Marshal Badoglio, Army Chief of Staff Mario Roatta, and Generals Ubaldo Soddu and Visconti Prasca. As usual, the de facto dictator of Italy, Il Duce, also sat in on the meeting.

At the offset, both Ciano and Jacomoni pressed for immediate military action that was strongly opposed by Badoglio and Army General Soddu. Badoglio pointed out that the Italian military attaché in Athens had provided a report of a well-armed Greek military force as well as a well-established anti-Italian mindset on the part of the general Greek populace. Jacomoni also pointed out that the population of Ciamuria (Southern Albania) was very approving toward Italy and would welcome military intervention.

"Minister, I beg you to reconsider this move," Badoglio pleaded. "We are in no position to invade Greece. The season is already getting late and the rainy period will begin in a matter of weeks. We don't even have the right type of uniforms. If we encounter any sort of resistance, the results could be disastrous."

"Nonsense, Marshal," Ciano countered calmly. " As you just heard, Minister Jacomoni feels the resistance will be token at best. Two hundred Italian bombers over Athens will dull the spirit of the common Greek rather quickly. I firmly believe the entire operation will be useful and easy."

For the first time at the meeting, Benito Mussolini raised his head and spoke. "Gentlemen, I have something to add to all of this. While I have some reservations about our military's present ability, I believe Ciano to be right. I approved a large sum of money to certain Greek officials that should make the day that much easier for us. I would also like to take an action that would coincide with Herr Hitler's present plans, without first informing him. It would place our country on a like plane and even out the scales, so to speak."

Badoglio let his head drop as if conceding defeat. He looked over at General Soddu, the officer that would command Italy's Army, and shook his head in silence. Soddu returned the stare with a worried glance. It was as if the two old warriors knew what was in store for their country.

"Then it's decided," Ciano piped up with renewed confidence. "We will put the plan into effect and begin our strategies for the first attacks. This must be put together quickly, certainly within the next ten days. I am aware that weather is a factor, so let's get going at once."

Badoglio and Soddu again exchanged apprehensive glances. They had already studied the long-range weather forecasts that predicted an abnormal amount of rain and possibly snow. The combination of nature's potential preview of winter ostensibly rattled their military-oriented minds. Each settled back into his chair and stared straight ahead.

Chapter Six

> "The Pope? How many
> divisions does he have?"
>
> *—Joseph Stalin, 1935*

Saturday, November 16, 1940
Private Quarters of Pope Pius XII,
The Vatican,
Rome, Italy

Two of Pope Pius XII's closest confidants were present on this dreary Saturday afternoon in the Pontiff's private quarters inside the Vatican. Both persons just happened to be Germans. Both Sister Pascalina Lehnert and Father Robert Leiber, S.J., were long-time confidants of the head of the Roman Catholic Church. Sister Lehnert was officially considered the pope's housekeeper and had served in that capacity since 1918 when Pacelli was papal nuncio in Munich. Leiber was the pope's unofficial private secretary. During his relatively short tenure as pope, both had played significant roles in the administration of his papal duties. Pius XII was acutely aware that both figures were extremely loyal to both him and to the Holy Church and valued their opinions on an elevated basis.

Tea had been served a few moments earlier by one of Sister Lehnert's German nuns, from the same order, Sisters of the Holy Cross, Menzingen Order. Along with another sister of the same sisterhood , the three were the only females allowed to work inside the Vatican at the time.

Sister Lehnert offered the pope and Leiber a cracker but both declined. The pope's furrowed brow indicated he was worried about something important. At last, he spoke.

"I have asked you both here to have an important conversation. It is a matter that is quite troubling to me and I know you will both be as honest with me as possible."

Both shook their heads in agreement as the pontiff continued.

"I have been under great pressure to make some official statements about Hitler and the Nazis' treatment of the Jews. Many of our cardinals and bishops, as political emissaries from several countries, have sent messages to that effect. Since you are both German, I imagine you see the dilemma I now face. If I come out deliberately against the Nazi regime, I have no idea what they might do or just how many people will suffer. I certainly want to do what's right for the Holy See, but this predicament is quite tricky."

"Yes, Holiness, I totally agree," Leiber replied. "Hitler doesn't take into account the fact that there are 40 million Catholics in Germany and also a high percentage of his military. He feels they are completely dedicated to National Socialism and to nothing else. While most Catholics might be indifferent to Jews in general, if the Vatican chastises the Nazi regime for its treatment of Jews, it could easily sway German Catholics."

"I have heard rumors, Holiness, of the deportation of Jews to concentration camps," Sister Lehnert inserted. "It is my guess that you have proof to back up these rumors, right?"

"That question is still unsettled, Sister. I have a number of reports and the evidence seems overwhelming. But, until it is verified, it is difficult for me to act. I want what is best for our Holy Catholic Church, which must survive under all costs. I have been a believer in political negotiation and diplomacy since I served as nuncio in Germany and still feel this is the best course to follow."

"What about the Vatican itself, Holiness?" questioned Leiber. "If Hitler decides to act against us, would you be safe here? Is Mussolini close enough to Hitler to avert a disaster?"

"Good point, Father. I am not as worried about my own safety as that of our Holy Church. Remember, several former popes have been abducted and the church survived. I am prepared to resign my role as pope if the need should arise. Then Hitler would only be abducting a lowly priest with little real value."

Sister Lehnert shuttered, "Please don't speak like that, Holiness. You are scaring me."

The pope touched the end of her habit and said in a reassuring tone, "It is my hope that it will not come to that. But we must be ready if and when such a day arrives. I have jobs for both of you to begin work on. Father Leiber, I want you to visit a number of the churches and monasteries around Rome and prepare them for the possibilities that lie ahead. If Germany occupies Rome, as I feel it might, then the Jews will undoubtedly be persecuted. I want to be able to offer them sanctuary should the need arise. All this must be done unofficially, without any written authorization. Most of the Church's leaders in Rome know your status with me and I doubt if many will question our motives. If they do, simply have them call me personally to confirm. I doubt that many will call, but it will be good to give them the option."

"Yes, Holiness, I agree with you on that."

"And you, my dear Sister. I have an important job for you."

Sister Pascalina Lehnert bowed her head as the pope continued. "I want you to begin organizing a campaign around Rome to bring in additional supplies to the Vatican. These would include clothes, beddings, foods and anything else associated with Jews moving into our properties. I want this done as quietly as possible, with no fanfare. Just increase our outside orders and use our Vatican trucks for hauling. No one searches our trucks and I doubt if anyone will notice more trucks delivering goods than is usual. You can use your sisters to help if necessary, because what I am asking is a big job. I know you can get it done as efficiently as possible."

Sister Lehnert flushed as she answered, "Certainly, Your Holiness. I am pleased you have such confidence in my limited abilities. I will start at once."

"Not before we finish our tea and crackers. I think I might have one of those now."

The sister handed the tray containing the crackers first to the pope and then to Father Leiber.

"I made these myself from my grandmother's old recipe," she beamed. "It has been in my family for more than five generations."

"Delicious," the pope declared. "You could have easily been a *bäcker.*"

"Our order is filled with good cooks and bakers, Holiness. We were taught early on that many things can be accomplished through proper handling of the stomach."

"Good thinking," the pontiff replied. "I will keep that in mind for the future."

The three friends chuckled lightly and continued their light repast. The meeting had served as an excellent use for the dismal weekend day.

Monday, December 2, 1940
Offices of the General Secretary of the Central Committee,
Communist Party of the Soviet Union,
The Kremlin,
Moscow, Russia

Joseph Stalin sat at his desk and contemplated his next words. Across from him sat Soviet Prime Minister Vyacheslav Mikhaylovich Molotov, his protégée and close friend. The pair was discussing Germany's failure to reply to their country's written counterproposal about the Soviet Union's potential entrance into the Axis Pact that had been presented more than a week earlier in Berlin.

"I fear we have worn our welcome thin with the Nazis, Vyacheslav Mikhaylovich," the Communist leader stated pensively. ""As you are aware, I entered these negotiations with mixed feelings."

Molotov nodded his agreement.

Stalin continued. "We must face the fact that the Germans hate and fear us and will eventually attack us. Our ideologies are much too different for us to co-exist. Our current non-aggression agreement and trade pact were simply tactics to give both our countries what we needed at the time. The changes we made last week were minor in nature and should have evoked a quick response. I don't think we will hear back from them."

"You might be right, Iosif Vissarionovich," Molotov concurred. "The German military victories in Western Europe have almost placed them at our doorstep. I believe it is time for us to take the steps to insure the safety of Mother Russia."

"Exactly what I am thinking. We must begin making our preparations. But we must be careful in doing so. Nothing big at first, just small deployments that won't attract undue attention. I'm sure the Nazis have informants who report our every move."

"The same as we do, Iosif Vissarionovich," Molotov chuckled. "It's like a children's game where one child observes the other then tells the parent in order to get the other in trouble."

"Except that the stakes here are considerably higher, my old friend. The very existence of our country will hang in the balance. No telling what the cost will be in Russian lives and property," the Soviet leader continued. "I fear it will be a great sacrifice for everyone involved."

Molotov again shook his head. "I will begin immediately. I will order production of our aircraft to be increased as well as most of the larger weapons and guns. The

Germans cannot begin an attack until next spring, so that should give us some time. Let's hope the weather cooperates and doesn't provide them with a dry season until then."

Stalin pressed a button and a male secretary appeared from outside the office. He gestured to the uniformed man who quickly disappeared. Moments later, he reappeared with a tray containing a bottle of Stalin's favorite drink, *Kizlyarka*, and a pair of glasses. Made from grape pomace, the strong liquor had an alcoholic content of 45 per cent and packed an incredible wallop. The secretary placed the tray on Stalin's desk and disappeared.

"So it's your *Kizlyarka*, is it?" Molotov remarked with a smile. "That stuff is so strong I can only drink a small amount. I wonder what it does to my stomach."

"We only need a small amount for our toast, Vyacheslav Mikhaylovich. This wouldn't be Russia if we didn't toast our upcoming victory, would it?" Stalin poured a small amount into both glasses.

"You are right as usual, Iosif Vissarionovich. I am not thinking clearly."

"To our people and our armies," he raised his glass.

"Our people and armies," Molotov chimed. "Let us all be victorious."

The two old friends swallowed the brandy and looked toward a map of the Soviet Union that hung along Stalin's office wall.

Sunday, December 8, 1940
Mussolini's Home,
Villa Torolina,
Via Nomentana, 70,
Rome, Italy

Even though the days in December were growing shorter, they somehow seemed much longer to Benito Mussolini. Italy's war in Greece was already a terrible mistake and had gone badly for the Italians since the first shots were fired. The Greek Army had fought tenaciously for their homeland and that fact had cost Italy dearly both in men and equipment. Italy's commanding general Soddu had already been replaced and the many of the country's newspapers were calling for the head of Mussolini's son-in-law, Count Galeazzo Ciano.

How can they call him 'The Most Hated Man in Italy' mulled the Duce? He was doing what he thought was best for our country. He's an intelligent, passionate person who has given his life for Italy. Surely some degree of sanity will return things to normal for our country. I can't put my finger on a solution; events are simply happening too fast. Our German friends are basking in their country's success and we are now regulated to playing second fiddle to them. Thank God it's almost Christmas. I love Christmas and the feeling it portrays. Most bad things take a back seat to the birth of Christ. At least, that's the way it supposed to be. Oh well, at least it's not my head that is being called for. That's something to be pleased about. As far as Galeazzo is concerned, he simply must take care of himself. All he needs is some sort of military victory and the complainers will be quieted... But where? And when?...

Mussolini looked up as his wife Rachele approached with a glass of white wine and offered it to her husband.

"What do you have for me this afternoon, my dear? A surprise?"

"You looked so forlorn when I first saw you I decided to try the *Lacryma Christi* here," she remarked, pointing to the yellow-gold liquid in the glass. Somehow I associate the tears of Christ with people who are troubled."

"It's not a bad association, Rachele, even if Christ was crying about the Bay of Naples. Your intention is good."

"I hope you enjoy it, Benito."

"If you wouldn't mind getting me the bottle. I'm a bit thirsty."

"I'll be right back."

I am a fortunate person to have someone like her. She brings some peacefulness to my life. I wish Galeazzo and Etta were closer; he could really use her comfort right now.

The leader of Italy returned to his batch of newspapers and their troubling contents.

Tuesday, December 10, 1940
Office of the Secretary of War,
Munitions Building,
21st and C Streets,
Washington, District of Columbia

Now in his second term as Secretary of War, Harry Lewis Stimson seemed preoccupied as he stared at a communication he had just received. Seated across from him was four-star General George C. Marshall, the Chief of Staff for the United States Army. The two had been in a conversation for nearly fifteen minutes when they were interrupted by Stimson's private secretary who deemed it prudent to interrupt. The secretary handed Stimson a page of paper and withdrew.

Stimson read and then reread the communication and handed it to Marshall. The top army officer studied it for several minutes and passed it back to Stimson.

"It seems to point to a slow German buildup in Poland and along its western borders," Marshall said evenly. "That could only mean the Nazis intend to invade Soviet Russia at some point."

"So much for international agreements," Stimson countered. "We all had misgivings when the German-Russian Non-Aggression Agreement was announced. We thought that Stalin was dallying for time and it certainly looks as if his time is running out."

"Yes, Mr. Secretary. I believe you are right. But this won't be as easy for Herr Hitler as it has been so far. The Russians have a large force and will be fighting in their homeland. I also question the fact that it is now winter in Russia; Germany will find it tough going in that bleak environment."

"Like Napoleon, I suppose," Stimson smiled.

"Correct, Mr. Secretary. I am impressed."

"I read a bit while I was governor general of the Philippines in the late 20's. I haven't had a lot of chance to put what I learned to use."

"Good thing the British were able to fend off the Luftwaffe this past summer. That probably changed Hitler's mind about attacking Britain."

"And made him consider Russia as a target," Stimson surmised.

71

Marshall nodded and moved toward a large map that was positioned on a wide double easel. He glanced intently at Eastern Europe and finally spoke. "I wouldn't want to be a German general with the task of conquering the Soviet Union. It is perilous at best and almost impossible to imagine. It could easily spell the beginning of the end for the Third Reich."

Stimson considered the general's words and replied, "I certainly hope you are right, George. For the sake of the entire world, I hope that you are right..."

Wednesday, December 18, 1940
Abteilung Landesverteidigungsführungsamt,
Oberkommando der Wehrmacht,
Wünsdorf, Hanover,
Lower Saxony, Germany

German Chancellor Adolf Hitler watched intently as the leaders of the German Wehrmacht (OKW) discussed his country's upcoming military action. The head of the Oberkommando des Heeres (OKH, or German Army High Command), the army commander in chief, Field Marshal Walther von Brauchitsch, stood alongside army general staff chief, Franz Halder. The conversation was evenly stated, with both veteran officers voicing their beliefs that the Soviet Red Army could be defeated in two or three months and that by the end of October the Germans would have conquered the whole European part of Russia. The invasion of the Soviet Union was originally tagged as Operation Fritz, but as preparations began, Hitler renamed it Operation Barbarossa, after Holy Roman Emperor Frederick Barbarossa (whose reign was from 1152–90), who sought to establish German predominance in Europe. The plan was also called Directive 21.

After listening for several minutes, Hitler interrupted the dialogue. "Are you quite sure we won't have any trouble with the Bolsheviks? I don't want to make a mistake here. Our plans have gone well, but this is a major undertaking. Like our true Germans, the Russians believe in fighting for their homeland."

"The numbers don't lie, Fuhrer," the half-bald von Brauchitsch replied. "We have studied their strength and we outnumber the Red Army almost 2 to 1. We have more equipment and better trained soldiers that now feel they are invincible. Nothing can stop us once the order is given."

"And have the reconnaissance flights into Russia continued without problems?"

"Yes, Fuhrer. The Soviets have been willing to let us fly into their airspace without attacking. We have been doing that for several weeks and have not observed any Soviet buildups along the borders."

Hitler thought to himself. *I am sure that the pig Stalin expects us to wait until the war with Britain is concluded before we attack him. That would make sense. But I have a good feeling about this and we must attack while no one expects us to do so. If our analysts are correct about the numbers, I believe we will have won before the winter can play a big part. Blitzkrieg has worked for us superbly so far and there's no reason to think it won't this time.*

He returned his attention to the waiting officers. "Continue your preparations for the attack, gentlemen. Unless you hear to the contrary, we will attack next spring as planned. I want no delays or postponements on this plan. Do you understand?"

Both Generals shook their heads in agreement. Operation Barbarossa was now in implementation.

Friday, March 21, 1941
Red Army Headquarters,
The Kremlin,
Moscow, Russia

All of Russia's top military leaders who had survived Joseph Stalin's purges of the Red Army's top officers were gathered with the Soviet leader at the Kremlin. They could tell from the onset that the Soviet Premier was in an apprehensive mood. The group included General Chief of Staff Georgy Zhukov, Deputy Commander of the Operations Directorate of the General Staff Marshal of the Soviet Union Semyon Budyonny, Marshal Semyon Timoshenko, and Red Army General Markian Popov.

Stalin began. "Comrades, I have called you here today for a most important reason. Our spies in Germany have sent word of unusual German military activities in recent weeks. Nothing really specific, but taken as a whole it seems the Germans are massing unusual numbers of equipment in Poland and elsewhere. If they don't intend to invade us then why send in all the large guns and equipment. They need only send in the troops to man these guns and the invasion would be a reality."

"Moving troops quickly is the easiest part," agreed the heavily-mustached Semyon Budyonny from his chair. It can be done in a matter of days. Having the proper equipment for an invasion takes much longer. I fear you are correct, Iosif Vissarionovich. The Huns are up to something, there is no doubt about it."

The remainder of Russia's military elite shook their heads in agreement.

Stalin continued. "I have expected something like this for several months. You are all aware that we have stepped up our production of tanks and weapons in case of such an attack. I am prepared to order further increases if this meeting agrees to do so.

I am also happy to report that the first flights of the new Yak-1 fighter aircraft have been successful and we are now in full production. This activity has been closely guarded and will come as a surprise to the Germans. Also, the new MiG-1 will be ready for tests within a month. If it proves successful, we will have a high altitude fighter to defend against bombers."

"Do you intend to call up our reserve armies?" Ukrainian-born Marshal Timoshenko questioned. "It would seem the correct thing to do."

"That would also send a signal to Germany that we are onto their intentions, Semyon Konstantinovich. I would prefer calling up key officers first and then the bulk of the reserves when they are needed."

"Isn't that taking a big chance?" Budyonny injected. "We could be ready for an invasion if our reserves were in place."

"They could easily step up the invasion date if they saw that happening," Stalin returned flatly. "No, I think it better to build up slowly. That way we could do it on our own terms as opposed to doing it because we are being attacked."

No one at the meeting questioned Stalin's reasoning so the Soviet leader continued. "Beginning immediately, I will start the officer call up. I will also order our factories to step up their production to maximum assembly. If we are correct about the Germans, they will attack us with everything they have. They might have some initial success but I believe the will of the ordinary Russian will prevail in the end. We have a great country with a remarkable past and we do not give in easily when provoked. We will call this our Patriotic War and our exploits will rewrite Russian history."

A Red Army soldier entered carrying a tray with small glasses filed with vodka. He passed out a glass to each officer seated at the table and quickly left the room.

"Comrades," Stalin rose with his glass in hand. "I give you Mother Russia and her long history of just wars. May she survive and prosper."

The group rose and raised their glasses. Each uttered, "To Mother Russia." They clinked glasses and patted each other on the shoulders. Finally, Semyon Budyonny looked around and barked out loud, "Isn't there more vodka? That little bit was quite good."

The uniformed soldier was already through the door with a bottle of Moskovskaya Osobsya vodka in each hand. He was warmly greeted by the assortment of Soviet generals. It was thus assured the meeting would run as long as the vodka held out.

Chapter Seven

> "It is not heroes that make history,
> but history that makes heroes."
>
> – *Joseph Stalin*

Thursday, May 1, 1941
Golf Club of Rome,
Rome, Italy

Count Galeazzo Ciano and Benito Mussolini sat dejectedly in a room off the clubhouse of the Golf Club of Rome. A half-drunk bottle of *grappa* sat on a small circular table between the two men.

The debacle of the Greco-Italian War was now behind them due mostly to the intervention of German troops sent in by a furious Adolf Hitler to save face for the Axis powers. Hitler was also upset that this usage of German troops intended for his secretive Russian campaign forced a minor change in schedule for the now-primed Wehrmacht.

"Times are grave, Galeazzo, I am beginning to think we have little hope for the future. First Taranto when the British used their ridiculous airplanes to sink our ships and then our country's nonsensical foray into Greece and the disastrous results there. I can't be seen in public for the stares and mutterings of many, including my ministers. I am forced to escape to a place like this golf club to seek a little peace and quiet."

Ciano thought for a minute and replied. "I was at fault in Greece, Duce. I underestimated the intensity of the Greek army and the will of the Greek people. I had thought they would roll over once we attacked."

"They rolled over *us*, Galeazzo. Our armies offered little resistance."

Ciano nodded his head and remained silent. *Is my father-in-law going to replace me because of my actions? If so, what am I to do? This could be disastrous for my career, not to mention my social life. Right now I get all the women I want and Etta doesn't seem to mind. Maybe I am worrying about nothing; the Duce doesn't seem to be in a really foul mood.*

77

Mussolini gathered himself and spoke again. "You must bring *every* important matter to me personally, Galeazzo. I want no more decisions made without my complete approval. I am very serious about this. Do you understand me?"

"Perfectly, Duce. You have my assurance." *What is he talking about? He approved the invasion of Greece and attended the pre-war meeting of all the generals. I should never have said that Greece was my fault. He will use it against me if it ever comes to that. I must be more careful from this point on.*

Mussolini refilled his glass with *grappa* and gestured to Ciano to do the same. The younger minister reached for the bottle and poured himself a healthy portion. For some reason, the *grappa* never tasted so good.

Sunday, May 11, 1941
Private Dining Room,
10 Downing Street, Westminster,
London, UK

A series of bombs fell in the near vicinity as Prime Minister Winston Churchill finished the last of his dinner and signaled for a waiter to remove the dishes and napery. With him in his role as minister of defence were members of the country's war cabinet. These included Sir John Anderson, Lord President of the council; Anthony Eden, Britain's Foreign Secretary; and Lord Beaverbrook, holder of several offices but, most importantly, Minister of Aircraft Production.

"That's rather heavy bombing for the second consecutive night in a row," observed Anthony Eden. "It's a wonder none have found their way here."

"We have history on our side," Churchill responded, reaching for a cigar. "We've been here at #10 Downing for more than 250 years and are still in one piece. I have a feeling if the Jerries want to bomb us they could do so quite easily. For some reason we are not on their target list and that's perfectly all right with me. I don't even bother with the bedroom they set up for me underneath the structure. I fear if we did get hit it would all come down on me if I were down there."

The other ministers smiled at Churchill's humor, not totally convinced he was joking.

"You are all quite safe here, gentlemen. Rest assured."

Lord Beaverbrook took the occasion to speak. "I have the figures here, Prime Minister. I believe these are what you asked for." He handed some papers to Churchill and copies to the other ministers.

Churchill glanced at the numbers and paused. After a few moments, he shook his head emphatically and produced a heavy draw from his cigar. "You have done a miraculous job, Max. I seriously doubted you would come out with these results. But these numbers speak for themselves. You haven't fudged a bit, have you?"

"Not one single bit, Prime Minister. I had my office verify them as of yesterday. You see to the right the extended figures of what we intend to produce for the year."

Churchill studied the papers and spoke again. "So we will have nearly 2500 new Spitfires by the end of the year and more than 3000 up-to-date Hurricanes."

"Yes, Prime Minister."

"What about the medium and heavy bombers?" Anthony Eden questioned. "Have we concentrated on building fighters at the expense of the Bomber Command.?"

"Not at all," Lord Beaverbrook replied matter of factly. "Page three will show you that 1941 will see almost 2000 modern Wellington mediums and more than 400 combined Halifax, Manchester and Stirling heavy bombers. Of course, the numbers rise dramatically in 1942 and the years after."

"Gentlemen, I want you all to hear this. I have just received word from Bomber Command that we are bombing the City of Hamburg as I speak. This isn't a token raid, but the beginning of a payback for Hitler's actions against London. Hamburg is a vital target, a large port and U-boat pens that provide daily attacks on our shipping. The nearby oil refineries are also important to the German war effort."

"It will be interesting to see how the Germans react to having their cities bombed, Prime Minister," Sir John Anderson reflected.

"Exactly, Sir John. Payback is often more defining than the initial act. Let's see how eager the Germans are to follow their leader once the word of these bombings spread throughout the country."

"I'm not convinced he cares all that much," remarked Churchill. "He has them under his thumb to the extent that they do as they are told. They have little to say about matters. If they object, they are arrested and more."

The British leaders sat back and reflected on the conversation. Lord Beaverbrook's figures had arrived at just the right time.

Tuesday, 22 June, 1941
Offices of the Fuhrer,
Wilhelmstraße 77,
Berlin-Mitte, Germany

The final papers for the implementation of Operation Barbarossa had been signed during the past two days and the orders for the most massive attack Nazi Germany had ever formulated had been given. Adolf Hitler sat by himself in his massive office. Barbarossa called for three of Germany's great army groups to smash over the frontier that divided the Soviet Union from Poland and Germany. One hundred-fifty Wehrmacht divisions and nearly three million German soldiers were involved along with three thousand tanks and numerous heavy guns. Another 3,000 aircraft of the Luftwaffe were ordered to support the army's ground operations and attain aerial superiority over the fighting.

I have assembled the greatest army that the world has ever seen. They are the best trained fighters that exist anywhere. I know the possible consequences of fighting a two-front war but our blitzkrieg has been so successful that I can't see the Russians holding out for long. Our Panzers will strike fear into the hearts of the Russian peasants. After this, the world will see that the Third Reich has become a reality. Germany will take her rightful place as the leader of the world and all nations will acknowledge our Aryan superiority. This is an historic day for everyone involved. I feel a sense of fulfillment and a feeling of peacefulness I have not experienced in quite a while. I wonder how long it will take for the first reports to be assessed.

Tuesday, June 22, 1941
Offices of the Foreign Minister,
Communist Party of the Soviet Union,
The Kremlin,
Moscow, Russia

Soviet foreign minister Vyacheslav Molotov finished reviewing the document in his hand and stepped in front of a battery of microphones that had been hurriedly assembled by Radio Moscow only hours after the first German soldiers crossed the Soviet borders. After a brief introduction, the second most powerful leader in the Soviet Union addressed untold millions of Russians spread over the now invaded country. His remarks would set the tone for the immediate future of his country.

He said in part…

"Today at 4 o'clock in the morning, without addressing any grievances to the Soviet Union, without a declaration of war, German forces fell on our country, attacked our frontiers in many places, and bombed our cities – Zhitomir, Kiev, Sevastopol, Kuanas and others… an act of treachery unprecedented in the history of civilized nations… Our people's answer to Napoleon's invasion was a Patriotic War…The Red Army and the whole nation will wage a victorious Patriotic War for our beloved country, for honour, for liberty … Our cause is just. The enemy will be beaten. Victory will be ours!"

The great bear that is Mother Russia thus gave notice to the world that she intended to defend her soil to the last man.

Tuesday, June 24, 1941
Mussolini's Offices,
Palazzo della Farnesina,
Via della Lungara,
Rome, Italy

It was a year and two weeks to the day that Italy had officially entered World War II as a member of the Axis Powers. The move was undoubtedly an act of political opportunism prompted by Benito Mussolini's feeling that the war would soon end and the Italian *Regio Esercito* (Royal Army) would be called on to do little or no fighting. His closest ally, Nazi Germany, was now racing through Russia with seemingly little resistance and was already calling for an early end to the war. A year earlier, Mussolini had simply felt that if he didn't commit to the confrontation, his beloved country would be left shorthanded when the spoils of war were distributed.

The news arrived that France had just surrendered to Germany this very day was a bit of icing on Mussolini's rather bare cake.

Members of his *Comando Supremo* (Italian High Command) had been summoned to his offices. Chief of Staff Marshal Ugo Cavallero, General Vittorio Ambrosio, commander of Italy's Second Army, and a small number of additional staff officers attended.

"What news do you to bring me about your meeting with our German allies?" Mussolini began in a weary voice. "For a change, I hope you have some good news."

"Duce," Cavallero answered, "North Africa looks promising for the future. The *Afrika Korps* are now firmly in place along with our motorized Ariete and Trento Divisions. The great German general Rommel is in charge and intends to push the British back into Egypt. He has already won several battles and seems destined for many more. Most of the ground troops involved are Italian, a total of six divisions. When we succeed, Italy will once again become a feared opponent."

"Have we been able to eliminate our supply problems for these units? I have seen us fail in the past because we had no food or ammunition for our troops."

"Improvements have been made, Duce. I won't say that all complications have been removed, but our troops are well-equipped for the present."

"Things are better than before, Duce," General Ambrosio agreed. "And the spirits of our men are also improved. A couple of easy victories was all it took. If the siege of Tobruk is successful, we will have additional victories for our side. Operation Skorpion was recently concluded there and another panzer division, the 15th Panzers, has recently arrived. The British have tried counter attacking, but with only limited success. If we can continue to keep the British contained, the area will become ours in a matter of weeks."

"I have heard that before, General Ambrosio. And somehow the expected results do not materialize."

Ambrosio remained silent, and Mussolini continued his invective. "I want the British pushed out of Tobruk and I want it done sooner than later. Am I understood?"

Both Italian leaders nodded their agreement.

"Thank you for coming, gentlemen. I know you have tight agendas. I appreciate your candidness."

Both generals and their staffs concurred and took their leave. Mussolini swiveled his chair and stared at a large map of the Western Desert Campaign that sat on an easel to the left of his desk. He studied the map for several minutes until returning to the paperwork on his desk.

Sunday, December 7, 1941
The President's Private Study,
White House, 1600 Pennsylvania Ave,
Washington, District of Columbia

First Lady Eleanor Roosevelt had finished hosting a Sunday luncheon at the White House and immediately walked into her husband's private study on the second floor. It was shortly after 1:30 and she found the president sitting with his long-time advisor, Harry Hopkins.

Hopkins rose to greet the first lady and was shaking hands with her when the door burst open. Behind the door was Secretary of the Navy, Frank Knox, in a state of near hysteria.

The president looked up at Knox who attempted to keep his voice level. "Mr. President, the Japanese have attacked our fleet at Pearl Harbor a few minutes ago. Our first reports indicate hundreds of Japanese fighter-bombers. We already know there is significant damage on Battleship Row. Admiral Stark at the Navy Department is trying to determine the consequences of the attack. All I can tell you is that it is bad, really bad..."

The president remained calm as others began entering the room with dispatches. Among them was Louise Hackmeister, the White House's chief switchboard operator. Roosevelt told her in a level tone, "Get Grace over here and have her set up some sort of receiving office. There needs to be order around here. It will get worse before it gets better." Louise shuffled off with an additional list of key personnel that needed to report to the White House. She would have the entire list called within 15 minutes.

Twenty minutes later, one of Roosevelt's secretaries, Grace Tully, appeared. She began taking calls in the study but quickly changed to the president's bedroom to avoid the din and general mayhem that surrounded the president's study. She was put into contact with Admiral Stark who began relaying a series of fragmentary reports from Hawaii. Tully took the notes by shorthand and then typed them into a readable form for the president. She was surrounded by a host of military figures including Marine General Thomas E. Watson, Roosevelt's personal physician Admiral Ross McIntire, the president's naval aide Captain John Beardall, and Presidential Secretary Marvin Hunter McIntyre. The group watched intently as Tully performed her duties and followed her every move.

Three hours later, Tully was again summoned to the president's study. He was now alone, seated at his desk with neat piles of notes all relating to the past few hours. He lit a cigarette and addressed the anxious woman who stood in front of him with her steno pad in hand.

"Sit down, Grace: I'm going before Congress tomorrow. I'd like to dictate my message. It will be short."

Roosevelt began.

> "Yesterday, December 7th, 1941 - a date which will live in infamy - the United States of America was suddenly and deliberately attacked by naval and air forces of the Empire of Japan.
> The United States was at peace with that nation, and, at the solicitation of Japan, was still in conversation with its government and its Emperor looking toward the maintenance of peace in the Pacific.
> Indeed, one hour after Japanese air squadrons had commenced bombing in the American island of Oahu, the Japanese Ambassador to the United States and his colleague delivered to our Secretary of State a formal reply to a recent American message. And, while this reply stated that it seemed useless to continue the existing diplomatic negotiations, it contained no threat or hint of war or of armed attack.
> It will be recorded that the distance of Hawaii from Japan makes it obvious that the attack was deliberately planned many days or even weeks ago. During the intervening time the Japanese Government has deliberately sought to deceive the United States by false statements and expressions of hope for continued peace.
> The attack yesterday on the Hawaiian Islands has caused severe damage to American naval and military forces. I regret to tell you that very many American lives have been lost. In addition, American ships have been reported torpedoed on the high seas between San Francisco and Honolulu.
> Yesterday the Japanese Government also launched an attack against Malaya.
> Last night Japanese forces attacked Hong Kong.
> Last night Japanese forces attacked Guam.
> Last night Japanese forces attacked the Philippine Islands.
> Last night the Japanese attacked Wake Island.
> And this morning the Japanese attacked Midway Island.
> Japan has therefore undertaken a surprise offensive extending throughout the Pacific area. The facts of yesterday and today speak for themselves. The people of the United States have already formed their opinions and well understand the implications to the very life and safety of our nation.
> As Commander-in-Chief of the Army and Navy I have directed that all measures be taken for our defense, that always will our whole nation remember the character of the onslaught against us.
> No matter how long it may take us to overcome this premeditated invasion, the American people, in their righteous might, will win through to absolute victory.

I believe that I interpret the will of the Congress and of the people when I assert that we will not only defend ourselves to the uttermost but will make it very certain that this form of treachery shall never again endanger us. Hostilities exist. There is no blinking at the fact that our people, our territory and our interests are in grave danger.

With confidence in our armed forces, with the unbounding determination of our people, we will gain the inevitable triumph. So help us God."

Roosevelt had delivered the entire message without hesitation or second thoughts. Only the last sentence, provided by Harry Hopkins, was added to his original text. The message was delivered to Congress the following day. The entire statement took slightly over seven and one-half minutes to read.

Sunday, December 7, 1941
Wolfsschanze (Wolf's Lair),
Führerhauptquartiere,
Forest Gierloz,
Rastenburg, Poland

It was quite an ordinary Sunday afternoon for Adolf Hitler at his headquarters in North Prussia. He was sitting comfortably in his office when an excited aide knocked on his door and entered. Hitler looked up with uncertainty on his face.

"Fuhrer, this has just been received," the assistant offered. He handed the message to his leader. Hitler took the paper and read its contents.

"Thank you. You may go," Hitler remarked evenly.

The officer saluted smartly and departed the room. Hitler put the communiqué down on a nearby desk and stared intently at a large world map along a side wall.

So our Japanese allies decided to attack the Americans on their own without informing me. From the sound of it, they did a pretty good job. Now their weakling American president will really have his hands full. This might turn out to be quite a blessing for us given our present problems in Russia and the new counterattack the Soviets began yesterday.

Since this was a surprise attack, the Americans are undoubtedly unprepared to go to war. It will take the United States years to build up their forces and by then the Japanese might have come out of it victorious. The Japanese Kwangchow Army numbers in the millions and they have been extremely successful in China. That should keep the Americans and their Jewish lackeys busy for years. This is good news for us. We can't lose the war at all. We now have an ally that hasn't been conquered in 3,000 years.

The British will also suffer since their Asian possessions will be threatened. That will be good for our European War, even if it is not succeeding as I want at this time.

I don't know if the Americans will even declare war on Germany because it wouldn't be in their best interests to do so. Our position seems even stronger now than before. But, I must get back to Berlin immediately and confer with our General Staff.

He pushed a button to summon his car. His personal dissatisfaction with the events of yesterday was now replaced by a sense of jubilation brought on by the actions of the Japanese Empire.

Monday December 8, 1941
Prime Minister's Private Study,
10 Downing Street, Westminster,
London, UK

For the past few hours, Winston Churchill had found himself slipping into a dejected state of mind. He had wrestled with the events of the past day and found himself more than blameworthy in his mind. He had played and replayed the facts and still came to the same conclusion. He could have certainly forfended the disaster that America had suffered at Pearl Harbor the previous day or at least lessened the degree of destruction to some end.

The problem stemmed from the fact that Great Britain had broken the Japanese Navy code JN-25 a number of months before. Through its code breakers at Bletchley Park, the British were able to tell much of the plans of the Imperial Navy and its bellicose intentions. But this intelligence data was not shared with the United States and was the source of Winston Churchill's current dilemma.

I fear I have made a terrible error in not sharing what we knew with the Americans. Our data might have prevented the deaths of so many men and the incredible loss of ships by the American navy.

But, I must remain fixed on my primary duty---saving our island from the onslaught of the Huns. I regret I only have met Mr. Roosevelt once and I don't feel our meeting went well. Our people have gotten back to me that he considers me a loudmouth and a drunk. Well, I might even agree with him on the former.

The real problem is that we need America in this war, and this dastardly attack by Japan will undoubtedly lead to that. That is about all I can really be thankful for at this moment. If the Americans had known of Japan's intentions, would they have acted differently? Probably so, but in what manner? That's all open for speculation at this point. I wonder if I will be judged badly in the future for my actions...only time will tell.

Satisfied he had exhausted all the plausible scenarios surrounding the attack, Britain's Prime Minister took a sip of the Graham's Vintage Character Port that he enjoyed immensely. He looked at the bottle with the stripped name of his wine merchant, Hatch, Mansfield and Co.

Nothing like a great port to calm me down a bit. Lucky we can still get these wines; they seem to be something of an indulgence, what with the war and scarcity of so many things.

Churchill settled back in his favorite armchair and continued to peruse the stack of files that had been given him earlier. He suddenly felt better about the whole matter of Pearl Harbor.

Chapter Eight

> "I only need a few thousand dead so that I can sit
> at the peace conference as a man who has fought."
>
> ---*Benito Mussolini*
> *to Italian Chief of Staff Marshal Badoglio*

Thursday, August 6, 1942
Italian 8th Army Headquarters,
Volgograd Oblast, Russia

Major General Giovanni Messe was a career soldier who had once been military secretary to Italian King Vittorio Emmanuele III. He had seen service in practically every Italian war sector and was generally considered by the Italian military as Italy's best general.

His present situation was not to his liking. His 8th Italian Army (also called *Armata Italiana* in Russia or AMIR) had been sent to Russia a month earlier at the behest of Benito Mussolini as a show of solidarity to Adolf Hitler. Some two hundred thousand Italian soldiers were involved in the massive attack that moved toward the Soviet stronghold of Stalingrad.

Messe was outspoken about the conditions and equipment of his troops but continued to follow orders of the German Field Marshal Gerd von Rundstedt, commander of Army Group South. He was weary when the news of a pending visit by Mussolini reached his headquarters.

"So, the Duce is coming to see for himself," he muttered to a group of subordinates. "That will be good for everyone here. He will see that we are in no condition to fight a better equipped army and perhaps he will see to it that we receive better food and some up-to-date equipment."

"I would be careful, General," one of his commanders warned. "Il Duce doesn't like to hear that things aren't going well. I know of a commander in Libya that was replaced because he told Il Duce the truth about how things were going."

"Thank you for your concern, Colonel Lagardi. I can handle myself in these situations. I have been at this for quite some time."

The colonel relented as Messe continued. "If something is not done, and sooner rather than later, we could suffer an incredible defeat here. The Russians are fighting for their homeland and they are good soldiers who are willing to fight under unbearable conditions. Our German friends might have underestimated their tenaciousness and overall ability to fight. We have been lucky so far, but I don't expect it to be that way forever. We have other weak armies around us, the Romanians and the Hungarians, and who knows what will happen to them in an all-out attack?"

The Italian officers remained silent, pondering their leader's words.

Messe was about to speak again when an adjutant came in with the news that Mussolini was at the front door of the headquarters.

"You are dismissed, gentlemen. I will reconvene our meeting after the Duce's visit."

Messe turned and walked to meet the Duce. They met inside the headquarters' main hallway.

"General Messe, good of you to receive me," Mussolini began, offering his hand.

"Always my pleasure, Duce. It is good to have you here with us."

"Where can we meet? The trip was tiring for me."

"Certainly. We can use my quarters. I have a nice ante-room for guests."

"Let's go then. I'll follow you."

The pair reached their destination in about five minutes. It was a large, formal house that had been taken over by the Italians.

Mussolini looked around and shook his head in satisfaction. "Nice, considering we are out in the country. You must be quite comfortable."

"I am indeed fortunate, Duce. My men are another matter."

"Let's sit down. Is there some *grappa* around?"

"I have a nearly filled bottle right over here." The general walked over to a serving cart and extracted a bottle and two glasses. He poured a generous portion of the brandy in each glass and handed one to Mussolini.

Mussolini sniffed the glass and nodded his approval. "Excellent, even on such a hot day, General."

General Messe pointed to a large sofa and Mussolini sat down. Messe took a seat at the other end as Mussolini began. "So, how are you progressing? Are the Russians now ready to give up?"

"Quite the contrary, Duce. These Russians are a hearty lot and seem determined to defend their country to the last man. I have seen few instances of a lack of Russian resolution. Even when we have the upper hand, they fight back for even a small amount of land."

"But they have been pushed back so far, their will to fight must surely be weakened."

"I have seen no such signs, Duce. As I said, their resolution seems to prevail throughout their ranks."

"What about our German allies. Do they still feel the end is near?"

"Duce, the Germans look down on us as inferior forces. They chide us about our lines of supply and will not share even necessary equipment and stores. It is not a pleasant situation."

Mussolini considered Messe's words and eventually spoke again. "I am not happy with the Nazi's attitude toward us, but there is little I can do about it. We need an important victory before the Germans will consider us equals."

"I agree, Duce. But the fact is we are a mop up force behind the German lines. The Romanians and Hungarians are in a similar position and do not seem to be strong fighting forces to me. If anything happened and the Soviets broke through the German lines, I doubt any of us are well enough equipped to stop them. The result could become disastrous."

Again Mussolini thought. "General Messe, I'm afraid you must make do with what you have. Our country is not in a position to do much else. You must make up with creativity whatever you lack in equipment and personnel."

"With all respect, Duce. An army cannot fight without provisions and correct clothing. It is okay right now, at the end of the summer. But once fall and winter set in, it will be much worse. I am not sure we can survive a winter under these conditions."

"As I said, you must make do with what we can provide. I will attempt to have more provisions provided, but our shipping leaves something to be desired. As far as uniforms and clothing, I will inquire as soon as I am back in Rome as to what is being done to provide you with winter clothing."

"Thank you, Duce. Any help will be appreciated."

"And, General, one more thing. No more defeatist talk from you, especially around your men. We need a positive outlook from everyone if we are to emerge victorious. Do you understand?"

"Yes, Duce," Messe replied compliantly. "I'll make sure to do as you wish."

"Good," Mussolini replied, standing up. He finished the grappa and handed the glass back to Messe. "I want to go to our troops and install some spirit in them. The men always seem to enjoy it when I visit them. You know how that is."

"Yes, Duce. They will enjoy your visit."

Mussolini walked to the door and exited the room. Messe followed behind as Mussolini's cadre of staff officers immediately surrounded him. Mussolini turned around and gave Messe a quick grin and waved his hand. He was quickly whisked away as Genera Messe stood in the doorway.

I wonder if he will try to help us. He seemed genuine but he is a politician and not a soldier. I wonder if I went too far in telling him the truth about our situation. Messe continued to watch the progress of the Duce's party as it slowly disappeared in the distance.

Thursday, September 4, 1942
Fr. Rodi's Room,
Gregorian University,
Piazza della Pilotta, 4
Rome, Italy

A soft knock on his door awakened Fr. Michael S. Rodi from a peaceful sleep. He walked to the door and opened it to find another priest, Fr. Bosworth, an American priest who also worked in the Secretariat of State for the Vatican.

"Sorry to wake you, Father, but Father Leiber sent me to fetch you."

"I understand, Edward," he replied using the priest's first name. "It must be something important for him to send you in the first place."

Rodi dressed quickly and the two set out for the nearby Vatican. They went immediately to Father Leiber's office where the German prelate was busy writing a note by hand.

"Sorry to have gotten you out of bed, Michael," Leiber stated. "But it is important as you might have guessed. Father Bosworth, thank you too. Now you can get back to your work."

The other priest departed and Father Leiber motioned for Rodi to take a chair. "Michael, we have a problem with one of our passport couriers who has been arrested by the Italians. I need someone to go to the Regina Coeli and try to get him out. I have a feeling that a Vatican representative will be able to convince the authorities they have the wrong person. I have prepared a letter that the pope has signed to that effect for you to take with you."

"Regina Coeli…Queen of Heaven?" Rodi questioned."

Father Leiber smiled, "Of course, you wouldn't know. Sorry for my mistake, Michael. The Regina Coeli was formerly a convent during the 17th Century. Napoleon's forces occupied it when Rome was under French control and the Carmelite nuns took it over when the French left. The new Kingdom of Italy confiscated the complex and turned it into a prison. The final work wasn't completed until the beginning of this century. It is located right off the river and directly across from the Ponte Mazzini. It is close to the Vatican. You can get into it using the Lungara Street entrance."

"Thanks for the history lesson, Robert. Things like that are good to know."

"The poor person in custody is named Vicente Liuzza, and the details are here in the letter. Read it before you go in so that you are familiar with the facts in the case."

"I'm on my way. I hope the Fascists are impressed with the fact that the Vatican never sleeps."

Leiber smiled again as Father Rodi left the room. He was confident that his American protégé could handle the matter.

93

Regina Coeli Prison
Via della Lungara, 29,
Rome, Italy

It was nearly three o'clock in the morning as Father Michael S. Rodi made his way through the unguarded entrance of the Regina Coeli Prison. The place was in good shape and, with the exception of the crisscrossed iron bars in the windows, bore little resemblance to a prison.

Rodi entered the building and was met by a sleepy *sergente* (sergeant) who looked up and observed the priestly robes of his visitor.

"What is it you want, Father?" the man questioned.

"I want to see someone in charge," Rodi answered briskly. "And I want to see him right now. A gross injustice had been done and must be sorted out."

"The *capitano* is sleeping and I don't want to disturb him," was the reply. "He doesn't like being disturbed when he is sleeping."

"I am here at the direction of the pope," Rodi increased his volume and waived the paper in front of the man. Do you want to keep the pope waiting?"

The mention of the pope sent a shiver over the non-commissioned officer's face. He looked at the priest and the waving piece of paper in his hand. He decided it was better to awaken his captain than suffer the wrath of God.

"I'll go and get him. Wait here."

Rodi smiled and let out a sigh of relief. He had hoped his ruse would work and was pleased his mission was going as planned.

After a few minutes, the *sergente* returned immediately followed by a *capitano* who was still buttoning his tunic. The captain looked at him and frowned. "So you are the pope?" he said icily.

"Only the pope's emissary," Rodi returned. "An injustice has been done and the Holy Father wants its rectified at once. I know you understand." He handed the letter to the officer and stepped back a bit.
The *capitano* took the sheet of paper and began reading. He finished the letter and flushed. He turned to the *sergente* and ordered, "*Sergente* Boasberggio, go and get the prisoner named Vicente Liuzza. It seems we have made a grave error." The

94

sergeant looked hopelessly at the officer and left the area.

An embarrassing silence ensued as both Rodi and the *capitano* looked awkwardly at each other.

Five minutes later, the *sergente* returned with a disheveled man in his mid-fifties in tow. He handed over some papers to the captain.

"Please sign here, Father Rodi," the captain said evenly.

"Of course. I am happy to do so." Rodi quickly signed the form and patted Signore Liuzza on the shoulder.

"We regret the error, *signore*," the *capitano* professed. "It won't happen again."

Rodi glanced at the Italian officer and turned to leave. He grabbed Liuzza's arm and escorted him out of the prison.

Out on the street, the pair walked almost a block before Liuzza stopped and asked, "What did you say to get me released?"

"It was what the pope said that counted," replied Rodi. "He sent a note to the authorities that you were a cousin of his on a mission of honor for your family. He asked the Fascists to please ignore the circumstances of your arrest since it would involve making your mission public and would be an embarrassment to his family."

Liuzza's face lit up when he heard Rodi's explanation. "*Il papa* did not tell untruths in the paper, my dear Father. We are all members of his family. Even though I acted foolishly, I am glad the Lord in heaven saw fit to rescue me."

Rodi peered at the figure, not fully understanding. He took the man's outstretched hand, shook it once and left. If he hurried, he could still grab a few hours' sleep before his daily routine began in earnest.

Wednesday, November 18, 1942
Headquarters, German Sixth Army,
Southern Russia,
Russian Soviet Federative Socialist Republic, Russia

At 52, General Friedrich Paulus knew he was in *the* battle of his long military career.

The fact that Adolf Hitler had changed his original orders that called for seizing the oilfields of the Caucasus, to capturing the namesake city of his hated rival Stalin, was difficult for Paulus. But the Panzer expert and commander of the Sixth Army had followed his Fuhrer's orders and was now embroiled in a bitter fight with the Red Army. Heavy support by the Luftwaffe had allowed the Wehrmacht to push their foes into narrow zones along the west bank of the Volga River. The seemingly productive effort had come at a great cost, both in men and equipment.

Paulus realized he was in a difficult position. His supplies were running low and the Luftwaffe was becoming less dependable as it encountered heavy losses of its own.

He pondered his choices as he lay in a tent that served as his headquarters. *The Russians are up to something. The last few days they have offered only token resistance and that worries me. Either they are depleted and about to give up on the city or they have withdrawn most of their soldiers and are about to mount a counterattack. If they do attack, where they attack will be critical. Our Italian and Romanian allies fight hard but their equipment is outdated. Same for the Hungarians. I doubt any of them could stop a large counteroffensive. If that happens, we could easily find ourselves surrounded and outnumbered.*

I pray that the Soviet commanders are not fully aware of our weaknesses. I must radio Berlin again for more fuel and ammunition. They simply must make us a priority or we will be in even more trouble. Some of my Panzers are idle as they await fuel and that makes them merely defensive weapons. I just hope I'm not too late on this.

He called for his orderly and gave the necessary instructions and lay back for a few hours rest. It was not a peaceful sleep.

Tuesday, January 19, 1943
Villa Number Two,
Anfa Hotel,
Casablanca, French Morocco

The secretive meeting between President Franklin D. Roosevelt and British Prime Minister Winston Churchill was supposed to include Russian leader Joseph Stalin but Stalin had declined due to the military complications that enveloped his country. Free France was represented by Generals Charles de Gaulle and Henri-Honoré Giraud. De Gaulle had initially declined the invitation but quickly reconsidered when informed by Churchill he would withdraw his support for de Gaulle and his French government that was operating from Great Britain if de Gaulle did not attend.

There was no announcement in the press of any of the three countries. No sitting American president had ever been to Africa nor had any U.S. President ever left the country during a time of war.

Due to the importance of the conference, both Roosevelt and Churchill approached the meeting as old friends.

It was the fifth day of the conference and a great deal had already been accomplished. A number of strategic military objectives had been agreed upon, including the destruction of the German U-boat patrols in the Atlantic Ocean and the launching of combined bombing missions against German and Italian forces. It was also decided that the Allies would initially invade Sicily rather than another part of Europe.

The palm trees swayed in a meaningful breeze around the villa as the participants and their staffs took their places at a long table. The topic for discussion on this fine January morning was the eventual surrender of Germany.

"I believe it is important that we agree on the wording of any statement regarding surrender by the enemy," Churchill stated. "We must get the message across to this monster that we are totally united in our resolve."

"I couldn't agree with you more, Mr. Churchill," Roosevelt followed. "In fact, I have thought about this for the past few days. I recall a scenario from our own Civil War. Brigadier General Ulysses S. Grant sent a note to the Confederate commanders of Fort Donaldson and Fort Henry in Tennessee and used the phrase, 'unconditional surrender' in his message. That phrase has stuck with me for all these years. I feel that language would be totally appropriate in this case."

"Well said, Mr. Roosevelt," Churchill agreed. "It makes the perfect point." Both French leaders nodded their agreement to the precise language.

"We should also make clear that the policy of unconditional surrender does not entail the destruction of the populations of the Axis powers, but rather the destruction of the philosophies in those countries which are based on conquest and the subjugation of other people," Roosevelt continued.

"Rightly so," Churchill added.

"But, of course," de Gaulle commented in a thick French accent.

Sunday, January 31, 1943
Offices of the Fuhrer,
Wilhelmstraße 77,
Berlin-Mitte, Germany

It was apparent to everyone around the Fuhrer that the Nazi leader's nerves were frayed. When news was received that was negative Hitler would respond with wild outbursts and rants that would continue for several minutes.

Such was the case with the urgent communique from the Sixth Army that had just reached Hitler's headquarters. It stated bluntly that the Commander of the Sixth Army, General Friedrich Paulus, along with his general staff, had just surrendered to elements of the Red Army.

The surrender followed a series of radio broadcasts between the general and Berlin where he had repeatedly asked permission to surrender his army, "in order to save the lives of remaining troops." Hitler had unequivocally replied, "Surrender is forbidden. Sixth Army will hold their position to the last man and the last round and by their heroic endurance will make an unforgettable contribution toward the establishment of a defensive front and the salvation of the Western World."

Hitler had promoted Paulus to field marshal the same day, knowing that no German field marshal had ever been captured alive. He fully expected the beleaguered 6th Army commander to commit suicide to protect the honor of his rank.

The surrender cast a pall over the entire offices of the Fuhrer. Hitler went into a private room and emerged some time later. He was still ranting, almost shouting. "How can one be so cowardly? I don't understand it…What is life? Life is the Nation. The individual must die anyway. Beyond the life of the individual is the life of the Nation… So many people have had to die, and then a man like that besmirches the heroism of so many others at the last minute. He could have freed himself from all sorrow and ascended into eternity and national immortality, but he prefers to go to Moscow!"

No one dared approach the leader of Germany. Hitler's secretary, Christa Schroeder, immediately sent for Hitler's personal physician, Dr. Theodor Morell.

Thirty minutes later, the figure of Dr. Morell emerged from the hall outside Hitler's offices. Of average height, Morell wore heavy rimmed glasses and was profoundly overweight. His white Nazi uniform with accompanying gold braid reminded Hitler's staff of that of Reichsmarschall Herman Goring. For his part, Goring confided to friends that he thought Morell was reminiscent of a ringmaster at the circus and the Reichsführer shunned the physician's company.

"Go right in, the Fuhrer's waiting," informed Schroeder. "I hope you can calm him down."

"Yes, yes. I'll certainly do that," the doctor quipped. He entered the room that served as Hitler's private office.

"Good afternoon, my Fuhrer," Morell gushed, throwing a Nazi salute at his leader. "I understand you are not feeling well today."

"It's the constant bad news that I receive, Doctor. It would make anyone sick."

Morell took Hitler's hand and felt his pulse. After a few moments he shook his head and pronounced, "This is no good. Your pulse is abnormal."

Hitler looked at the doctor and shouted, "I already know that, you fool. Give me something to calm me down."

Morell selected a combination of morphia and hypnotics and administered the drugs to Hitler. After a few minutes, Hitler turned and said, "Your magic has worked again. I feel more relaxed already."

"That is good, my Fuhrer. I am always available to you."

"We have had some really bad news, Herr Doctor."

"Yes, Fuhrer?"

"Our 6th Army has surrendered at Stalingrad. They had been ordered to fight to the last man."

Dr. Morell was unable to speak.

"Germany has its heroes and its villains. General Paulus is no hero. I shouldn't have made him a field marshal. I will not make that mistake again and my generals should take notice."

Again Morell remained silent.

"You may go, Herr Doctor. I am well again."

The corpulent physician quickly zipped his bag shut and departed the office. This time he neglected to give the Nazi salute.

Chapter Nine

"In a manner never known before, the Pope has repudiated
the National Socialist New European Order...
Here he is virtually accusing the German people of injustice towards the
Jews and makes himself the mouthpiece of the Jewish war criminals"

— *Reich Security Main Office,*
following Pius XII's 1942 Christmas Address

Friday, February 5, 1943
Mussolini's Offices,
Palazzo della Farnesina,
Via della Lungara,
Rome, Italy

It was a day that Benito Mussolini knew was coming. His son-in-law, Count Galeazzo Ciano had become too much of an embarrassment to him and his government. Ciano's outspoken efforts toward seeking peace with the enemies of Italy had finally prompted this move on the part of the Duce. Mussolini had endured such goings-on since France had fallen to the Germans, but now it was time to take action.

He summoned Ciano to his offices and offered him a seat.

"What are you going to do now?" Mussolini started, seemingly uncomfortable with his question. "I'm sure you have some inkling of what I'm talking about. I am going to have to change my entire cabinet. You must resign as foreign minister."

"I understand, Duce, and I share the reasons for your decisions. I do not intend to raise the least objection to whatever you propose."

Mussolini paused, concentrating on his words. "In my opinion, you have several options. First, there is the governorship of Albania. You always enjoyed the place."

"No, Duce. That won't work. I would be going as an executioner and hangman of those people to whom I promised brotherhood and equality. It would make me sick."

"Then, there is also the Ambassador to the Holy See. You have good connections at the Vatican and might be able to help our country in that role."

Ciano thought for a while and responded. "That might be all right. The Vatican is a place of rest and could easily open up possibilities for the future. What happens to me is in the hands of God, and the ways which Providence chooses are at times mysterious. I will take the Vatican post."

Mussolini studied the younger man before he spoke. Satisfied his son-in-law's answer was sincere, he spoke again. "So it shall be, Galeazzo. I am sorry it has come to this."

Ciano chose not to answer and walked to the door. He shook his head affirmatively as he departed Il Duce's office.

Monday, February 8, 1943
Private offices of the pope,
The Vatican,
Rome, Italy

When Father Michael S. Rodi had learned that his foray into the Italian prison was but a test to see just how he handled himself, he was slightly taken aback by the news. Father Robert Leiber informed him shortly after the undertaking that the man he freed was actually a member of the Italian underground that had gotten drunk and found himself in jail. The underground had contacted the Vatican to see if it could help in the matter.

Leiber chose Rodi to get the man out of prison to give his protégée some experience in dealing with the Italian police. If Rodi passed the test successfully Father Leiber had more important things in mind for the young American priest.

"The Roman underground is not well organized," Leiber informed. "They will ask our help a great number of times in the future. They have limited resources and we must be ready to help whenever we can."

"I wasn't aware of any local resistance, Robert. I'm not sure what they are doing."

"There isn't a great deal they can do right now, Michael. But, if and when the Germans decide to occupy Rome, they could play an important role in what happens around here. They can take up arms while the Vatican's hands are tied. We have only the Swiss Guards who carry arms, and there aren't very many of them to guard our city."

"I will help in any way you see fit, Robert."

"Things are beginning to sort out in Italy. Ciano is now the ambassador to the Vatican and that means the cabinet is being shaken up. More changes are in the offing, and I'm not sure they will all be positive," Leiber opined. "You will be called on whenever necessary. I believe it might become a game of cat and mouse for us. The Germans are far from stupid, and we must be even smarter in the actions we take. Many people will be affected by our decisions."

Rodi pondered his benefactor's words and realized the possible far reaching effects of the Vatican's dealings. He also realized he would be a part of anything important that occurred in the future.

Saturday, July 24, 1943
Grand Council Chamber,
Palazzo Venezia,
Rome, Italy

Located in Central Rome, just north of the Capitoline Hill, is the 17-century-old Palazzo di Venezia, the former papal residence that now houses the seat of the Italian Government. The plain medieval structure is also the home of Italy's Grand Council, the legally constituted governing body of the country. Its six-story external tower juts prominently into Central Rome's relatively flat environment.

All 28 members of the Grand Council were in attendance, nattily attired in the black Fascist uniforms of their party. Mussolini entered the building keenly aware of the fact that his government was in trouble. Included among the council members was Count Galeazzo Ciano, the country's former foreign minister.

Il Duce correctly perceived a hostile environment. Few of his ministers looked him directly in the eye and a small number of his detractors seemed to utter soft denunciations.

I must be straightforward and not show any weakness. I have survived for many years and this is just another bump in the road. I have appointed most of these men here and they owe me their existence. Our country is in mortal danger right now and I am the only one who can save her. I am prepared for all this, but I am sure Grandi and his henchmen have also organized.

He took his normal seat and nodded to Carlo Scorza, the Secretary of the Fascist Party, to start the roll call. Then, with all members noted as present, he began his lengthy discourse in defense of his actions.

"The war has come to an extremely critical phase. The invasion of the national territory, which everyone thought was quite out of the question, even after the United States had broken into the Mediterranean, has actually come to pass. The peripheral war on the African coast served the purpose of making impossible the invasion of the country. In a situation like the present, all open and hidden opposition to the Facist regime is leagued against us and there has already been considerable demoralization even in the Fascist ranks, particularly among those who have a vested interest in the present setup and are afraid that their personal position is in danger. At this moment I am easily the most disliked and, in fact, the most hated man in Italy."

Mussolini rambled for the next thirty minutes and eventually ended. A period of discussion followed with council members speaking for and against some of Il Duce's points.

When Dino Grandi took the floor, Mussolini's fate began to wobble. Grandi criticized the activities of the Fascist Party and in particular its leadership. He called for the King of Italy to step forward and assume his responsibilities. His rhetoric produced a desired feeling of uneasiness among the council members. Even Count Ciano spoke, and ended by declaring himself in agreement with Grandi's position.

Mussolini remained silent, suddenly realizing his dire situation. Next, Grandi made a resolution that called for a vote. Minister Scorza immediately called for the vote.

When it was concluded, nineteen (including Count Ciano) had voted for it and seven against it. Minister Suardo abstained and Minister Farinacci voted for a resolution that he himself had authored.

Mussolini rose and pronounced, "You have brought the regime into crisis. The meeting is adjourned." It was now 2:40 a.m. Scorza attempted to give the signal for the ritual 'Salute to the Duce,' but Mussolini stopped him. "No, I excuse you from that!"

The ministers filed out of the council room in silence.

The day following the Grand Council vote, Benito Mussolini, leader of Italy, arrived at the Villa Ada for his normal 20-minute meeting with Italy's king. On previous visits, he normally updated Victor Emmanuel III on the current state of affairs.

This late afternoon was different, and Mussolini arrived unshaven and in a state of grogginess. He followed the monarch into the drawing room where the king, in his marshal uniform, began speaking.

My dear Duce," he started in an nervous tone, "it can't go on any longer. Italy is in pieces. Army morale has reached the bottom and the soldiers don't want to fight any longer. The Alpine regiments have a song saying that they are through fighting Mussolini's war…"

The King then recited in Piedmontese dialect, several verses of the song.

Finishing, he continued again. "The result of the votes cast by the Grand Council is devastating. Nineteen votes in favor of Grandi's resolution and four of them cast by holders of the *Collare dell'Annuziata* (Italy's highest decoration). Surely you have no illusions as to how Italians feel about you at this moment. You are the most hated man in Italy; you have not a single friend left, except for me. You need not worry about your personal security. I shall see to that. I have decided the man of the hour is Marshal Badoglio. He will form a cabinet of career officials in order to rule the country and go on with the war. Six months from now we shall see. All Rome knows what went on at the Grand Council meeting and everyone expects drastic changes to be made."

"You are making an extremely grave decision," Mussolini shot back. "If you provoke a crisis at a time like this the people will believe that, since you are eliminating the man who declared war, then peace must be at hand. You will strike a serious blow to the morale of the Army. The crisis will be claimed as a personal triumph by both Churchill and Stalin, especially the latter, whose antagonist I have been for the past twenty years. I am perfectly aware that the people hate me. I admitted as much last night before the Grand Council. No one can govern for so long and impose so many sacrifices without incurring bitter resentment. Be that as it may, I wish good luck to my successor."

Mussolini signaled to his private secretary, Nicolò De Cesare, to leave. They made their way to the doors of the villa where a group of Carabineri was standing. He approached the group.

"I place you under arrest Benito Mussolini," the group's leader declared. "His Majesty has charged me with your personal security."

Mussolini made no protest and started toward his waiting car. "No," the Carabinieri officer pointed to an ambulance parked nearby. "You must get into this." Mussolini answered meekly, "As you wish." He and De Cesare entered the vehicle along with a number of armed Carabinieri policemen.

Three days later, Mussolini was taken aboard the Italian Corvette *Persefone* to the Island of Ponza, the largest of the Pontine Islands off Italy's western coast in the Tyrrhenian Sea. He later was moved to La Maddalena on Northern Sardinia and finally onto the 6000-foot high Campo Imperatore Hotel on the Gran Sasso Mountain in Central Italy's Abruzzo Region.

Wednesday, August 11, 1943
Private offices of the pope
The Vatican offices
Rome, Italy

Pope Pius XII was involved in a serious discussion with Cardinal Secretary of State Luigi Maglione and his principal advisor, Father Robert Leiber, S.J. The pope was disturbed about a Curia meeting the week before that pointed out the fact that German threats against the Vatican had been growing for the past few years.

"The Italian government fears there will be an invasion of the Vatican now that Mussolini has been overthrown," Maglione spoke flatly. "I believe this is all quite possible. The entire country is in madness right now and there's no telling what will happen. I fear for your safety, Holiness."

Pius pondered the statement and replied. "I must agree the danger is real, Eminence. We must begin to prepare for such an eventuality. Father Leiber agrees that we must take some action, and sooner than later." Leiber nodded his agreement.

"I want you to oversee a special project," the pope ordered. "I want a special floor built here in the Vatican where we can safeguard all my personal letters and records. When it is completed, place everything you feel important there and we will all sleep much better."

"I will start immediately, Holiness. I know just the place. No one would ever suspect this location."

"Tell as few people about it as possible and only use our most trusted workers," warned Leiber. "If the wrong persons get wind of this, we could easily be compromised."

"Yes, Father. I understand how important this is."

"And, Eminence. One more thing, "the pope declared. I want you to immediately draw up a plan in case I am abducted or killed. I want you to call a meeting of cardinals to choose a successor and insure our Holy Church will have the leadership it deserves."

Maglione's head dropped but he quickly nodded his agreement. "It will be done in a matter of days, Holiness."

"Good. Then leave me with Father Leiber to discuss some personal matters."

"Of course, Holiness."

The cardinal departed and Leiber moved closer to Pius XII.

"It is my hope that the cardinals will select Maglione as my successor. He is the only person that knows enough to deal with the Germans. He had done a good job as Secretary of State."

"I agree, Holiness. Bringing in someone new in such a crisis wouldn't bode well for either the Vatican or the Holy Church."

"I intend to have some private meetings with some of the cardinals to let them know of my position," the pope continued. If there were any real problems, I would be able to see them before they convene."

"Yes, Holiness. That sounds like a smart idea to me."

"I am glad, Robert. You don't always agree with my positions."

"This time I agree fully, Holiness. I can assure you of that."

"Now Robert, there are a few things I want to go over with you..."

Thursday, September 9, 1943
South of the Pyramid along the Via Ostiense,
Rome, Italy

Carla Capponi was twenty-four, unmarried and a recent inductee into the Italian Communist Party (PCI). On this morning, she had joined other Italian patriots in a futile effort to keep the German Army from entering the Eternal City. Various elements of the Italian Army, without direct orders and with little actual leadership, had taken stands at certain key junctions of Rome and were providing stiff resistance to the advancing units of the Wehrmacht.

The attractive, green-eyed young woman was determined to do her part in keeping the German army from occupying her beloved city. The fighting was intense along the Ostian Way. To her surprise, the Italian units seemed to have the upper hand. Carla and other women in the group of partisans were ordered to care for the wounded and dead. It was immediately apparent that the number of dead was growing with each passing hour.

The sound of nearby machine gun fire caused Carla to look up. Within seconds, another wounded man was brought to the makeshift aid station that had been hastily set up. As the man was turned over, Carla was surprised to see the collar of a priest on the wounded man. A heavy stream of blood was flowing from his chest and the man was breathing with great labor.

Carla applied some cloths to the affected area that caused the wound to bleed less profusely, but it was soon apparent that the person was near death.

She leaned close to his mouth as the man attempted to speak.

"Tell the Vatican that I was shot," he whispered weakly. "I am in God's hands..."

He gasped a short breath and was gone. Carla made the sign of the cross over him and covered his face. She reached into his coat and removed his identification. She placed the document inside her blouse and vowed to give it to the authorities--- provided she survived her present predicament.

She returned to her duties as additional Italian soldiers appeared to reinforce the bedraggled defenders of the City of Rome.

Friday, September 10, 1943
Offices of the Secretary of State,
The Vatican,
Rome, Italy

Father Michael S. Rodi, S.J., had taken to heart the news of the young priest's death the day before. The priest, a German Jesuit named Wolfgang Saux, was one of his assistants in the ongoing task of supplying Rome's churches and convents with food and supplies. Saux was also the person that helped Rodi with his German whenever the circumstances permitted. The two had grown close during the past months. *My friend's death makes all this personal*, he pondered. *Wolfgang just happened to be in the wrong place at the wrong time. How many others will be caught up in this madness? I must be careful to watch where I go when I leave the Vatican. It would be foolish to get caught in a similar situation when our work is so important to so many unfortunate people.*

⁓

Friday September 10, 1943
Offices of the General Secretary of the Central Committee,
Communist Party of the Soviet Union,
The Kremlin,
Moscow, Russia

Joseph Stalin was extremely pleased with the successes of Russian forces against the German Wehrmacht in the war termed by his country as "The Great Patriotic War." He had summoned Vyacheslav Mikhailovich Molotov, the Soviet Union's Foreign Minister, to his offices to discuss the current situation that existed in Italy.

Russian intelligence sources had accurately informed Stalin of the Italian Communist Party's progress and Stalin saw an opportunity to further inflict damage on German forces active in Italy. He was particularly interested in Rome and its environs.

"Come in," Stalin beckoned to Molotov. "Have some good vodka with me."

Molotov acknowledged the gesture and poured himself a heavy shot from a bottle on a nearby table. "What no *Kizlyarka?*" He took a sip and pronounced the liquid, "Excellent. As good as I have had."

Stalin smiled and took a seat on a small sofa. Molotov followed and sat in a covered chair to Stalin's right. Not one to linger, the Soviet leader got right to the point.

"I see an opportunity for us in Italy, Vyacheslav Mikhailovich. Our reports suggest a certain laxness on the part of the Italian people. Their resistance efforts so far are nothing to speak of and the Italians generally seem satisfied with the status quo. We need something to get Italians started, to ignite their fire, in a manner of speaking."

Molotov smiled at his leader's choice of words and replied. "That might not be too difficult. The ICP has a number of loyal followers. I'll look into it."

"Nothing should be too difficult for the person who was the hero of the Winter War and who has a homemade bomb named after him."

Molotov smiled again. "Who would have thought such a simple invention would receive so much attention. I am humbled by it all."

"Just thank heaven that you thought of it and not the Finns," Stalin shot back. He raised his glass toward Molotov and finished the vodka. He rose and returned to his desk where paperwork was piled high in several stacks.

Saturday, September 11, 1943
Hitler's planning room
Berghof,
Berchtesgaden, Germany

SS-Standartenführer (Colonel) Otto Skorzeny stood in front of the Fuhrer and reported that all was ready for the Gran Sasso raid. German intelligence had finally pinpointed Mussolini's location after the dictator's arrest almost two months earlier in Rome. The Duce's captors had moved him from place to place to frustrate any attempts at rescue.

Skorzeny addressed Hitler in an authoritative tone. "Mussolini is definitely at the Campo Imperatore Hotel at the top of Gran Sasso massif. It is a ski resort that is highly favored during the winter. It is only accessible by cable car and that makes his captors think he is safe. Major Mors and General Student have planned an airborne assault by paratroopers that should take everyone by surprise. We will use our DFS 230 Gliders that are completely silent in their approach. Our informants tell us Mussolini is guarded by a couple hundred Carabinieri guards, but I don't expect them to give us much trouble. The element of surprise will be our greatest weapon."

Hitler thought for a moment and replied. "Good, Skorzeny. You will accompany the commandos. I will hold you personally responsible if anything happens to the Duce."

"I understand, Fuhrer. He will come to no harm. You have my personal guarantee."

"You will fly him to Rome and then on to Vienna. I want him to set up a new government in Northern Italy and take back control of the Italian military. You stay with him every step of the way. It is vitally important to the Third Reich that this mission succeeds."

110

"I understand the importance, Fuhrer. You have my word."

"Get on with your duties, Skorzeny. You are dismissed."

Skorzeny executed a Nazi salute and departed the room. Hitler permitted himself a brief smile as the dedicated officer left the room.

Monday, September 13, 1943
Hitler's conference room,
Wolfsschanze (Wolf's Lair),
Rastenburg, East Prussia
Germany

Adolf Hitler was still visibly upset when he summoned SS-Obergruppenführer Karl Wolff to his operations room at the Wolfsschanze. Wolff was a top SS officer and the ideal personification of what an SS officer should be. Blonde, a bit over six feet tall and possessed of incredibly blue eyes, Wolff had become a confidant of Hitler over the past few years. He had been appointed liaison officer between Hitler and the SS in 1939 and that opportunity had presented the Darmstadt-born Catholic-schooled officer rare access to Hitler himself.

Wolff frequently ate breakfast with the Fuhrer after the two had walked along the rock-strewn paths of the glistening forest of fir trees that concealed the Fuhrer's bunker from view. During these sessions, Wolff was able to offer his leader frank points of view without ever challenging Hitler's authority, a rarity among Hitler's top officers.

SS-Obergruppenführer Wolff was just recovering from a bout with a gallstone and had just returned to active duty. The sight of his friend settled Hitler who welcomed Wolff warmly. He congratulated the general on his new posting in Italy and railed against the King of Italy and the pope. Finally, he managed to get to the point. The two were next to a long table that stretched across the room that was completely void of chairs. Both Field Marshal Alfred Jodl and General Field Marshal Wilhelm Keitel were in attendance.

"I have a special mission for you, Wolff," Hitler began. "It will be your duty not to discuss it with anyone before I give you permission to do so. Only the Reichsführer (Heinrich Himmler) knows about it. Do you understand?"

"Of course, my Fuhrer…"

"I want you and your troops to occupy Vatican City as soon as possible, secure its files and art treasures, and take the pope and the Curia to the north. I do not want him to fall into the hands of the Allies or to be under their political pressure and influence. The Vatican is already a nest of spies and a center of anti-National Socialist propaganda.

I shall arrange for the pope to be brought either to Germany or neutral Liechtenstein, depending on political and military developments. When is the soonest you think you'll be able to fulfill this mission?"

Stunned by Hitler's order, Wolff managed a weak reply. "Fuhrer, I am sure that such a mission would take time to organize. I cannot give you a firm timetable right now. I think I must transfer additional SS units as well as some police to Italy that would include some units from the southern Tyrol.

There is also the need for translators in both Greek and Latin to go over the files we will discover. The artwork is another matter."

He paused, and then continued. "The earliest I can see this coming together would be in four to six weeks."

Hitler looked directly at Wolff and barked, "That's too long for me. This must take place while we still have control of Rome. Rush the most important preparations and report developments to me approximately every two weeks. You may go now."

Wolff departed, his mind churning with possibilities.

Abduct the pope? This is sheer madness.

Something like that could turn all of Italy against us, not to mention the whole of Catholicism…I'm not even catholic and I think it's a bad idea…I must find a way out of all this…Pius XII is a powerful man, one that it is said can capture a person's soul… The Fuhrer seems intent on going through with this, no matter what… If I could do something to impair this irresponsible plan, maybe the pope would be grateful…

Meanwhile, Adolf Hitler thought of a touch that would immediately sweeten the pot for the troubled SS officer.

"Have Wolff promoted to *Hochster SS* (Highest SS) and *Polizeifuhrer* (Police Leader)," he ordered. "That will place him just under Himmler in the SS. He is just the person to rein in Mussolini. The Duce will undoubtedly seek more independence from our National Socialism policies unless he is impeded."

Chapter Ten

"Go ahead, calumniate! Some mud will
always stick where you have slung it!"

*— Attributed to the Jesuits
during the smear Mussolini campaign in Italy*

Saturday, September 25, 1943
Private offices of the pope
The Vatican,
Rome, Italy

Pope Pius XII had summoned his cardinal secretary of state the day after the news confirming that the establishment of the Italian Social Republic was reported in most of Italy's daily newspapers and Italian radio.

Cardinal Luigi Maglione had hurried to the pope's private offices. When he arrived, he found Monsignori Giovanni Battista Montini and Secretary of the Roman Curia Domenico Tardini already present. Moments after his arrival, Father Robert Leiber also arrived at the behest of the pope.

"We're sure everyone has heard the news," Pius began. "Mussolini is back in Italy and a new government has been set up in Salò."

"Salò?" questioned Tardini. "I heard about the government but I have no idea where Salò is located."

"I am told it is a small town on Lake Garda, near Brescia," the pope replied.

"At least the scenery will be pretty," Montini offered.

"Yes," Pius agreed. "I believe so."

"Why there, Holiness?"

"The fascists control most of the area around Lake Garda," Leiber inserted. "The Duce certainly couldn't come near Rome. He would immediately be rearrested and I don't believe he would escape this time around."

"How does that affect us, Holiness?" Maglione asked.

"We don't believe it does," the pope answered. "We in Rome are now occupied by the Germans who are also guarding Mussolini in his new location. The Bosch wouldn't bring Mussolini back here and infuriate the people who threw him out. We would be foolish to recognize the ISR and I doubt that many countries beyond the power of the Axis alliance will either. The ISR can't be much of a factor and, at this point, Herr Hitler has his hands full elsewhere. He won't be able to devote much time or attention to Mussolini.

And, there is also the question of the Italian surrender to the allies. The rumor is that Badoglio wants to declare war on Germany right away. That would lead to an interesting turn of events. "

"Will the Germans occupy The Vatican now that they are here?" Monsignori Montini questioned.

"Not unless we do something to provoke them," Pius responded. "And, we don't intend doing that unless we are put into a corner and have no other choice."

"The Nazi's haven't caught on to our supply missions as of yet," informed Father Leiber. "We are moving supplies each day to the churches and seminaries which have taken in the Jews around the city. As long as the trucks have the Vatican name and emblem on their sides, they are given free passage. The number of Jews persecuted grows each day and our supplies are some of the churches' only means of survival."

"I believe we have taken in more than three thousand so far," Cardinal Maglione informed.

"I bet the number is even higher," Tardini inserted. "We even have more than two hundred young Jews that have been added to the Swiss Guards."

"Yes," the pope replied. "We can almost double the guard in the most conspicuous places. It should have a steadying influence on our German friends."

"There's a bit of irony, having Jews and Nazis standing next to each other at the entrances to the Vatican," Leiber smiled. "That white circle around us never felt so comfortable."

"Yes," Cardinal Maglione agreed. "But I must admit I am a bit uneasy when I leave the Vatican."

"You will not be harmed in a Vatican vehicle, Eminence. I can assure you of that," Pius added forcefully. "I have the assurance of the man who will soon become the German Commander in Rome, General von Stahel. He is Catholic and respects the church and its leaders."

Cardinal Maglione greeted the pontiff's news with a sigh of relief. He returned his attention to the pope's stacked desk and additional items that were to be discussed.

Sunday, September 26, 1943
Offices of the SS, Villa Wolkonsky,
Via Ludovico di Savoia,
Rome, Italy

The stately, multi-storied and politico-enhanced building that was the home of the German diplomatic mission was named after the Russian princess that had lived on the site during the 1830's. Villa Wolkonsky also housed some offices of the Nazi SS.

Two Jewish residents sat in front of SS Obersturmbannfuhrer Herbert Kappler, chief of security for the SS, with their eyes firmly fixed on the thirty-six-year-old. The Jewish representatives were Ugo Foà, the leader of the Roman community and Dante Almansi who represented the national Jewish union.

Kappler had developed a plan that he thought might offset the eventual Nazi intention of arresting and deporting the city's Jewish population.

After a cordial reception, Kappler suddenly became much more forceful.

"You and your coreligionists are Italian nationals, but that is of little importance to me," he intoned. "We Germans regard you only as Jews, and thus our enemy. And we will treat you as such. But it is not your lives and the lives of your children that we will take---if you fulfill our demands. Within thirty-six hours you will have to pay fifty kilograms of gold. If you pay, no harm will come to you. In any other event, 200 of your Jews will be taken and deported to Germany, where they will be sent to the Russian frontier, or otherwise rendered innocuous."

"That seems like a lot of gold," Foà remarked in a low voice. "We are not rich people in the ghetto." Kappler did not move or answer.

They rose to leave and Kappler added a final insult. "Mind you, I have already carried out several operations of this type and they have always ended well. Only once did I fail, but that time a few hundred of your brothers paid with their lives."

The two Jews swallowed hard, but said nothing. They quickly left the office to return to their homes in the ghetto. As they walked along the way, the men talked. They were both outraged with the ultimatum the Gestapo chief had demanded. But as they continued to move their minds quickly considered the choices they had in the matter.

"The offer is really not so bad," Foà eventually spoke. I just said that to see what the pig would say. I have done some gold trading and I believe that 50 kilograms of gold amounts to about $55,000 dollars in value. Given we have some 12,000 Jews to consider, that sum is only about $5.00 per Jew. Not at all unreasonable."

"Quite reasonable, Ugo, under the circumstances."

"Yes. But the problem is getting the gold they desire. Most of the affluent Jews I know have already gone into hiding and are unreachable. What are left are mostly old people who have little to give. I'm not entirely sure we can raise the full amount."

"I might be able to go to another source," Almansi offered after a brief pause.

"And just who would that be?"

"The Vatican. I have good contacts there and they have plenty of gold. 50 kilograms would be nothing to them."

Foà thought for a moment. "If we must, it would be most unique in our people's history. Our people will give what they can, and God will provide for us for the remainder. We must keep our faith."

Almansi nodded and they continued walking. Even if the circumstances were dire, there was now a ray of optimism for the ghetto Jews of Rome. It was a faint, glimmering hint of hope with a golden hue.

Monday, September 27, 1943
German Military Headquarters,
Fasano, Italy

Two weeks has passed and SS Obergruppenführer Karl Wolff reminded himself of Adolf Hitler's order to prepare a plan to occupy Vatican City and kidnap Pope Pius XII. Even though his opposition to the plan increased daily, Wolff dutifully set in motion the first aspects of the ludicrous order. Prior to reaching his new headquarters in Fasano, he stopped in Rome and met with the German Ambassador to Italy, Rudolph Rahn. The paunchy, thick-browed career diplomat was repulsed at the idea but finally agreed with Wolff that he would take the matter under consideration.

Wolff had decided that if he were forced to invade the Vatican, the move would be conducted on a high-level military basis with great precision.

To that end, he developed a detailed plan. Initially, some two thousand of his men would seal off all existing exits of the Vatican. Next, German forces would occupy the Vatican's popular radio station. Once in control, arrests of the pope and all the cardinals within the Vatican would follow. These holy men would then be bustled off in cars and trucks to Northern Italy before any Italians or Allies could react. The entire caravan would speed to Bozen and Munich and then into Liechtenstein unless the final destination was changed.

Another part of the scheme called for the German troops to conduct a room to room search for any German deserters, political figures or Jews that had taken refuge in the Vatican. A special force of 50 hand-picked men would, at the same time, round up all the Vatican's treasures---gold, paintings, sculptures, foreign currency, books and records.

Wolff outlined his plan to Field Marshal Albert Kesselring, another German top officer who did not endorse Hitler's order. "Sheer madness," Kesselring commented. "The Fuhrer has not considered the repercussions of such a move. It could turn all the Italians against us in one stroke."

"I agree, Field Marshal. But I have been ordered..."

"There must be a way to avert such an action. We must come up with something."

"I have already thought about it since I first received the order. I don't have any idea..."

"Let me think about it, Wolff. I will get back to you. Now that your headquarters are here in Fasano, you are right next door."

"One more thing, Field Marshal. What do you think of the SS taking over the administrative function here in the occupied zone?"

Kesselring considered the matter and answered Wolff directly. "I am a soldier. I consider the proposal an ideal solution. I will pass it by my staff and let you know."

Wolff contemplated. *Excellent, if this actually takes place. It might make the matter of kidnapping the pope somewhat easier to prevent. I just hope it all comes through.*

Monday, September 27, 1943
Offices of the Secretariat of State,
Palazzo del Governatorato,
The Vatican,
Rome, Italy

A draft had been prepared on directions from Pope Pius XII that was immediately sent to Renzo Levi, the Jewish colony's immediate contact with the Vatican.

It stated that the pope himself had authorized a loan in coins or ingots of "any quantity of gold you may need."

The document also spelled out that the loan could be repaid in installments, with neither a time limit nor any interest due.

October 6, 1943
New Headquarters of the SS,
Via Tasso, 155
Rome, Italy

The Jewish community of Rome was able to raise the gold without any outside help. After receiving the gold raised by the Jews, Kappler wasted no time sending the takings to Berlin. The recipient was Obergruppenführer Ernst Kaltenbrunner, second in command of the SS. Kaltenbrunner's reputation was that of a staunch intelligence chief that had shown little interest in the overall Jewish problem that was facing Kappler at any moment. Kappler hoped that his superior's resolute reputation in the intelligence sector might be a factor that would sway his judgement. Kappler also included a letter that showed his feelings on the purported Jewish roundup for the City of Rome.

118

The letter said flatly that the deportation of the Jews would be a mistake. Kappler pointed out that the SS would lose all chances of gathering intelligence information from Jewish contacts that were known to have contacts with the Allies and with recognized Jewish financial groups abroad.

As an afterthought, Kappler also cabled his superior in Berlin and reminded him of Generalfeldmarschall Albert Kesselring's (Commander-in-Chief South) approval of using the Jews of Rome as labor for building his defensive positions.

Four days later, a cable was received at Via Tasso 155 that spelled out Kaltenbrunner's displeasure and disinterest with both the gold and Kappler's arguments.

It read:

```
GROUP XIII/52
BERLIN to ROME
RSS 256/11/10/43
QGL on 6556 kcs            1902/15 GMT        11/10/43
1955/156


To KAPPLER. It is precisely the immediate and thorough
eradication of the Jews in ITALY which is the special
interest of the present internal political situation
and the general security in ITALY.  To postpone the
expulsion of the Jews until the CARABINIERI and the
Italian Army officers have been removed can no more
be considered than the idea mentioned of calling up
the Jews in ITALY for what would probably be very
unproductive labor under responsible direction by
Italian authorities.
The longer the delay, the more Jews who are doubtless
reckoning on evacuation measures have an opportunity
by moving to the houses of pro-Jewish Italians or
disappearing completely (18 corrupt) ITALY (has been)
instructed in executing the RFSS orders to proceed
with the evacuation
of the Jews without further delay.

KALTENBRUNNER. Ogr.
```

The two close friends strolled around the columned elegance of the Generals Hall, a focal point in the renaissance castle that was home to the feared *Schutzstaffel* (SS) element of the Nazi Party. Forty-three-year-old Heinrich Luitpold Himmler, the Reichsführer of the SS and one of the most prominent leaders of the National Socialist Party, walked closely with Obergruppenführer Karl Wolff, his trustworthy friend and the third ranking officer of the SS.

Even though he was six months older than Himmler, Wolff considered himself Himmler's protégé. The pair had seen each other through a number of experiences and Himmler judged Wolff to be totally devoted to him and to the Nazi Party.

"So the Fuhrer has informed you of his plan to kidnap the pope?" Himmler asked softly.

"Yes, he has. I must admit I was totally incredulous when I first heard the order."

"And have you changed your mind?"

"No. Not really. I just have no idea as to how to proceed. That's why I came here to ask your advice. I have a basic outline finished, but that's all."

"Thank you for the courtesy, Wolffchen," Himmler replied using his pet name for Wolff.

"This is a delicate matter. It must be handled with great care."

"You are in agreement with the plan?" Wolff asked apprehensively.

"It is necessary that the pope and the Catholic Church be expelled from Rome," Himmler explained. "In my mind, Catholics rank just under Jews in the visualizations for our Third Reich."

"I believe the pope will soon come out against our treatment of the Jews and that could become extremely harmful to our cause."

"Weren't you brought up as a Catholic?" Wolff questioned.

"Yes I was brought up a strict Catholic and even attended Catholic school. That was also long ago. Right now, I am a convert and proponent of the Third Reich and both the Jews and Catholics are our enemies. I know you see that," professed Himmler.

Wolff nodded but chose not to speak.

"This war will force us to take important steps to advance our cause, and I agree with our Fuhrer that the pope is a definite liability. He must surely be dealt with. Kidnapping him seems to be an ideal solution to our problem. We can say that we are saving him from the allies and no one will know the difference. Our real problem is the Red Army that might just overrun all of Europe. The Russians are our natural enemies and must be stopped---at all costs."

Wolff thought to himself. *Even Himmler has bought into this insanity. Maybe I was foolish to come here in the first place. I'm no better off than I was before. The Fuhrer's insistence on an immediate plan presents a number of obstacles and I am caught in the middle. I must do something even if it is to disobey the Fuhrer's order. I must think about all this clearly. One mistake and I know Hitler will have me shot even though I know he likes me personally.*

Thursday October 14, 1943
Offices of the German Ambassador to the Vatican,
Villa Wolkonsky,
Via Ludovico di Savoia,
Rome, Italy

Events concerning the deportation of Rome's Jews as well as the ultimate safety of Pope Pius XII had generated a loosely formed curious mixture of German diplomats and military leaders with similar viewpoints. Either singularly or collectively, the faction firmly believed it was in Germany's best interests not to deport the local Jews and were willing to make their feelings known. Led by Germany's Ambassador to the Vatican Ernst von Weizsäcker, the group included German Chargé d'affaires to Italy and an additional legation member, Albrecht von Kessel. Also there were top German military leaders General Reiner Stahel, the Commandant of Rome, and Field Marshal General Albert Kesselring.

A number of attempts to persuade Berlin to affect a different course proved futile. A telegram to the personal attention of Foreign Minister Von Ribbentrop, agreed to by several of the group, stated their position.

It read:

> Oberstumbannfuhrer Kappler has received orders from Berlin to seize the 8,000 Jews resident in Rome and transport them to Northern Italy, where they were to be liquidated. Commandant of Rome General Stahel informs me he will permit this action only on approval of the Herr Reichminister for Foreign Affairs. In my personal opinion it would be better business to employ Jews for fortification work, as was done in Tunis, and, together with Kappler, I will propose this to Field Marshal Kesselring. Please advise.
>
> Möllhausen

The reply by von Ribbentrop was swift and scathing. Von Ribbentrop furiously demanded why someone in the Reich's foreign ministry had used the word 'liquidate" in an official document, one that had been sent to him personally.

Word of the message leaked to Himmler who accused von Ribbentrop of overstepping his authority.

A letter from Adolf Hitler to Kappler settled the matter. In it the German leader said that the Roman Jews were indeed going to be deported and that von Ribbentrop "insists that you keep out of all questions concerning Jews."

Friday, October 15, 1943
Hitler's operations room
Wolfsschanze,
Rastenburg, East Prussia, Germany

SS Lieutenant Colonel Eugen Dollmann was in pursuit of his own formula to dissuade Adolf Hitler from taking certain actions that would affect Rome's Jewish population and the City of Rome itself. His failure a few days earlier to persuade Hitler to bypass Rome through a letter from Benito Mussolini was still fresh in his mind.

The letter from Il Duce pointed out the Allies' advance toward Rome after their landing at Salerno and implored the Fuhrer to defend Rome street by street. Mussolini included the hallowed confines of the Vatican in his plea. Dollmann further argued that were the Jews deported and the pope kidnapped, "general chaos might reign in the city, a horrible spectacle for one of the world's greatest cities."

In the end, Hitler found little credence in Il Duce's argument or Dollmann's contention of potential bedlam in the City of Rome. Both of his pre-orders were then considered to be in effect.

But Dollmann was determined to suggest another possibility, an evacuation of the city, with the Fuhrer. He was bolstered by his own belief that he was one of the very few people who came into close contact with the Fuhrer without falling prey to his hypnotic influence. Hitler fixated on the eyes of anyone to whom he was speaking. Those who could withstand this stare were acknowledged, while others who withered were either devastated by Hitler's rantings or quickly dismissed.

Field Marshal Albert Keitel also sat in on Dollmann's meeting with the German leader.

Hitler began with "The field marshal has told me that you are doubtful about the possibility of staying in Rome and that you would prefer to evacuate the city. Why does an old Roman like you see it this way?"

Dollmann reacted to the Fuhrer's statement with a steady explanation that included some historical facts. He said that he was fearful of an uprising by the Roman Resistance as well as the fact that mass deportations of Jews might cause the Vatican to break its silence and chastise the action. He pointed out that the Allies were already bombing outlying areas of the city and might conceivably target some of Central Rome. Priceless art treasures potentially would be destroyed in defending the city. And finally, there was the ongoing problem of feeding the city. Military activities would severely cut the flow of foodstuffs into the city and present additional problems.

123

With a curious look that included a degree of surprise, Hitler responded, "This evacuation which you advise, how do you suppose it can be carried out? Undoubtedly you have thought about it. Or do you perhaps think that I should restitute Rome to the traitors from the south where the King and his government have fled as compensation for their violation of their agreement and their word of honor?"

Dollmann coolly countered with two alternatives. The first was to place the city under the International Red Cross. The second, Dollmann fervently believed, was to extend the Vatican's control over the city.

Hitler was taken back by the latter suggestion and realized full well what such an action would mean to his old friend Mussolini. In his mind, such a move was simply out of the question.

"Have you spoken with Ambassador Weizsäcker about all this?" Hitler asked with a thick air of suspicion.

Dollmann said no and Hitler spoke again. "We are in Rome now and I think we shall stay in Rome."

Dollmann knew he had exhausted his possibilities. *I have tried everything I could think of and nothing has worked. The only hope we have left is that the blackmail scheme will run its course and the papacy will be spared. I pray for this course of action, both for Germany and for the Holy See.*

Chapter Eleven

"Just for today I'll adapt to the circumstances, without
asking for the circumstances to adapt to my wishes."

— *Pope John XXIII*

Friday, October 15, 1943
Archbishop's residence,
Istanbul, Turkey

Angelo Guiseppe Roncalli was officially the Roman Catholic apostolic delegate
to Greece as well as the head of the Vatican's diplomatic mission to Turkey. His
posts were considered secondary in the church's hierarchy; in fact, they were small
Roman Catholic communities in countries that were predominantly non-Catholic.

But Roncalli took advantage of his post as the war spread throughout Europe. He
began issuing fake baptismal certificates to be used in helping Jews escape the
ravages of the Nazis. He used his diplomatic nuncio status to insure that hundreds
of these fake certificates found their way to parish priests throughout Europe who
in turn passed them on to secreting Jews.

Rumors of Roncalli's successful undertakings reached the Vatican and Pope Pius
XII decided to find out about the archbishop's activities for himself. He conferred
with Father Robert Leiber and the pair decided to send someone who would attract
little attention to meet with Roncalli. Leiber suggested Father Michael S. Rodi and
the pontiff quickly agreed.

"He will attract little attention, if any," Leiber assured the pope. "He will just be
a young priest on a bit of a holiday during these trying times. He can catch the
Simplon-Orient-Taurus Express in Venice which will take him right to Istanbul. It
is an elegant train. I wouldn't mind taking the trip myself."

"Your services are needed here, Robert," replied the pope. "You can make the trip
after the war ends."

"Yes, Holiness. I wasn't totally serious anyway."

"We know, Robert. We know."

Saturday, October 16, 1943
Offices of the SS,
Villa Wolkonsky, 155
Via Ludovico di Savoia,
Rome, Italy

The stately, multi-storied and portico enhanced building, Villa Wolkonsky, was the home of the German diplomatic mission. It was named for a Russian princess that had lived there during the 1830's. Villa Wolkonsky also housed some offices of the Nazi SS.

Lights in the building had burned all night as recently promoted SS Oberstrurmbannfuhrer Herbert Kappler readied his men for their upcoming action. The possessor of steel-gray eyes and a dueling scar down his cheek that seemed to pulsate when he was uncomfortable, Kappler was also the person credited with tracking down Benito Mussolini. He was considered Adolf Hitler's most experienced Gestapo officer in terms of dealing with Jews.

The time had officially been set as one hour before sunrise for the arrest and deportation of Rome's Jewish population. Even though Kappler wasn't in agreement with the plan, he was a loyal Nazi and followed his orders faithfully.

His second in command, Hauptman Erich Priebke listened intently as Kappler detailed the operation.

His opposition was apparent as he spoke. "This is another example of gross political stupidity of people in Berlin who do not understand local conditions here in Rome. The Jews here are poor, orderly and act like sheep. They present no real problem. Arresting them will only provoke hostile actions that we do not need at this time. Himmler should see that, but he is blinded by his prejudice."

Priebke nodded his agreement to his superior's diatribe but remained silent. He had witnessed firsthand the benign Italian disposition to the city's occupiers and agreed that the situation should be left alone. But, like Kappler, he believed that orders were orders and should be followed no matter the cost. He was also aware that these Jews were the only known Jewish descendants of the people who lived in Rome at the time of Christ and had lived on the banks of the Tiber River for nearly two millennia. They numbered nearly 12,000 according to Fascist records that the Gestapo had reviewed.

~

Saturday, October 16, 1943
Just outside the Jewish ghetto,
Rome, Italy

The first shades of morning were just beginning to materialize when SS Obersturmbannführer Herbert Kappler gave the order to begin the roundup of Rome's Jewish population. Due to the fact that there were limited SS personnel to carry out Berlin's order, a number of Wehrmacht soldiers had been assigned to augment Kappler's SS contingent.

Seasoned veteran of Jewish deportations SS Hauptsturmführer (Captain) Theodor Danneker was Kappler's main instrument for gathering the Jews. A year earlier, Danneker had organized and executed the *Rafle du Vel' d'Hiv* of Jews in Paris, considered to be highly successful by Germany. The insidious Paris raid opened the door for Hitler's actions in Rome.

For the present, Danneker had brought with him 14 officers and NCO's and thirty soldiers from the Waffen SS Death's Head Corps, one of Himmler's mobile killing squads. Most of the soldiers were tall, blonde and absolutely without conscious.

It had started raining, and, during the next few hours, Danneker's crack soldiers located and arrested more than 1,000 Jews in the ghetto and loaded them onto trucks that conveyed the hapless people to the nearby *Collegio Militare,* a military school fronting on the banks of the Tiber.

Some of the trucks coming from various parts of the city stopped at Saint Peter's Square while their drivers observed that historic section of the city.

~

Saturday, October 16, 1943
Pope's private chapel
The Vatican,
Rome, Italy

The pope was at prayer in his private chapel when the *maestro di camera del papa* (chief chamberlain of the papal household) entered and said, "Your Holiness, you have a visitor. It seems most important."

The pontiff considered the interruption and the seriousness of his servant's face. "I will go to my private study. Meet me there," Pius XII answered.

In a few moments, the pope entered. Seated in front of him was Italian Princess Enza Pignatelli Aragona Cortes, with whom the pope was familiar through her charitable workings. Princess Pignatelli was in a highly agitated and extremely nervous frame of mind.

She rose as he entered. "Your Holiness, you must act immediately," the woman began excitedly. "The Germans are arresting the Jews and taking them away. Only you can stop them."

"But the Germans promised not to hurt the Jews after the gold was given," Pius replied. "I don't understand…"

He picked up a phone on a nearby table and called Cardinal Maglione. After a brief conversation, he placed the phone back in the cradle.

He walked toward the door and motioned for the princess to follow.

"I'll do all I can," he said, taking her hand. She bowed slightly and left the room. The pope walked to a window and looked out the window. His worst fears had finally come to pass. He could see a number of German vehicles massed in areas not far from the Vatican.

Are we to be next? he pondered. *Is all my work in keeping our Holy Church safe from this insanity to be in vain? I must begin to think about our people here in the Vatican as well as all the clergy in and about Rome. So many lives …*

Sunday, October 17, 1943
Count Ciano's private suite,
Oberallmannshausen,
Starnberg,
Bavaria, Germany

The brisk wind from the northeast brought the realization of oncoming winter to the inhabitants of the pristine villa located near the shore of Lake Sternberg in Bavaria. Count Galeazzo Ciano and his wife Etta and their three children had been the 'guests' of Adolf Hitler and the Nazi Government since their secretive departure from Italy on the morning of August 27th. That fateful morning some three weeks ago had been orchestrated by the SS after the Cianos had received information that Marshal Badoglio had given orders for Ciano's arrest to Chief of Police Carmine Senise. Senise was sympathetic to Ciano and delayed the arrest.

Ciano's wife Etta had counted on Hitler's fondness for her in soliciting the escape from Italy. She had talked to German officials in Rome who took the matter to the Fuhrer himself. Hitler was happy "to save the blood of the Duce" but hesitated about Ciano. He eventually granted Etta's wish but remarked, "Etta would be pleased at an opportunity to get rid of her husband."

Nothing could be further from the truth. Etta Mussolini Ciano had taken to heart the events surrounding her father's downfall and her husband's expulsion from his position. She had suddenly become a caring wife and mother. Genuinely fearful for the lives of her family, she had reached out to the German leader knowing he held a soft spot for her. Etta had no way of knowing that Adolf Hitler considered Galeazzo Ciano a traitor to his country and his party.

The escape plan was simple yet required exact timing. Etta had the children put on double sets of clothes and led them out of the apartment on the pretense of a walk. As they neared the nearby Piazza Santiago de Chile, a black American automobile pulled next to them. Two Germans inside the vehicle motioned for them to get in and the car soon sped off.

Meanwhile, Count Ciano followed their departure immediately. Wearing large, green-tinted sunglasses, he walked briskly to a slowly moving car that had its door open. Ciano jumped in and the car raced away before the startled Carabinieri guards could react.

Both vehicles sped to Rome's Ciampino Airport where a Junker 52 waited with its engines running. The Ciano family quickly climbed aboard and the aircraft was soon airborne. Etta had been told that the plane would first fly to Munich for lunch and then on to Spain.

SS-Brigadeführer und Generalmajor der Waffen-SS Karl Wolff met the plane upon its arrival and informed the Cianos that they would be receiving ration cards for food and clothing. Realizing the problem, Ciano turned to Etta and muttered, "My God! I think they are planning on keeping us here for some time." His despair was lessened when he saw the luxurious villa that the family was to occupy.

The appointed host for the Cianos was pie-faced SS Sturmbannführer (Major) Wilhelm Höttl the deputy group department head of Department VI (Foreign Secret Service). Höttl was responsible for the visitor's everyday needs and became quite friendly with Galeazzo Ciano.

129

Ten days after their arrival, Etta requested a meeting with Hitler through Obergruppenführer Ernst Kaltenbrunner, director of the Reich Main Security Office, who had visited the Cianos two days after their arrival.

After talking to Etta, Kaltenbrunner arranged for her to meet with Hitler on August 31. The meeting was disastrous. Etta immediately explained to Hitler that she thought the war is already lost. The only thing to do is to make a separate peace with the Russians." Hitler ranted, "Nein! Nein! Anything but that! I shall never negotiate with the Russians, madam. You cannot marry water with fire. Peace with them is impossible!" The conversation ended quickly.

Life at Oberallmannshausen became almost unbearable. Bad food, unfriendly personnel and constant surveillance by the SS took its toll on the Cianos. The pair even contemplated suicide since they now thought of themselves as prisoners of the Germans.

Meanwhile, Kaltenbrunner had placed Hildegard Burkhardt Beetz, the 22-year-old wife of a Luftwaffe major fighting in Russia, with the Cianos. She spoke flawless Italian and felt immediate empathy for the forlorn couple.

A radio broadcast informed the Cianos that Mussolini had been freed and had been brought to Germany. Etta saw this as a perfect chance to appeal to her father about her husband and arranged to see him at the residence that had been provided for him in Hirschberg.

Mussolini dearly loved his daughter and finally agreed to meet with Ciano. This meeting took place several days later. The two met cordially, with Ciano explaining his position relating to his vote at the Grand Council. Mussolini appeared to accept the explanation and Ciano agreed to return to Italy and work in whatever capacity the Duce desired.

Hitler, however, saw many problems with Mussolini's forgiveness. Mostly, he feared Ciano's influence in the new Fascist Republican Party and the Duce's unwillingness to prosecute his son-in-law. Ciano's diaries, now believed to exist by the German hierarchy, were also a cause for the Fuhrer's alarm.

Kaltenbrunner had a plan of his own. It was a four stage plot that called for Ciano to reveal the hiding place of his Foreign Office records, so the SD could seize them. Then Ciano would be quickly taken to Switzerland with Edda and his family. Frau Beetz would accompany them.

Once safe in Switzerland, Ciano was to turn his diaries over to Beetz. Finally, Beetz would return to Italy and deliver them to SS-Gruppenführer Wilhelm General Harster, commander of the SD in Italy under General Karl Wolff.

Adolf Hitler nixed the plan the day before it was to be put into effect.

Friday, October 21, 1943
Private office of the pope
The Vatican
Rome, Italy

A messenger had just delivered a note to Pius XII from Cardinal Luigi Maglione.

The pope opened the note and read:

> *Restauro completato.*
> *Si può stare tranquilli.*
>
> (Renovation completed. You can rest easy.)

The pope recognized Cardinal Maglione's scribbled hand and crumpled up the paper. He placed it in a small clay container on his desk and lit the end. The paper caught quickly and was soon ashes.

I am glad that's finished. I am also elated that the diplomatic corps has stated that should I be forced to flee Rome, they would ask to accompany me. That is a noble gesture but I still intend on staying in Rome no matter the circumstances.

Saturday, October 22, 1943
Westbound aboard the Simplon-Orient-Taurus Express,
Belgrade, Yugoslavia

The past few days were probably the most hectic in the entire life of father Michael Sins Rodi, S.J.

After being informed of his mission to visit Archbishop Roncalli in Istanbul, Rodi had hurriedly gathered his meager belongings and packed for the trip. He was told to secure a Vatican passport for the trip as well as a sizeable amount of money to turn over to Archbishop Roncalli upon his arrival.

Excitement filled the young priest as he contemplated his assignment. *I am pleased with what has happened to me here in Rome. Now I am being given a more important role in the work of the Holy See. I haven't even heard of this fellow Roncalli but I'm sure he must be doing something important. Robert said to find out everything about his 'certificates' and bring some back with me. Certificates? Robert would not say more in case I was ever interrogated on my way to Istanbul. This is quite mysterious but I love being involved. It makes me feel as if I am really contributing to the Vatican's efforts in this horrible war.*

After the long train ride, Rodi arrived in Istanbul without incident and went directly to the residence of Archbishop Roncalli. He was received immediately by the prelate and greeted warmly.

"So you are the young fellow that Rome chose to send to talk to me," Roncalli said cordially. "I wondered when word of my actions would reach the Vatican. You must be an important person to come all this way just to talk to me."

"Quite the contrary, Your Excellency. I might be the *least* important person in the Vatican. Besides, I have something to give to you." He handed the valise with the money to Archbishop Roncalli.

Roncalli took the satchel, peered inside for a moment and turned to his visitor. "No matter, Father. I am delighted to receive you. I don't have many visitors from the Holy See here in Istanbul."

"It seems to be a beautiful city, Your Excellency."

"Istanbul is a wonderful place. I've actually grown quite fond of it since I first arrived. And the diplomatic community is actually first rate. I have made many friends here."

Rodi thought about his mission but decided against bringing it up so early in their conversation.

Roncalli caught the hesitation in his young visitor and brought it up himself.

"So, what is it you want from me, young priest? We can sit here all afternoon in idle chatter, but I sense you have something important to ask me."

"Yes, Your Excellency. Thank you for being so direct. I was sent to ask you about your 'certificates' whatever they might be. That's all I was told."

Roncalli sat back and smiled broadly. "I figured as much. The timing on this is perfect."

"I don't understand. Please explain this to me if you will."

"Certainly, Father…"

"Rodi, Your Excellency. I'm actually an American Jesuit."

"Your Italian is excellent. I would have thought you an Italian."

"My teachers at the Gregorian would be glad to hear you say that."

"And I would be happy to tell them," Roncalli stated freely.

"Now, can we talk about your certificates?"

"Most assuredly, young priest. Let's sit and I'll have expresso brought in."

It took the archbishop nearly an hour to explain. As soon as the war began, he was made aware of the efforts of the Nazis to ferret out any and all Jews from a number of countries in Eastern Europe. For some reason, the Jews' pleas had made their way to him and he had decided to do something about it. In the face of such adversity he had figured the Good Lord would not mind if he issued fake certificates of baptism for individuals in these countries. His first efforts were successful and soon he was sending these 'certificates' to numerous parish priests in a number of countries. He also cleverly designed the certificates so that there were many different versions and thus untraceable by the Germans. Roncalli estimated that he had sent nearly two thousand certificates since he had started.

He also further explained that he had also sent immigration certificates to Palestine through the Nunciature diplomatic courier. The Sisters of Our Lady of Zion were used as couriers for Hungarians Jews for certificates and visas.

Rodi had the foresight to ask Roncalli for copies of these documents and the archbishop readily agreed. He provided a large number of each and placed them in a Vatican pouch and handed it to Rodi.

"Maybe someone at the Vatican will now take note. I requested help some time ago but heard nothing in reply."

"These will be put in the hands of the Holy Father himself," Rodi assured. "He has already helped a great number of Jews and I'm sure these documents will augment that cause. Why, we already have a number of Jews in the Swiss Guards."

Roncalli smiled at the news. "I have always respected His Holiness, and your news adds to my esteem. This horrible business of war sometimes brings out the greatness of men, and our pope is an example of that..."

"And you yourself are to be lauded, Archbishop Roncalli. Your work is helping save thousands of lives."

"I am nothing more than a simple parish priest, Father Rodi. I am doing what my heart says is the correct thing to do, nothing more."

"You are too modest, Archbishop. I will insure that the pope knows that much about you."

"Thank you, my young friend. I am most grateful. Now that we have concluded our business, I will have you shown to your room so that you can refresh yourself. We are going to the best Turkish restaurant in Istanbul. I want you to rest a day or two and then you can make your way back to Rome."

"But, I believe I should leave immediately, Archbishop."

"Nonsense, my young friend. Here in Istanbul, I am the boss and I think you should take a few days to enjoy the city. You might never be here again."

As his reflection of the past events ended, Rodi glanced out of the window of the car and saw a sign with an arrow pointing in the direction the train was heading. It said, Belgrade 2.

This has been a wonderful experience for me and a great benefit for our church. It amazes me that a man like Roncalli is stationed in a place like Istanbul. I wonder if the church could make better use of his talents and cleverness.

134

He settled back as the train began decreasing its speed as it neared the main station in Belgrade. Rodi could see the devastation caused by three years of war on the city. Burned-out buildings dotted the landscape and a heavy concentration of Wehrmacht soldiers was apparent as the train came to a stop.

The train's conductor passed swiftly through the cars giving note of the passport search that would immediately follow.

An SS untersturmführer (2nd lieutenant) with two soldiers, an unterfeldwebel (sergeant)and a schutze (private), both brandishing MP 40's eventually appeared at the door to his wooded compartment.

"Papers," the officer barked, taking note of Rodi's roman collar. "Are you a priest?" he asked in German.

"Yes. I work in the Vatican for the pope."

"The SS Officer said nothing and examined the papers. "These appear to be new. Have they just been issued?"

"Yes," Rodi answered truthfully. "This is my first excursion outside the Vatican since I arrived."

"You said excursion. Was your trip for business or pleasure?"

"Mostly pleasure," Rodi answered, slightly more nervous than at the beginning of the meeting. "I had never been to Turkey and the chance presented itself so I took it."

"What is in your satchel?" the Untersturmführer questioned.

"Nothing much. I was only there a few days," Rodi replied reluctantly.

The SS Lieutenant noticed the hesitation and suddenly ordered, "You will open the bag immediately. Let's see what nothing much actually is."

Rodi felt the beads of perspiration around his neck. *Stiffen up now, this is no time to get the jitters. This must just be routine, that's all.* He quickly opened his leather satchel and displayed the contents. The Vatican pouch was resting atop some papers and caught the SS Officer's eye. "What's that on top," he inquired. "That's a diplomatic pouch isn't it?"

"Yes, you are quite right. The Archbishop of Istanbul is a friend of the pope and sent him a personal greeting. I am just the messenger carrying it back to His Holiness."

135

The officer considered Rodi's answer and said, "What's in the message?"

"He did not say. I am not in a position to question an archbishop."

Again, the German officer considered Rodi's response. The officer glanced at his two men who held their machine guns in the ready.

"It very well may be a book of prayers to settle a bet," Rodi offered. "As I told you, the two are close friends. The Archbishop did mention something about settling a wager with the pope."

"This has the Vatican seal. It must be considered a diplomatic article."

"I don't know about such things," Rodi replied. "I am but a simple priest on holiday doing the Archbishop of Istanbul a favor by carrying this back to Rome. I don't think the pope would take kindly to someone opening the pouch."

The officer thought for a moment considering his options.

Finally, he handed the pouch back to Rodi. "Here. Take this back. I cannot break the international rules of diplomacy for no reason. I'm not so sure about the clergy wagering on things, I thought priests were above gambling. Besides, I am a Catholic myself and don't want any trouble with the church."

"God bless you, Lieutenant," Rodi proclaimed, making the sign of the cross in the man's direction. "We are all God's children." The SS Lieutenant nodded to the two soldiers and quickly departed the compartment.

Rodi sat back and brushed off the beads of perspiration that had also formed on his forehead.

That was a little too close for my liking. Good thing I told the truth, well almost all the truth, and he decided not to open the pouch...That could have been devastating... I must remember all the details to tell to Father Leiber. It might help him in the future...

Chapter Twelve

"We have always held to the hope, the belief, the conviction that there is a better life, a better world, beyond the horizon."

— *Franklin D. Roosevelt*

Monday, October 25, 1943
Oval Office,
The White House,
1600 Pennsylvania Ave,
Washington, District of Columbia

The Oval Office had been moved almost ten years earlier to the southeast corner of the West Wing to provide more light for the president and his staff. Windows on both the east and south bathed the room in luxuriant sunlight on cloudless days.

On this particular fall day, President Franklin Delano Roosevelt met privately with the United States Ambassador to the Vatican, Myron C. Carter, a wealthy industrialist who had been Roosevelt's personal representative to the Vatican since before the war.

Taylor had asked for the appointment after receiving a coded message from his assistant, Harold Tittmann, who had remained in the Vatican.

"Mr. President, Tittmann was again asked by the pope about Rome's status as an open city."

Roosevelt frowned and replied, "We've been down that road before, Myron. You know I want to bypass Rome but the British don't feel the same way as I. Since London was bombed unmercifully, they feel that any capital city should be treated in a similar manner."

"I realize that, Mr. President. So does the pope. This time he is asking if the Allied advance might circumvent Rome and thus oblige the Germans to retreat. He is also keenly aware of what might happen if the city was left without any police protection.

I believe he is also fearful of any Soviet presence near the city. He has told me in confidence that he fears the Russians and their way of thinking more than anything else at this time."

Roosevelt thought for a moment, but continued to listen.

"His best hope would be for an agreement between the Allies and the Germans for an immediate take-over of power throughout Rome. He is even considering mobilizing the Swiss Guard."

"I'm just unsure of what we can do right now, Myron. Our advance seems to have stalled for the moment and our commanders have their hands full. At this time, I don't think they are even considering what might happen to Rome in the future.

I will promise you this much. I will talk to my advisors about the possibility of making the Vatican an independent neutral state. That would insure that every precaution would be taken to safeguard Vatican property during any assault on Rome. If this can be arranged, General Eisenhower will be notified and the word will be passed down to the field commanders.

I know this is not what the pope has asked for, but we are only part of the Allied front and must respect the British on this matter."

Taylor nodded, realizing that the president was indeed caught in a ticklish predicament. *He wants to help; He simply cannot risk offending the British... If I were in his position, I'd probably do exactly as he has... I will tell Tittmann to tell the pope, off the record of course, that Roosevelt's hands are tied... That will leave the door open if anything else comes up that we can act upon...*

Tuesday, October 26, 1943
Private offices of the pope,
The Vatican,
Rome, Italy

Upon returning to the Vatican, Fr. Michael S. Rodi was immediately given another assignment by Fr. Robert Leiber. "I want you to go to the Curia and see a Monsignor Hugh O'Flaherty. He is an Irish priest who has something of a mind of his own. He has put together a rather intricate network of people who are finding homes and shelter for both Jews and escaping Allied prisoners. This won't be an official visit. Just introduce yourself to him and tell him you have heard about his work. You two might be of use to one another one day."

"Certainly, Robert. It sounds like fun."

"Fun, indeed. Need I remind you of the seriousness of our work?"

"No, Robert," Rodi answered contritely. "I didn't mean…"

"I know, Michael. It's your enthusiasm, that's all." He smiled at the young priest.

"Now, get yourself over to the Curia. Get back to me whenever you can."

It only took Rodi a matter of minutes to reach O'Flaherty's office. Judging by its size, Rodi reckoned that the Irishman held a senior position in the Curia.

Told to wait, he settled in a chair outside the monsignor's office.

A few minutes later, a smiling bulbous-nosed priest wearing dark rimmed glasses opened the door and offered his hand. "I'm Hugh," he said warmly. "What can I do for you?"

"I'm Michael," Rodi returned. "I wanted to meet you in person."

"Well then, let's have you in," O'Flaherty replied, gesturing into his office.

Rodi entered and found a clustered workplace. O'Flaherty moved some papers to clear a space on his desk.

Rodi began the conversation. "I have heard about your work in this office. I wanted to learn more about it."

"And just why should I tell you, my young visitor?"

Rodi wasn't prepared for the question but gathered himself. He decided to stretch the truth a bit. "The person I work for works at the direction of the pope and told me the pope wants to know more about your operation. He couldn't come himself, so he sent me. Please don't be offended, everyone in the Secretariat is impressed with your efforts. I just want to get the facts straight and make my report."

O'Flaherty considered Rodi's response and decided the likeable young priest was trustworthy.

"Okay, lad, I'll bring His Holiness or whomever up to date. It doesn't seem to be much of a secret anyway." He paused, and then started again. "It all began when I started visiting Italian POW camps some time ago. I was trying to let the families know about the men captured. I would inform them of their whereabouts and injuries.

I got to know a number of these men and then I decided to help some of them escape. The plan worked and I was able to find places for them to stay. More people came to help out and we developed something of a network. Now that the Jews are being rounded up, we really have our hands full. We have people hiding everywhere, in places that are hard to imagine. We even had a hideout located next to the SS headquarters building when we first began.

Even though I used a variety of disguises, word got to the Germans that a priest was running this escape network. The Gestapo finally figured out it was me. They tried to assassinate me, but failed. I realized that as long as I stayed inside the Vatican I was safe."

Rodi looked with wonderment at the determined priest behind the desk. His admiration for the Irish priest had grown steadily since he first sat down.

"You are familiar with the white line outside St. Peter's Square?" O'Flaherty asked casually.

Rodi nodded affirmatively.

"You can thank me for that," the monsignor continued. "The Gestapo chief, I believe his name is Kappler, had it painted. He informed mutual friends that if I crossed the line, the guards had orders to shoot me. I am now forced to meet my contacts on the stairs of St. Peter's," he added laughing.

"How many people have you helped so far?" Rodi questioned, hoping for an answer.

"I don't keep an exact number, but I know it is in the thousands. And, there are many more to be helped. With the Allies bombing around the country, I expect the downed airmen numbers to increase."

"Is there any way we can help?" Rodi asked.

Monsignor O'Flaherty smiled again, thought for a moment, and finally replied. "We are able to scrounge everything we need at this point. Tell the dear Holy Father that I am grateful for the offer and that I will call on him if it is ever necessary."

"I will do that happily," Rodi answered. "It will be my pleasure."

"Go with God," O'Flaherty finalized.

"And also with you."

Wednesday, October 27, 1943
Villa Napoleon overlooking the Porta Pia,
Rome, Italy

Baron Ernst von Weizsäcker, Nazi Germany's newest ambassador to the Holy See, held his current post through his own choice. Formerly the *Staatssekretär* (State Secretary) of the German Foreign Office and number two to Foreign Minister Joachim von Ribbentrop in the party's hierarchy, Weizsäcker was a prominent member of the German nobility that had grown weary of Hitler's foreign policy. He resigned his former position and asked to be sent to Rome. In the back of his mind was the notion that such a posting might somehow lead to his mediating a separate peace between Germany and the Western Allies. It was apparent to the career diplomat that the Roman Catholic Church would play an important part in any possible facilitation.

The grey-haired, aristocratic-looking 61-year old was also a practicing Catholic and was sickened when General Wolff informed him of Hitler's plan for the invasion of the Vatican and the abduction of Pope Pius XII. He considered the consequences of such an action to be detrimental to both German Catholics and the German people. He knew that something must be done to thwart the fiendish scheme that had been ordered by his Fuhrer.

He called a meeting to discuss the options. Included were General Wolff, Colonel Eugen Dollmann, the SS liaison to Field Marshal Kesselring, and Weizsäcker's secretary, Albrecht von Kessel. At the last minute, Eitel Möllhausen, the half-French consul who replaced German Ambassador to Italy Rudolph Rahn following Rahn's automobile accident, was also invited.

The mood was somber as Weizsäcker began. "We need to do something to prevent the Fuhrer's plan to invade the Vatican to take place. I feel it would be a catastrophe and turn the Italian people against us. So far, our occupation has had little opposition. I want to keep it that way."

"Precisely," Wolff added. "Even though I have started things in motion, to appease the Fuhrer, I have stalled on certain important parts of the plan. I intend to continue delaying as much as I can without placing myself in danger."

After a brief silence, another spoke out. "We must inform the pope of our plan," Consul Möllhausen advised. "Once he is informed, he can, in a sense, be blackmailed."

"Blackmailed?" questioned von Kessel."

"Yes. Blackmailed. Telling him of the plot would force him to remain silent about the genocide our leader has contrived. Pius is under pressure from many to speak out publically about our actions. The blackmail would be for his own good. Also, in order to increase the pressure on him, other Vatican officials must be told that the pope would jeopardize the Church as well as the clergy that have asylum in Churches and monasteries."

I will ask Ambassador Rahn to contact the Fuhrer about the invasion plan. He can point out the negatives and maybe buy us some additional time regarding his order to kidnap the pope."

"That's a good idea," Wolff added. "Even a few weeks would help a great deal."

"Then it's settled," Möllhausen replied. "Dollmann here will inform General Kesselring of our meeting. I trust he will be pleased."

Dollmann nodded his agreement. The German officers and diplomats sat back in their chairs and pondered their choices. At length, General Wolff stood and prepared to leave. They filed silently out of the small conference room. No one in the room bothered to give the Nazi salute as they departed.

Monday, December 27, 1943
Offices of the General Secretary of the Central Committee,
Communist Party of the Soviet Union,
The Kremlin,
Moscow, Russia

Joseph Stalin had just returned from his Christmas holiday and was reading intelligence dispatches at his desk in his private office in the Kremlin. The productive tripartite Tehran Conference was already almost a month behind him and his Christmas meeting with Latvian Communist leader Janis Kalnburzins had also proved quite fruitful in settling some internal problems in that country. His attention was diverted when a uniformed figure entered the room and approached his sofa.

He observed Alexander Nikolaevich Poskrebyshev in his uniform as a Major General in the Red Army.

He is a vital piece of our party's inner workings and is indispensable to me personally. Even though he looks like a peasant, there is something almost noble about him. I like him personally and I trust him implicitly. I wouldn't have anyone else doing his job.

Poskrebyshev's actual title was Director of Administration of the General Secretary, a most important post during wartime. He was also Stalin's personal secretary. Anything that Stalin received first passed through the hands of the stocky man' with protruding eyes.

Poskrebyshev handed Stalin another intelligence document that had just been received.

"So it has finally happened," Stalin remarked. "I knew it would happen someday. I just didn't know when."

"Yes," Poskrebyshev replied. "That is if our information is correct. We have had false reports before and this could be another such time."

"I don't believe so, Alexander Nikolaevich," Stalin rejoined. "This report cites the *RRG (Reichs-Rundfunk-Gesellschaft)*, German State Radio, as the source. It must be a major happening since they are claiming that Hitler is alive and not dead as first reported. We didn't even know about the first reports of his death."

"We are still processing incoming reports. The initial reports might well be there."

"Make sure the first deputies get a copy of this as soon as possible. They should be informed and quite happy about it."

"Bulganin will be the happiest. Of that I am sure."

Stalin smiled and agreed with a nod of his head. "I must return to these reports, Alexander Nikolaevich. I believe they will be the death of me yet."

"I only give you the important ones," Poskrebyshev returned.

"For that I am eternally thankful. I should give you another medal."

Chapter Thirteen

"In this state of mind, which excludes any falsehood, I declare that not a single word of what I have written is false or exaggerated or dictated by selfish resentment. It is all just what I have seen and heard."

— *Galeazzo Ciano*
December 23, 1943, Cell 27, Scalzi Prison

Saturday, March 11, 1944
Saclzi Prison,
Via Carmelitani, 20
Verona, Italy

The 17th Century Baroque style former Catholic Church had been used as a prison since 1883 and housed a number of Italian political prisoners including Count Galeazzo Ciano, former foreign minister of Italy. In Scalzi Prison, he was simply inmate #11902.

Ciano had been in prison since mid-October and had not fared well. His airy, cold and damp cell had brought a recurrence of his asthma as well as the return of chronic pain to his ears. He had begged his wife Etta to send him warm clothing, sweaters, an overcoat or fur coat and a cap. His food, however, was another story. He had been allowed to utilize the sizeable amount of money he had on his person when he was arrested. Ciano therefore ordered his meals from Verona's top restaurant which delivered the food each day.

Etta Mussolini Ciano had been an infrequent visitor to the prison and had attempted to intercede with her father on Ciano's behalf with no success. Mussolini was resigned to the fact that his son-in-law's fate was sealed and chose not to become involved.

Ciano was settled in isolation cell #27 and was permitted few visitors. His one consolation was that his diaries were now outside the reach of the Third Reich. Penned for several years beginning in 1939, these memoirs detailed numerous meetings between Bento Mussolini and Adolf Hitler, as seen from Ciano's

145

perspective. They also included an insight into Italy's difficult voyage into the waters of war and the rationale behind many important decisions that were made that affected Italy. In Ciano's opinion, disclosure of these writings could be beneficial to the Allied powers and everyone outside the German axis of power.

Ciano's wife Etta had been successful in smuggling the diaries out of Italy and into Switzerland where they were being held in a safe place. Ciano held out the faint belief that somehow these diaries could be the key to saving his life. He also harbored the notion that his writings would one day provide financial assistance to his wife and children.

The tribunal that would decide the fates of Ciano and the other defendants finally convened on Saturday, January 8, 1944 in the music room of the *Castelvecchio*, a Veronese fortress located on the banks of the Adige River.

The verdict in the 14th Century castle was never in doubt. The prejudiced tribunal found the defendants guilty and sentenced each of them to death by a firing squad. The date set for the execution was January 11, 1944 in the early morning.

Meanwhile, Hildegard Burkhardt Beetz had become close friends with Galeazzo Ciano. Her friendship with the Ciano family and her close ties with Obergruppenführer Ernst Kaltenbrunner, director of the Reich Main Security Office, allowed her the opportunity to visit Ciano in Scalzi Prison. She took and delivered notes to Etta from Ciano and developed a deep, personal feeling for the condemned man. On several occasions, Beetz used her German connections to help Ciano inside the prison and was even part of a plot, without Hitler's knowledge, to rescue the young diplomat from his incarceration. The plot, Operation Conte, was to disguise two German SS men as Italian Fascists and overpower Ciano's guards and free him. Ciano would then be flown to Hungary where his old friend, Count Sandor Festetics, would receive him. Adolf Hitler would then be told that Fascists rescued Ciano. In the end, Hitler learned of the plan. He quickly nixed the idea and with it, Ciano's last chance for survival.

Frau Beetz made a final visit to Scalzi and met with Ciano. She found him calm, resigned to his impending fate. She had hidden a phial that she supposed contained potassium cyanide in her dress and handed it to Ciano who had asked her to get the poison for him. She also made him promise not to take the contents of the vial until word had been received about the status of a possible pardon for Ciano and the other prisoners.

Ciano slumped down on his bunk and addressed the attractive woman. "You know I am not afraid of dying, my dear friend. I will not give that satisfaction to Hitler and Mussolini. It seems absolutely useless. I want to die as an Apostolic Roman Catholic so it will be necessary for me to go to confession and receive Holy Communion. Can you use your influence and get Don Chiot to visit me? They wouldn't refuse a visit by the chaplain, would they?"

Hildegard Beetz was near tears as she answered, "I'll certainly do what I can Galeazzo. I will go now and talk to the General Command. I'll be back as soon as I know anything."

After Beetz departed, Ciano lay down on his bunk and considered his choices. A feeling of hopelessness and despair engulfed his mind.

I don't want to be shot in the back in the morning. I don't want to give this joy to Hitler and others. I'm not sure if I can resign myself to the ice of the bullet in the neck. I feel it! I feel it! And I don't want it…I can't bear it…I won't have it…I will cheat the execution squad by swallowing the potassium chloride sweet Hildegard so kindly brought me…

Moments later, he swallowed the contents of the small phial.

I must be dying; my heart is beating so violently, he thought. After a minute or so, he realized his heart was again beating in its normal rhythm. *Is this dying? What, I am alive, very alive…* Ciano considered what had happened and sunk even lower into the mattress. *I'm not even able to kill myself…this is most surely the end…I am doomed to the firing squad.*

Around six o'clock, the bells of a nearby monastery reverberated throughout the old prison.

Chaplain Don Chiot gathered the condemned men in General Emilio De Bono's cell. The 77-year-old Fascist summoned his courage and said to the others, "Boys, let's give the last salute on this earth to the Madonna, whom we will see in paradise."

All agreed and recited the Angelus as a group.

At nine o'clock, a small group approached Ciano's cell.

"It's time," Scalzi Superintendent Sergio Olas pronounced.

Count Galeazzo Ciano rose and walked out of his cell. He was immediately manacled. A series of stops at the remaining prison cells produced the remainder of the five prisoners who were to be executed.

Ciano turned to Don Chiot and said evenly, "Yes, we have all erred; we are all swept away by the same gale. Tell my family that I die without rancor toward anyone."

A police van, with the prisoners inside, drove through the nearly deserted streets to Fort Procolo's firing range, just outside Porta Catena, one of Verona's ancient city gates. Five wobbly wooden folding chairs were lined up against a wall. A prisoner was assigned to each chair. Ciano's chair was so unsteady that he fell and had to be helped up again. Both Ciano and De Bono asked for their chairs to face the firing squad but were denied.

Twenty witnesses stood and watched the spectacle. Thirty federal policemen raised their old Carcano M91 rifles and waited for the order to shoot. They were in two rows, fifteen paces behind the chairs with the front row kneeling.

Police Commander Nicola Furlotti yelled "Fire" and the salvo sounded. The wild firing was totally inaccurate and none of the prisoners were killed. They lay screaming as a few more shots were fired in their direction. Even though Ciano had been hit five times in the back, he was still alive. Furlotti rushed up and fired two pistol shots at Ciano's temple. The prison doctor examined the men and found that some still had pulses and Furlotti returned and shot each one again.

The will of the tribunal and Benito Mussolini was officially imposed.

Tuesday, March 21, 1944
GAP Central Headquarters,
Via Marco Aurelio,
Rome, Italy

The *Gruppi di Azione Patriottica* (GAP) had been formed seven months earlier through the initiatives of the Italian Communist Party at the insistence of the Kremlin. Because of the successes of the French Resistance in deterring the Nazis, the GAP utilized similar techniques in its attempt to harass German troops occupying Rome and other parts of Italy.

GAP's present headquarters was in the basement of a building on the Via Marco Aurelio. The space also served as the group's bomb-making facility. A physicist and his wife were the GAP members in charge of producing the bombs for the operation.

Carla Capponi (code name Elena) was one of the loyal Communists that made up GAP. She had participated in a number of forays that GAP had planned and was delighted to be included in this upcoming operation.

148

She stood mesmerized as the commander of GAP Central, Carlo Salinari (code name Spartaco), outlined the plan for an attack on a large column of German soldiers. To her right was another young GAP member, a Sicilian medical student at the University of Rome named Rosario Bentivegna (code name Paolo). The bespectacled Bentivegna was one of the group's leaders as well as a person Carla found quite handsome.

"These soldiers follow the same route each day. They return from their duties around 2 o'clock and march back through the Piazza di Spagna to their barracks. They sing loudly all the way in a boastful manner a German victory song that only the pig Germans could enjoy.

We have watched them for several days, and their route is always the same. Along the way, they pass through a narrow street that leads up a hill. They will be marching uphill and that will be to our advantage."

He paused and produced a large map of Rome. A small street had been singled out with a red circle. Carla strained to see the name of the street.

"This is the Via Rasella, and this is where we will catch the Huns. We have had help from the British in planning this attack. Our mutual plan is to steal a rubbish cart sometime tomorrow from behind the Coliseum and fill it with explosives. The cart has two silver iron trash cans on a four-wheel chassis. It will be parked alongside the Palazzo Tittoni, about one-third of the way up the Via Rasella. The bomb will have 18 kilograms of TNT and should do great harm to the Germans. Your leader, Paolo, will be dressed like a street cleaner and will set off the fuse when the troops start up the street. We think that 50 seconds is time enough for the soldiers to reach the spot where the bomb will explode. A number of you will be waiting on the south side of the Via del Boccaccio," he continued, pointing to a spot on the map. "You, comrades, will act as lookouts and will fire four 45 mm mortar shells into the German ranks once the bomb has exploded. If all goes well, you will all exit through the tunnel at the Via del Traforo.

We want to kill as many of our enemy as possible. It will make a definitive statement and show the world that the GAP is totally serious about inflicting grief on our enemy.

I will show each of you where you will be stationed and you will pick up your weapons around noon the day after tomorrow. I'm sure you will have questions, but save them for when we go over the final details."

Carla observed Bentivegna and sighed as the meeting broke and the group drifted to other parts of the basement. The young leader seemed preoccupied with the plan as it had been explained.

He is most brave and will be in the most danger during the attack…I hope he survives along with the rest of us…It would be a shame if he is killed…This is the most serious undertaking our group has ever tried… I just hope everything works as planned. We will need a great deal of luck to be successful…

Thursday, March 23, 1944
Papal main kitchen,
The Vatican,
Rome, Italy

For some time, the pope's main kitchen off the papal residence had become Father Michael S. Rodi's favorite watering spot. Rodi had discovered a most delightful tea and had availed himself of the great pleasure of brewing a pot whenever the chance arose.

The tea was called Formosa Oolong and, according to the head cook, was one of the finest produced by the island located a little over 120 miles from the coast of China. Rodi had even looked up the mysterious sounding tea in the Vatican's library and found that it was made from special grade mountain leaves that were larger than most tea leaves. The leaves were dark brown in color and included stems. The aroma was nutty and floral and contained peach and carrot flavors that emerged during preparation.

The Vatican seemed to have a good supply of the Formosa Oolong, a fact that Father Rodi considered when he determined that the tasty liquid would be his favorite for the rest of his life.

He was consuming his second cup of the morning when he noticed another young Italian priest seated at a small table in a corner of the room staring blankly at the wall. *Why it's Father Rabasca, my friend from the university.* The two had become friends and shared many candles with their late studying.

Rodi walked over to the priest and greeted him warmly. "Tony, nice to see you again. Have you heard anything from Günter lately?"

Father Rabasca looked up, nodded negatively, but remained silent.

"What's the trouble? You look worried. Can I be of help?"

"I don't think so Michael," Rabasca replied. "But maybe I should tell you about it. I need to tell someone, it's really beginning to get to me."

150

"By all means, let's hear all of it."

"I have a younger cousin, Fredo. He was still in school until the Germans came. He became disillusioned and joined the Italian Communist Party with some of his other friends."

"That's not so bad, Tony. Many students feel the need to join causes. This one just happens to be contrary to what your country believes in right now. You shouldn't worry. It is probably just a passing whim."

"You don't understand, Michael. I went to my aunt's house for the Sunday meal and Fredo was there. He was boasting to everyone about the party and what they intended to do to the Germans. He ranted and raved and even got down to some specifics."

"What sort of specifics?"

"Well it seems that he and some others have been getting instructions on how to make bombs and devices to use against the Germans. It all sounded quite sinister. My aunt and uncle were beside themselves. They tried to talk to Fredo but he wouldn't listen."

"Youths are like that sometimes, Tony. They usually grow out of it."

"But that's not the worst part, Michael. He also bragged that his group was already planning to ambush some German soldiers. He intends to kill them all."

Rodi was keenly aware of what such an action could mean. "Doesn't he realize that the Germans would seek revenge for such an action?" The Bosch would exact a heavy toll of Italians if the ambush were even slightly successful. We have all seen the warnings posted on the streets. It could easily turn into a bloodbath."

"I know," Rabasca replied dejectedly. "I know."

"Did he say when the ambush was to take place? And *where*?"

"No, he didn't. I don't think he knew. If he had known he would have certainly said so."

"We must go and see him, Tony. Maybe we can change his mind."

"I don't think so. He seemed pretty committed. He was almost fanatical."

151

"We will try in any case. Is he still living at his home?"

"No. He is staying with some of his communist friends. He only goes home for his meals, the dupe."

"Does that include lunch?"

"I believe so. His dedication hasn't affected his appetite."

"Can we go there now? It's nearing lunchtime."

"Of course. It's not far from here. It won't take us fifteen minutes to get there."

"Then let's get started…"

The pair rose and headed out a nearby door. Father Rabasca motioned to the left and the two habited men started toward one of the Vatican's rear entrances.

Their walk was brisk in the chilly October air and the twosome quickly reached their destination. Father Rabasca opened the door without knocking and walked into the living room that was just off the entrance hall. From the opposite direction an aproned figure emerged with a bowl she was stirring. Her face lit up when she saw her visitors included her favorite nephew along with another priest.

"Tony," she blurted. "Back again so soon? Can you stay for lunch?"

Rabasca turned to his friend and introduced him to his aunt. "This is Father Rodi who also works or the Vatican, Zia Antonella. And, yes, we can stay."

Her face lit up at the prospect of having two priests in her home at the same time. "Good," she replied. "It's almost ready. Fredo's already here in the kitchen. He's never late for a meal. But today he's in a foul mood… he's just sitting there, staring."

The two priests looked at each other but said nothing.

"Go and wash your hands," she ordered, pointing down the hallway.

Rabasca motioned for Rodi to follow and the two entered a bathroom off the hallway.

"She always makes me wash my hands," Rabasca stated. "Just like my mother does."

152

Rodi smiled. "All mothers do. It's part of their nature."

They finished and dried their hands. Rabasca led the way back to the kitchen where a decidedly dejected Fredo sat gazing straight ahead. Again the pair looked at each other.

"Hello, Fredo," offered Father Rabasca. "Why the big frown?"

Fredo said nothing and didn't acknowledge the question.

"Fredo?" Rabasca asked again. What's wrong?"

"Nothing," he replied in a low voice. "Just leave me alone."

"Come on Fredo. It can't be that bad."

"I said, let me alone."

Father Rabasca reached down to comfort his cousin, but the youth pulled away. The priest looked at his aunt who shrugged her shoulders in disbelief.

The priests took seats at the large rectangular table and Father Rabasca started the blessing. "Heavenly Father, bless this meal and us who are here to partake of your wonderful bounty. Guide us in our daily tasks and grant us your presence in our obligations. And Dear Lord, help Fredo in his hour of need…"

A tear appeared on Fredo's face that was soon followed by many more. He fought the feeling but suddenly gave in. "They wouldn't let me go along…said I was too young, too inexperienced… what do they know?"

Father Rabasca moved his chair closer to Fredo and reached out for his shoulder. "Tell us all about it Fredo. Don't be afraid."

"I'm not afraid," Fredo barked. "I'm more mad than afraid."

Father Rabasca waited for Fredo to continue.

"It wasn't supposed to be like this," he finally began. "We were all in this together." Father Rabasca looked over to Father Rodi, his face ashen.

"We all trained together and learned how to make bottle bombs and how to put the explosives together to make the most damage. We even practiced in an old field just outside town. We all reported this morning for the final instructions and three of us were told we weren't going because it was too dangerous."

Again Father Rabasca looked at Father Rodi.

"I know I could do it, I'm not afraid."

"Of course not, Fredo. I'm sure you are good at what you try to do," Rodi inserted. Now, tell us more about what it was you intended to do."

"We were to kill German soldiers, lots of them. It was all planned."

"Where was all this to take place?" Rodi asked again. "Where were the Germans to be killed?"

"On the Via Rasella. It is the perfect spot for an ambush."

Rodi looked at his fellow priest.

Rabasca thought for a moment and answered. "It is a short, narrow street that descends from the Barbarini Palace on the slope of the Quirinal, one of the Seven Hills of Rome. The Quirinal is the closest hill to the Vatican and quite close to the Trevi Fountain. It has tall buildings on each side, if I remember correctly."

Rodi spoke again to Fredo. "When is this attack supposed to happen?"

Fredo looked at the priest, unsure of whether to answer. "I'm no traitor," he said weakly. I've already said too much."

"Tell the father what he wants, Fredo," his mother commanded. "For the sake of God, tell him."

Fredo thought for a second and blurted out, "Sometime this afternoon. Whenever the troops come to the street."

Father Rabasca reacted first. He called to his friend, "We must take the Ponte Cavour to cross the river. Then go toward the Spanish Steps. Follow the Via Sistina and then in the general direction of the Trevi Fountain. Via Rasella is off to the right. We will ask someone."

Rodi nodded. Both priests were already on their feet and heading for the door. Fredo sobbed again as the pair left the room.

"Tony, it would be better for you to go to the Vatican and tell Father Leiber what you know," directed Rodi. "I'll go directly to the Via Rasella and see what I can do to stop this insanity."

Father Rabasca nodded to his friend and departed. Rodi went in the opposite direction toward the tiny Via Rasella. He had absolutely no idea what he would do when he arrived at the location.

Chapter Fourteen

"When facing such events, any honest soul is deeply pained
in the name of humanity and of Christian sentiments."

— *Pope Pius XII*
Vatican press release, Friday, March 24, 1944

Thursday, March 23, 1944
Near the Via Rasella,
Rome, Italy

As he approached the Via Rasella on the larger Via del Tritone, Father Michael
Rodi realized he had become very tired from his running. He slowed his pace and
tried to catch his breath. He had already asked for directions and was about to do
so again when a loud blast from a nearby street rattled the windows around him.

He dashed in the direction of the noise and suddenly the sounds of gunfire began
to echo through the area.

I must be close now, the sounds are getting louder.

He turned a corner to an incredible sight. Something was burning about midway
up the street and guns were firing without pause. He tried to get his bearings but
bullets whizzed all around his position.

Suddenly, a young woman appeared carrying an automatic rifle. Carla Capponi
paused as she knelt down beside him and observed his collar.

"*Sacerdot?*" (Priest) she questioned.

Rodi nodded. "*Si deve lasciare qui*" (You must leave here) she insisted.

This time Rodi nodded negatively. "*Cè bisogno di me.*" (I am needed.) He unwrapped a small stole from his coat pocket and placed it around his neck.

The woman nodded and was suddenly gone.

Rodi gathered his faculties and stood up. The firing was now more sporadic and the young priest made his way through the carnage. A number of bodies and body parts were strewn about and some of the corpses were still smoking. He started administering the last rites to those who were obviously dead and continued to do so for about ten minutes.

At one point, he found a young German soldier still alive but bleeding badly from a wound to his shoulder. Rodi ripped off his coat and began tearing it into pieces. He wadded up what was once the inner lining and placed it over the soldier's wound. The wound continued bleeding and Rodi realized if he couldn't stop the bleeding, the soldier would soon die. In a flash, the solution came to him. He removed the stole and tied it tightly around the bandage and shoulder. To his amazement, the bleeding soon stopped. Pleased with this development, he stood up to see who needed him next when he observed a German officer standing a few feet away.

SS Obersturmbannführer Eugen Dollmann looked in amazement at the priest. He approached the figure that was now kneeling while making the sign of the cross over a dead soldier. Rodi finished and moved to another prone figure whose leg had been blown off. Rodi knelt close to the soldier's head and whispered in his ear. The soldier groaned and moved his head slightly. The priest continued administering the last rites to several other soldiers in need. He finally looked up at the German officer standing over him, who declared, "Go on with your work, Father. There are many others who need your help here."

Rodi nodded and continued helping wherever he could. German medical personnel began arriving on the dreadful scene. Rodi pointed to several living soldiers and continued his efforts in administering to the dead.

Several minutes later, another officer approached him. "I am SS Hauptstrumführer Dittman" he pronounced. "I am Colonel Dollmann's aide. He wants to know who you are. He says we are in your debt and he wants to repay you for what you did."

"I am but a simple priest. Any priest would have done what I did," Rodi answered politely.

"Colonel Dollmann is used to getting what he wants, and he insists on learning your name. Do you understand?"

"I guess so," Rodi replied. "I am Father Michael Rodi. I am an American priest working at the Vatican."

"American? Your German is quite excellent. I would have thought otherwise."

"I had good teachers. They insisted I be correct in what I said."

SS Captain Dittman came to attention and clicked his heels. "I will give the information to Colonel Dollmann. I think you will hear from him."

SS Obersturmbannführer Herbert Kappler had been among the first to arrive at the scene of the massacre. As the German police attaché and commander of the security police in Rome, it was his job to supervise the investigation into what had occurred. But, he was not the first high ranking German officer to view the carnage.

Within minutes of the last shot, Major General Kurt Mälzer, the German commander in Rome often called the "King of Rome," arrived – having just polished off his usual wine-centered heavy lunch at the nearby Hotel Excelsior. He immediately ordered the nearby buildings in the area searched. Over 200 people from the neighborhood were then lined up against walls in the Piazza Barberini and made to hold their arms up in the air. Malzer, who was half-drunk and seemingly crazed by the incident, was eventually persuaded by cooler heads not to have all 200 people, mainly women and children, shot on the spot and the entire street blown up.

The bodies of the dead German policemen were covered with whatever was available but left in the exact positions where each had fallen.

"Someone will pay dearly for this," Kappler forewarned his subordinate when he was told that 32 German bodies had been counted so far. "This is an atrocity against our country. I am sure the Fuhrer will demand a high number of Italians be shot for each dead soldier."

Thursday, March 23, 1944
Private offices of the pope,
The Vatican,
Rome, Italy

Pope Pius XII was talking to Father Robert Leiber, S.J. when Father Anthony Rabasca was shown into his office. He offered his ring and Rabasca knelt as he kissed the symbol of the pope's authority.

"I have important news Holy Father," Rabasca explained excitedly. "Father Rodi wanted me to come here and tell Father Leiber what has happened."

Both men listened intently as the youthful priest continued.

Rabasca explained that he and Rodi had discovered a Communist plot to attack a German army unit that very afternoon and that Rodi had gone directly to the site to attempt to stop the attack from occurring.

The pope looked at Leiber and thanked Father Rabasca for his effort. He motioned for the prelate to leave.

Once they were alone, the pontiff addressed his close advisor. "This could be quite serious if Father Rodi isn't successful. Depending on the degree of the attack and its success, the Germans will be quite upset."

"Yes, Holiness. I would also expect reprisals against those involved. That could present a host of new problems," Leiber responded. "If the attackers are identified as Communists, the Germans will make it hell for them."

"And rightly so," the pope agreed. "But that's only part of the problem I foresee."

Leiber looked questioningly at his leader. Pius XII bowed his head and continued. "This could easily escalate the Hitler plan to invade the Vatican, that is, if our information about his order is genuine. Remember, we have never known whether the plan actually exists or is merely hearsay on the part of our intelligence people."

"There's no real way to know, Holiness."

"I know that. But we must continue our preparations for such an eventuality. The next few days will tell about how the Germans will react."

"We must just wait and see. And rely on the protection of our Lord."

"Our Lord will do what he can. We must increase our security around the Vatican. Can you please see that the guard is doubled starting tomorrow morning. More Swiss Guards with machine guns might fluster the Germans' mettle."

"I will see to it at once, Holiness. I will continue to send you reports as they are received."

The pope walked toward one of his windows and gazed at his beloved Rome.

What will happen next? Am I to be made a prisoner in my own city? This madness just had to come to an end.

Thursday, March 23, 1944
Field Marshal Kesselring's headquarters,
Monte Sorrate,
North of Rome, Italy

After inspecting the Fourteenth Army at Anzio, Field Marshal Albert Kesselring returned to his mountaintop headquarters north of Rome around 1900 hours.

He was immediately briefed on the Via Rasella massacre by his chief of staff, General Siegfried Westphal. Westphal, working with Colonel Dietrich Beelitz, Kesselring's Chief of Operations, had developed a full report of the incident in the period since the attack occurred. The Fourteenth Army commander, General Eberhard von Mackensen, was also at the briefing.

It was explained in some detail to the German commander that Adolf Hitler had been contacted and went into a rage upon hearing the news. It was further stated that Hitler intended to level a full quarter of the City of Rome, a reprisal that "would make the world tremble."

Westphal went on to say "The Fuhrer has demanded that we execute fifty Jews and Italians for every German killed. I talked to our people in Rome and they feel that number is excessive. But they agree the Italians need to be taught a lesson in order to scare them."

Kesselring thought for a moment and turned to von Mackensen. "Get the OKW *(Oberkommando der Wehrmacht)* on the phone. I want to speak to Jodl himself."

Several minutes later, the phone was handed to Kesselring. During the long conversation, Hitler's Chief of Operations (Alfred Jodl) agreed that a deterrent effect was in order and he also concurred that the German officers on the scene in Rome were correct regarding the Fuhrer's unreasonable number of Italians to be shot. In the end, the old Prussian militarist von Mackensen had offered a formula whereby only ten Italians would be shot and Jodl finally agreed to that number.

As soon as Kesselring hung up, he turned to von Mackensen and ordered, "Kill ten Italians for every German. Carry it out immediately."

The German plan for reprisals was now officially sanctioned.

Thursday, March 23, 1944
Gestapo Headquarters,
Villa Wolkonsky,
Via Ludovico di Savoia,
Rome, Italy

When the mass execution order reached SS Obersturmbannfuhrer Herbert Kappler he was already aware that he faced an immediate problem. Only *four* prisoners that had death sentences were available.

The number of dead Germans had reached thirty-two and the number of available prisoners was nowhere near that number. Kappler was aware of fifty-seven Jews who were scheduled to leave for Auschwitz and he added them to the list. Prisoners at either the Via Tasso or the Third Wing of the Regina Coeli Prison numbered 280, but some of these were women who were excluded from the list. Kappler ordered his men to make a thorough check of the records of all prisoners held at Via Tasso. The cards of these prisoners were arranged in three groups, *Spionage* (Spies), *Kommunismus* (Communists) and *Jude* (Jews). The question of substance to any of the prisoner's supposed crimes was never a factor in the final decision. Few were excluded from the fatal number.

He gave orders for his SS soldiers to round up as many Jews as they could find. A move that proved successful enough to inch closer to his eventual quota of 320. In fact, when the final count was made there were five extra unfortunates in the number. Kappler decided to include these Jews since they were already in his custody.

Kappler kept the actual numbers of condemned prisoners to himself and prepared to follow the Fuhrer's 24-hour mandate.

Next, he received word from General Wolff to delay the reprisals until the following day when Wolff would arrive from his headquarters at Fasano. Kappler thought about the general's request but decided to obey the Fuhrer's instructions instead.

Calls were made to his superior in Verona, General Wilhelm Harster, to line up additional authority for the act he was about to commit. He sought and received the consent of the Chief Justice General Hans Keller of the German Military Tribunal in Rome.

Sometime in the very early morning, Consul Eitel Möllhausen learned of Kappler's action and burst in on the Gestapo chief who was bent over his stack of cards. Kappler looked up momentarily and went back to the stack in front of him.

Möllhausen glared at the officer and motioned other SS soldiers out of the room. When the two were alone, the 30-year-old diplomat addressed the head of Rome's Gestapo without reserve.

"Listen Kappler, if I were in your place my conscience would tremble. I do not know how I would act. But I certainly would feel myself at a decisive turn in my life. What you are doing goes far beyond patriotism, war, or your duty to the fatherland."

"I am simply following the Fuhrer's orders," returned Kappler without hesitation. "I am a good soldier and true to my oath."

"Remember that one day you will be called to account not only before men but also before the tribunal of God," the German consul seethed. "I only hope he has pity on your wretched soul."

"Möllhausen, I can only promise you I will do what I am able to do. And this is what it is: For every name I write, I will think three times."

Seeing his words were useless, Möllhausen abruptly departed, slamming the door on his way out. Kappler shook his head and returned to his stack.

As the morning progressed, Kappler was still short of his quota. Another German soldier had just died, bringing the number of prisoners necessary to carry out his Fuhrer's orders to 330. While the number seemed almost impossible to fill, he continued at his thankless task. At one point, the SS Colonel even took to naming members of the Italian Military and the Carabinieri who had been involved in some part with Mussolini's arrest and expulsion. Included were aristocratic Piedmontese Colonel Guiseppe Cordero Lanza di Montezemolo and several members of his staff. Even Italian generals (64-year old Major General Simone Simoni, 58- year-old Brigadier General Sabato Martelli Castaldi and 55-year-old Brigadier General Darnado Fenulli) were added to his growing list.

As daylight broke, Kappler realized he had worked all night. He looked again at his total and was satisfied that he now had enough prisoners and Jews to fulfill his Fuhrer's orders. He straightened his uniform and went about the job of rounding up enough SS officers to fulfill his duty.

SS Obersturmbannführer Eugen Dollmann was still fuming when he returned to the small apartment he kept near the offices of the German Embassy.

I am disgusted both as a German and a human being. I know the Fuhrer has ordered the execution, but that doesn't make it any better. German officers should be able to think for themselves, not act as sheep being led to the slaughter. There must be something else I can do to stop this senseless act.

He suddenly realized that his only possible means to end the Fuhrer's order was the only person in Rome with enough power to act in such a dire situation ---Pope Pius XII.

I must go and see if the pope will see me or someone who could intercede with Kappler. I will change into civilian clothes. I know whom I should go and see. He will know what to do about this insanity.

He hurriedly changed and set out for his destination across the Tiber---a monastery in the piazza just below the windows of the papal apartments. The place was the location of the Order of Salvatorians and the residence of Abbot General Father Pankratius Pfeiffer, unofficially known as Padre Pancrazio. The silver haired priest was an old friend of Dollmann's, as well as the personal liaison with the German occupation forces. Father Pfeiffer was called 'the good padre' and had been helpful to Dollmann in the past. He was on particularly good terms with both Field Marshal Albert Kesselring and Generalleutnant Kurt Mälzer, Rome's military commander.

Dollmann was immediately ushered into Father Pfeiffer's small office where the old friends exchanged greetings.

"I know why you are here, Eugen." The Abbot General surprised his guest. "I don't know all the details but I am aware of the attack."

"It was ghastly, Padre. So many bodies and body parts scattered all over the street. It made me sick to my stomach."

"I can only imagine. Such happenings are not the work of the Lord."

"Exactly, Padre. That's one of the reasons I came to you."

Pfeiffer leaned closer waiting for Dollmann's next words.

"I expect there will be reprisals for what has happened, and I have not as yet been informed of what they will be. It is my hope that any reprisals will be contained within the framework of the Hague Convention.

The Fuhrer is beside himself with rage and is demanding a reprisal. Nothing had been decided as of yet, but I am certain something will soon be done. I believe that the Hague Convention provides for the execution of hostages. The situation could easily turn into a bloodbath if something isn't done soon."

"What would you have me do, Eugen? How can I help?"

"If you could go to the Vatican and tell them of my pacification plan to give us time to cool off the hotheads who want to destroy the entire area around Via Rasella and all the people who live there. I propose that we hold a funeral procession for the Germans who were killed in the attack. We would also bring to Rome the families of those soldiers killed and let them join the parade through the streets. That would make the Italians sympathetic to both the slain officers and Germany itself. Both the pope and Field Marshal Kesselring would address the people of Rome, with each calling for peace. This plan would buy us time, perhaps two or three days in which to placate the agitated state of mind that reigns among the ranks of many Germans."

Pfeiffer exclaimed, "Excellent! I am certain the Vatican will be enthusiastic. I will go at once and inform them." He smiled at his friend and placed his hands on Dollmann's. "I will try my best, Eugen. You have my word."

"Thank you, Padre." Dollmann felt himself beginning to smile. "I hope you are successful. Let's talk again tomorrow. Maybe things will have changed by then."

The two shook hands and Dollmann departed. He realized he had just played his final card in the high stakes game where many lives could potentially be forfeited.

General Mälzer's headquarters,
Excelsior Hotel,
Via Vittorio Veneto, 125
Rome, Italy

It was around noon when Generalleutnant Kurt Mälzer summoned SS Obersturmbannfuhrer Herbert Kappler to his headquarters in Rome's most fashionable hotel. In addition to Kappler, SS Sturmbannfuhrer Hellmuth Dobbrick was also sent for. He was the unfortunate commander of the SS Police Regiment

Bozen that had been attacked the previous day. Fortunately for Dobbrick, he had traveled the day before in his car to the training exercises and had just passed in front of the marching column on Via Rasella when the bomb exploded.

Mälzer questioned Kappler on the status of his list of potential retaliation victims and was told that it would be completed within the hour.

He turned to Dobbrick and made a short speech about the importance of the mission at hand and reminded both Dobbrick and Kappler that the mission had been ordered by Adolf Hitler himself. He also stated that it would now be his duty and also the existing survivors of Regiment Bozen to avenge their dead and wounded comrades. He next ordered the German major to immediately execute the 320 men that would be included on Kappler's completed list.

Incredibly, Dobbrick refused to obey his superior's order. "My men are not capable of such an action; you might even think of them as inept. We are all from the Tyrol, are mostly Catholic, and we have a number of beliefs that such an order would violate. I simply cannot in good conscience obey such an order."

Mälzer was shocked and momentarily unable to speak. At last he walked over to a telephone and called Fourteenth Army Headquarters and spoke with Chief of Staff Colonel Wolfgang Hauser. He asked that a detachment of troops be made available to carry out the Fuhrer's orders.

Hauser refused the request and replied, "It was the police who were struck; it is the police who must make the expiation."

Mälzer repeated Hauser's words to Kappler. Dumfounded by the turn of events, he told his subordinate, "It's up to you, Kappler."

Kappler was unsure of what to do. The thought of who would actually carry out the heinous order had never really crossed his mind. He had never killed anyone even though he had volunteered for frontline service some five times during his career.

He tried to get himself out of this difficult situation. His logic had no effect on the general who was also trying to avoid a calamitous situation.

Finally, Kappler was forced to give in. He agreed that if Mälzer ordered him to do so he would put his men at Mälzer's disposal.

"No," the commandant of Rome shot back. "As head of the Gestapo in Rome, you have the duty to set an example for your men. I order you to take control of this matter."

166

Kappler reluctantly agreed. However, in the back of his mind he thought *I have no right to ask my men to do what I myself am loath to do... I must call all my officers together and develop a plan... He looked at his watch and again considered. I only have eight more hours to do the Fuhrer's bidding.*

Mälzer was relieved that Kappler had finally agreed to carry out the Fuhrer's order. He wanted to wipe his hands of the whole affair as soon as possible. But, he decided, he would continue the genuine mourning of the men who were lost. He would have a drink later that night to their honor and courage.

SS Obersturmbannfuhrer Kappler's office,
SS Headquarters,
Via Tasso, 155
Rome, Italy

In another section of the 18th Century building that was the prison as well as offices of the SS in Rome, SS Obersturmbannfuhrer Herbert Kappler looked over the group that he had assembled.

All twelve officers under his command were present and seated even before the SS leader returned to Via Tasso. Unsure of the purpose for the meeting, they talked in hushed tones as their leader moved to the front of the room. They stop whispering as Kappler began addressing them in a most somber manner.

"Within a few hours," he started slowly, "three hundred twenty persons will have to be killed by you people seated here. This order is a direct result of the terrible attack on the Via Rasella yesterday by Communists and terrorists. As officers of the SS, you must all take part with no exceptions. This action is under the direct order of our Fuhrer and must be completed by 2030 tonight. I consider this order a symbolic necessity. It is indispensable to the maintenance of discipline."

The officers stirred and looked at each other as Kappler continued. "I must tell you that the commander of the police regiment that was attacked has refused to avenge his men and has been disciplined. Due to his cowardly refusal, we here have been selected to do the job and that decision is final."

Kappler paused to let his words sink in. This time no one moved nor spoke.

"Speed and security are our next concerns. You already know the timing involved. We must all act quickly and professionally. It is absolutely necessary that the executions be kept secret at all costs. No one can predict the reactions of the Romans if they were to discover what was taking place in their midst. The partisans could organize another armed assault like the one that just took place. The whole city could explode without notice," he warned.

"I know that executions are usually carried out by a firing squad in the prison yard at Fort Bravetta, but this is an exception. There are simply too many to be executed. What we need is something like a big grotto or cavern, in other words a large, natural death chamber. Does anyone know of any such place that is nearby?"

SS Hauptsturmführer Kohler spoke from the back of the group. "I know of such a place. It is about two or three miles from here on the Via Ardeatina. It is a network of tunnels among the Christian catacombs. I believe it is abandoned but I also think the Italian Resistance uses it to hide its vehicles. An informer recently reported it to me."

"You will go immediately and investigate its feasibility," Kappler ordered Kohler. "And report back to me as soon as possible."

He paused, consulted his notes and began again. "Now for the rest of you. Schutz, you will direct the executions and, Priebke, you will be the keeper of the list. You must insure that everyone named on the list is actually executed and vice versa." Both named officers acknowledged their tasks.

Around 0100, he made his way to the mess hall where he briefed his non-commissioned officers on the assignment ahead. SS Hauptsturmführer Kurt Schutz interrupted his conversation to inform Kappler that another member of the Bozen Regiment, "had just died."

That brings the number I must execute to 330. Where do they expect me to produce such numbers? I am already a bit lower by my last count and I am running out of options. If only I had more prisoners to choose from---or maybe more Jews. He pondered his next move and was happy to see that Kohler had returned from his mission to the caves.

"I took some Wehrmacht engineers with me," reported Kohler. "They felt it would be easy to seal the entrance with explosives. This would create a mass tomb."

"Good initiative, Kohler. We need more forward thinking like that."

Suddenly Kappler's attractive secretary, Katerina Schwarzer, appeared and handed the Obersturmbannfuhrer a newly typed list of prisoners. "There are ten more Jews on the list," she offered. "They were brought in a few hours ago."

168

Kappler studied the list and smiled. "We're almost there," he smirked. "It's just a matter of time."

Katerina smiled a knowing smile and departed. For a moment, Kappler's mind drifted to a thought of Katerina reclining in his bed.

It is good to think of something other than the executions for a moment. And Katerina provides just that hiatus. What a wonderful secretary she is...and a great lover as well....I am indeed a most fortunate man...

Satisfied he had enough officers for the task, Kappler neatly folded the paper with the names of the officers and placed it inside his tunic next to the list of prisoners who were to be shot. He was satisfied he had done his duty to the SS and the fatherland.

Chapter Fifteen

True Christianity today is not different from primitive Christianity ...
She remains what she has been since her foundation: always the same.

— *Pope Pius XII*

Wednesday, March 24, 1944
Mouther House of Order of Salvatorians,
Residence of Abbot General Father Pankratius Pfeiffer,
Piazza San Pietro adjoining papal apartments,
Rome, Italy

Padre Pancrazio's facial expression told the story of his hastily formed meeting with Pope Pius XII at the Vatican. The urgency of the situation had caused the Salvatorian Abbot to break protocol and ask to see the pope on short notice.

Pius agreed to see him after Father Pfeiffer pleaded with his staff to do so. The pontiff listened attentively to the priest who was Germany's official liaison to the Vatican and whose presence had aided a number of prior church-related problems that had arisen.

In the end, the pope decided that his silence would again be utilized in the name of a greater good for the future. He thanked Pfeiffer for his ongoing interest to bring peace to the children of God and expressed interest in finding out further details of the massacre. He pointed out to Pfeiffer that the Vatican's initial reports, although unverified, pointed to members of the Italian Communist Party as the perpetrators of the attack on the Via Rasella.

The pope also pointed out that the Communist Party was the indisputable enemy of the Holy See and was actively attempting to destroy the Roman Catholic Church and its members. He specified Albania, Bulgaria, Czechoslovakia and Hungary as well as Lithuania, Estonia and Latvia as countries where the Catholic Church was fighting for its very existence.

The pope promised Pfeiffer that the Vatican would make a statement on the matter that would be published in *L'Osservatore Romano*, the Vatican's semi-official newspaper, available around noon of the same day. He fervently hoped his words that would bear the headline, Carita Civile (Civil Compassion) would be taken to heart by all Romans and everyone interested in peace.

Pfeiffer had already called Dollmann with the bad news of the pope's unwillingness to get involved when the newspaper arrived shortly after noon. At first glance, the pope was true to his word. Father Pfeiffer eagerly read the following:

Carita Civile

We recall that on other occasions we have addressed ourselves to the grave times through which the country is passing. Now in these anxious hours we turn specifically to Rome.

Our appeal is made to the honest heart of the people, who have so admirably demonstrated their spirit of sacrifice and profound sense of dignity. Do not with violent urges shatter this attitude, which is so worthy of the virtues of our people. Every ill-considered act would have no other result than to end by injuring many innocent people, already too tried by anguish and privation.

All those upon whom it is incumbent to maintain public order have the task of assuring that it is not disturbed by any attitude whatsoever that might in itself be used as the reason for reactions that would give rise to effectively influence the minds of the citizenry-- -above all the clergy--- have the high mission of persuasion, pacification, and giving comfort...

Pfeiffer sighed and put the paper down. He thought passively. *Does the Holy Father have enough influence on his unwavering multitudes of supporters to fend off the possible reaction of Rome to what lay ahead?* He considered the possibilities. *If Pius is correct, disaster might well be averted. Romans have always thought for themselves and that is a positive. It is to their credit that history has shown that Romans have an ability to see the falseness of obvious scenarios.* A bible passage came to mind, from Romans 8:25. "But if we hope for that we see not, then do we with patience wait for it."

172

Adversely, Pfeiffer considered the alternative. *Should the pope's words fall on deaf ears, the City of Rome and the Vatican could easily be devastated. Chaos would reign and the Holy Church could be severely damaged.*

Father Pfeiffer reread the entire article and shook his head. This day was already proving to be persisting and seemed to the prelate to become even more so as the afternoon progressed.

Regina Coeli Prison,
Via della Lugara, 29
Rome, Italy

A line of Opel Blitz 3.6 Wehrmacht trucks with canvass tops used for carrying meat filled the narrow street that was Via della Lugara, home of Rome's largest prison, Regina Coeli. They had been ordered by the SS to transport the large number of inmates from the old prison located just off the waters of the Tiber River to an unspecified destination. The drivers would be told their destination once the trucks were fully loaded. Armed SS guards would be positioned on each vehicle and motorcycle escorts would precede and follow the caravan. A few similar trucks had also been sent to the 20-cell prison that the SS operated for special prisoners at the Via Tasso.

In an orderly fashion, prisoners were brought out of their cells and ushered into the trucks. Men, and male children (mostly Jews) were first loaded and then the remainder of the list that SS Obersturmbannfuhrer Herbert Kappler had assembled. The prisoners had neither any idea where they were being taken nor any inkling they were about to be executed. It is highly improbable that any of them had even heard about the attack on German troops at the Via Rasella.

At the Via Tasso, a number of problems were encountered during the loading. Several of the prisoners had to be carried out, their injuries from Gestapo torture too great to allow them to walk. Among these unfortunates was a 55-year-old priest, Don Pietro Pappagallo, the chaplain to the sisters of the Bambin Gesù Convent. Singled out by a German spy for his activities in support of the Italian Resistance, Pappagallo had been imprisoned. During his stay, he had been an inspiration for the other prisoners in Cell 13 of Via Tasso.

Also included were Colonel Guiseppe Cordero Lanza di Montezemolo whose face was swollen and his right eye almost closed from beatings he had received. He was assisted into the truck and the back canvass dropped and secured. The column of trucks was officially ready to go.

173

⌒

Site of the Ardeatina sand pits,
Via Ardeatina,
Rome, Italy

The route from Via Tasso to the Ardeatina sand pits brought the caravan to the Appian Way, Rome's storied road that was used by the Apostle Peter some twenty centuries ago. The trucks took the fork toward the old Roman Port of Ardea, but stopped after about a mile. The vehicles halted and the prisoners were let out. Upon seeing their surroundings, the prisoners realized that all hope was lost.

From among the group, a woeful cry materialized, "Father, bless us!"

Don Pietro Pappagallo suddenly thrust off his ropes, stepped forward and began to pray. His fatherly blessing brought comfort to nearly everyone who was about to die. His act of bravery was observed by his German captors.

It was close to 1530 when the additional trucks from the Regina Coeli arrived. The prisoners dismounted and were forced to stand in a large group with SS soldiers standing guard.

SS Oberstrumbannfuhrer Herbert Kappler barked orders at the SS officers and non-commissioned officers that he had assembled. He had already designated SS Hauptsturmführer Erich Priebke as the tally keeper and SS Hauptsturmführer Kurt Schutz as the officer within the caves directing the executions.

Kappler was not unaware of aversion to his orders by some of his officers. He had shrewdly designated a case of top cognac to be brought to the site. He offered generous portions to the officers who immediately began to imbibe the potent brandy.

Finally, the order to begin the process was given. Kappler had designated five-man platoons for the shootings. Each officer chose a prisoner, and, after Priebke had checked off each name, the officer escorted them back into the caves. At various intervals along the route, a German soldier held a torch to illuminate the nearly totally black space.

Well into the labyrinth that connected the central tunnel, another set of torches lit a small area. Here was Schutz, waiting like a primordial slayer. The prisoners were made to kneel and tilt their bowed heads to one side. Upon Schutz's order, "Fire!" each officer fired a single round. According to SS policies, the round was aimed at the neck at an angle that was meant to pass through the brain, supposedly insured an immediate, simple death for each prisoner. The dead Italians were left on the floor of the cave where they had fallen, then stacked one on top of the other.

Both Kappler and Priebke each took turns in the rotation. Kappler shot in the second platoon and Priebke in the third. Lifeless corpses were piled up as the stack steadily grew.

Soon the system began breaking down and before long the site had become a human slaughterhouse. The cognac began affecting the officers who became shoddy in their firing. More than one shot was required to kill several prisoners and sometimes the heads were blown completely off the bodies.

At one point, one of the SS officers balked at shooting. SS Oberstrumfuehrer Wetjen said to other officers, "Kappler gives the orders, but he doesn't have to carry them out."

Kappler heard the statement and then asked Wetjen, "Why have you refused to shoot?"

"I feel revulsion in my stomach," the younger officer replied.

Kappler looked at the officer and spoke. "The SS must conduct itself in a certain manner even if the orders are unpleasant. We have all taken an oath and that is paramount. I have been told to do this and I will follow my orders. You must also carry out the orders like a good soldier."

"You're right," Wetjen conceded. "But it's not that easy."

"Would you feel better if I was at your side when you fired?"

The officer nodded and Kappler put his arm around Wetjen's waist. Both Kappler and Wetjen then raised their PO8 Lugers and each fired at a kneeling prisoner.

Toward the end, the gruesome site within the caves reached horrific proportions. Only the fact that the German officers were now mostly drunk permitted the final executions. An additional five prisoners remained, due mostly to an inadequate numbering system on one of the lists. Kappler deliberated for several moments and then ordered the five prisoners shot.

At around 2000, the final shots were fired, some 30 minutes before Adolf Hitler's time limit was to expire. Many of the officers were soaked in the blood of their victims.

SS Hauptsturmführer Erich Priebke consulted his list again and tallied up the numbers. Some 335 Italians were accounted for, five more than the 10 for 1 ratio that had been ordered.

Kappler signaled to the engineers who had been waiting outside the caves. They prepared two explosions that would seal the caves from the outside.

After the explosions, Kappler ordered his men back to Via Tasso for dinner. Later that night, he attended another meeting of high-ranking officers at the Hotel Excelsior. It was decided at that time that a communiqué be issued by the German High Command that informed the world that in reprisal for the thirty-three men killed in the Via Rasella attack, 335 Italians were executed.

Saturday, March 25, 1944
Headquarters of the Wehrmacht,
Hotel Excelsior,
Via Vittorio Veneto, 125
Rome, Italy

It was early Saturday when the ranking officers of the SS and German diplomatic corps met in General Mälzer's suite at the plush Hotel Excelsior. Wolff, Kappler and Dollmann were joined by Consul Möllhausen. The topics of discussion were the executions of the day before and the new Hitler order that had just been received that involved the deportation of all men and their families between the ages of 18 and 45.

Hitler's new directive was the first item of discussion.

"Reichsführer Himmler called me a short time ago to have our Roman Ambassador to Rome Weizsäcker not publically condemn the deportations. He was also adamant that there be no mention of the reprisals against the Italians," Wolff began. "We talked a good while and he seemed open to our cause here. Before we hung up, Himmler agreed that the deportations could be postponed if Rome's influential people were in agreement. We sitting here *are* the influential people in Rome and I feel such an order from the Fuhrer is sheer madness."

"The number of troops an order like this would require is beyond our capability," Kappler spoke up. "We would have to get additional forces from Kesselring."

"Kesselring has his hands full," warned Möllhausen. "And I understand he is planning a new attack on the Anzio beachhead. There would be no soldiers left to implement the Fuhrer's deportation order.

Also, if this order would be put into effect, I feel the pope would have to come out publically against such an order. The Vatican has shown deference to our activities to this point, but a mass deportation of Romans to the north would be impossible for the pope to overlook."

"Good point. There is also the issue of logistics. Such numbers would clog all roads to the north and prevent their usage for military affairs," added Wolff. "It could lead to a military disaster."

Wolff had thought about this scenario for the past ten hours. *This whole war is turning against us and it would be smart to think of the future. If I show respect for Rome and all Italian citizens, it would go well for me if we lose the war. I certainly don't want to invade the Vatican and kidnap the pope, but if the Fuhrer orders it, I might have no choice but to obey. Depending on how Kesselring's tactics play out, another delay might just do the trick. I wonder if the pope would be open to seeing me in person. I know this is improbable at best, but if Weizsäcker is correct about the Vatican, there might just be an outside chance. I have heard a lot about Pius; meeting him in person would be most interesting...*

After arranging the details for the report to Berlin, the meeting adjourned. The German High Command would be informed that Rome's important persons were in agreement that the mass deportation of Italian men and their families should be postponed. The group felt that once the Anzio and Monte Cassino battles were decided in Germany's favor, such an undertaking could then be revisited.

Sunday, March 26, 1944
Santa Maria dell'Anima,
Via di Santa Maria dell'Anima, 64
Rome, Italy

It was a crisp Sunday morning and Father Günter Kempff was already a few minutes late in entering the confessional. A perturbed glance from an older woman waiting in line told the prelate he should be on time like any good German priest. Kempff acknowledged the look and took his small seat inside the confessional. He slid the window and the confession started,

"Forgive me, Father, for I have sinned."

The first few penitents were mostly older parishioners with the usual assortment of sins and Kempff dished out the normal penance for their actions, two Hail Mary's, an Our Father or two and on rare occasions, an entire rosary for something really out of the ordinary. It was the part of his weekly duty at the German Church of Rome that Kempff didn't enjoy. The sinner's anguished repetition had long ago forced him to endure the long hour before Holy Mass as a form of personal penance for his feelings.

Toward the end of his session, Kempff's attention was suddenly roused by a fresh male voice, much younger and crisper. Kempff sat up and leaned toward the opening where the confessor was kneeling.

The man's German was crisp and fluent and Kempff found himself paying attention to every word.

"And I participated in the killing of more than three hundred people a few days ago."

Kempff was startled and said, "What did you say, my son? Could you repeat that for me?"

"You heard right, Father. I killed more than three hundred people a few days ago."

"Are you a soldier? After all this is wartime and people are killed in war all the time."

"Yes, I am a soldier, but that is no excuse. These people were killed with their hands tied behind their backs…they were executed, I'm sorry to say."

Kempff thought for a moment then asked again, "Were you ordered to do so, my son?"

"Yes, Father, but that is no excuse. I personally pulled the trigger on many of the prisoners. I killed those men, and for that I am truly sorry. I haven't been able to sleep since the incident. That's why I am here…"

Kempff thought again. "Since you were following orders, I do not believe you were at fault, my son. I know this is hard for you, you sound like a reasonable man. A reasonable man would feel sorrow for such an act. It would be a normal reaction."

"War does not favor reasonable men, Father. It makes you susceptible to the basest forms of living. I abhor what I have done but I don't have the courage to disobey my oath to the Fuhrer."

"We must all do what our conscience tells us, my son."

"And, that's not all Father. There is something that might be even worse…"

"What could be worse than killing 300 men? I can't imagine…"

"I should not even mention it, Father. It is beyond my imagination."

Kempff wondered, *Should I probe any further?* His curiosity got the best of him and he continued, "It would do you good to let it all out, my son."

The voice on the other side of the opening paused for a moment. Then he slowly continued.

"Father, I will be asked to do something in the future that is against all I believe, all I have been taught, and everything my religion stands for…"

What could it possibly be? He sounds both frightened and lost at the same time.

The voice spoke again in a low whisper. "I have been advised that I will be part of a plan that would involve invading the Vatican and kidnapping the Holy Father." The voice trailed off as the last words stemmed from his lips. "I don't see how I can go through with it and remain a Catholic…"

Kempff was taken aback by the statement and struggled to come up with the correct response.

"Have you spoken to your superiors about this madness?" Kempff inquired.

"Yes, Father. I think they feel the same way about it as I do. But the order is supposedly to be direct from the Fuhrer. There is no questioning an order from him. I would be arrested and shot as a traitor if I didn't comply. I even heard that the general in charge is stalling for time since he is not in agreement with the Fuhrer."

Kempff remained silent and finally spoke to the young German.

"My son, your position is quite difficult to comprehend. You must think about the consequences of your act and how it will affect the Holy Church. Our pope means a great deal to millions of people around the entire world, not just to Catholics in your country and here in Italy. His demise would be a calamity…"

"I know, Father. I know."

179

"I will pray for you, my son, to our Holy Savior. I will ask that he guide you in your hour of need and allow you to make the proper decision.

The voice on the other side of the confessional's opening remained silent.

"Now you must make an Act of Contrition for your sins," directed Kempff. "You have no penance today, I feel your soul is already burdened a great deal. I absolve you in the name of Our Lord. Go now and seek the comfort that Jesus Christ brought to all of us."

As the person exited the confessional, the curtain on Father Kempff's enclosure briefly swept back. A uniformed officer had exited the confessional. All that Kempff had been able to distinguish was the explicit insignia on the man's collar. He shuddered when he recognized the double SS of the feared Gestapo. He sunk his head and pondered his next move. His attention was diverted as the next person entered the confessional. A familiar "Forgive me, Father," began the next confession.

Chapter Sixteen

"The Jesuits are a MILITARY
organization, not a religious order."

— *Napoleon Bonaparte*

Sunday, April 2, 1944
Gregorian University,
Piazza della Pilotta, 4
Rome, Italy

A week had passed since Father Günter Kempff's incredible confessional episode. The German prelate had wrestled with the confession every day since and had thought of practically nothing else. He was now sitting at the table with his friend Father Michael Rodi to a meal that the latter had prepared in the Gregorian University's kitchen. Part of the meal was a rich vegetable soup that Kempff was stirring while staring into space.

"You haven't touched your soup, Günter," observed Rodi. "The way you are stirring it will soon be cold. Aren't you hungry?"

"I haven't eaten much all week, Michael. It has nothing to do with your cooking."

"Something is really bothering you, my friend. You seem to be carrying a heavy burden."

"Yes, you are right Michael, a *truly* heavy burden."

"Would it do any good to talk about it? I would be happy to help…"

"I'm not sure the pope himself could help, Michael. The matter is quite involved and has dire consequences." Kempff thought to himself. *I cannot break the Seal of Confession, I would have to give up being a priest if I did…*

"I'm sure there's an answer to your problem, Günter. You just need to talk about it some more."

181

"That's just it. I can't talk about it to you or anyone."

A light went on in Rodi's mind as he suddenly realized his friend's predicament. *It is something he probably heard during confessions and he cannot break the Seal of Confession... This is serious... There must be a way to help...* He thought again and finally spoke.

"Günter, what if you discussed the matter in a purely hypothetical sense? You wouldn't have to be specific, and you could talk in general terms. Would that help?"

Father Günter Kempff considered his friend's suggestion and replied. "Yes, maybe that might work. Then I wouldn't be betraying..." His words trailed off in mid-sentence.

The apprehensive priest slowly began to talk, choosing his words carefully. "Suppose some information came into my possession that could easily change the direction of the war and the fate of our Holy Church. This information, should it become known, would be a great help in saving the Church."

My God, Rodi realized. *He really is on to something that is even more significant than I could have imagined. I must help him find a way to bring this all out in the open.*

Rodi spoke in a low voice. "Günter, what you have told me is quite serious; I see why you are so worried. Is there anything else, hypothetically of course, which you can add to what you have already said?"

Kempff considered Rodi's question and finally replied. "I don't really know. I have thought about this for the past week. I think there might be a solution but I can't figure it out by myself. Right now I'm too tired to think very clearly."

Rodi patted his friend on the shoulder. "I might just have an answer. Let's finish our meal here and then I want you to come to the Vatican with me. There is someone there I want you to talk to."

Kempff looked over warily at the other priest. "Maybe I have already said too much, Michael."

Rodi swallowed his now lukewarm soup and reassured his friend. "Nonsense, Günter. We have only spoken in a hypothetical sense. There is no harm in that."

The German priest looked over, unconvinced. He took a sip of the soup and pronounced, "This is almost cold. It must be warmed if we are to eat it." There was no hint of a respite from the deeply troubled cleric.

182

⌐∽

Office of Father Robert Leiber, S.J.
Secretariat of State,
Palazzo del Governatorato,
The Vatican,
Rome, Italy

The German Jesuit Father Robert Leiber had spent most of his Sunday afternoon trying to catch up on the pope's paperwork, a job that was not among his favorite tasks. When the door to his office opened, he was pleasantly surprised to see his protégé, Father Michael S. Rodi, with Father Günter Kempff standing just behind. When he observed the almost ashen face of Kempff, he realized something was wrong.

"Good day, fathers. What brings you here on a Sunday afternoon?" Leiber asked.

"We have something of a problem, Robert," Rodi answered. "And I thought you might just be the person to hear us out."

"I'll try and do my best. Let's have it."

"First of all, this is all hypothetical, Robert. That must be clear from the start."

"Yes, hypothetical," Kempff agreed. "That is important."

Rodi followed. "My friend here," he began, pointing to Kempff, "posed a purely suppositious situation earlier today at our noon meal.

A friend of his has been made aware of certain facts that would negatively affect both the current war and the Holy See if they reached fruition. Father Kempff had been greatly troubled by these facts and is at a loss as to what to do about them. When he spoke to me, theoretically of course, I thought it best that we come and visit with you."

Leiber correctly calculated in his mind that Kempff had heard something in the confessional that could hurt the Holy Church and was dumbfounded as to how to proceed. *This is a ticklish matter, and must be handled with great care. I wouldn't want to give advice to the German priest that would compromise his position as a confessor. If I only had more to work with, there might be a solution. I imagine what Michael has told me is all that Kempff has told him.*

Leiber's quick mind processed the information and finally responded. "I'm afraid I can't answer that. What you have told me is just too general in meaning. I would have to know more about it in order to make any suggestion."

183

Suddenly, a thought surfaced in his mind. *What if this has to do with the German plan to invade the Vatican and kidnap the pope? When the German diplomats came to see us about not speaking out about the German atrocities, they mentioned something about an order that Hitler had given. That would make sense... The diplomats were actually blackmailing us with the threat of an invasion... I might try asking Kempff certain questions that would not betray his seal... In that way, I might be able to get to the bottom of this...*

Leiber addressed Kempff in a soft, compassionate tone. "I want to ask you a few more questions. All you need do is move you head yes or no."

Kempff looked uncertainly at Leiber, and acknowledged the instructions.

"First of all, I presume the person supplying the information is German, correct?"

With a slight hesitation, Kempff nodded affirmatively.

"Good. That's a start."

"Do you know this person personally?"

Kempff nodded negatively.

Do you believe the information you received is genuine?"

Again, Kempff shook his head positively.

"Does the information involve the Holy Church and the Holy Father personally?"

Again, Kempff nodded.

"Was there any reference to Hitler in the information?"

Another yes. "Did the information provide any time for the events to happen?"

This time a negative nod.

"Do you feel there is a way around this information? That somehow this can be averted?"

Kempff hesitated, unsure of how to reply. At length, he shook his head positively.

"What measures would you take to prevent this from taking place?"

Kempff shook his head. No.

Leiber considered his next move. *This isn't going to be easy. I must take my time.*

He decided on a different approach.

"If I say a word, just nod again. Kempff shook his head okay.

"German diplomats."

No.

"German military."

Again, no.

German parishioners of your church?

Another no.

Leiber realized he was stuck. Who else could be a part of all this? He retraced his line of questions and finally had a thought.

"German SS. Gestapo."

This time Father Kempff's head rose slightly as he sighed.

He nodded his head slowly and then put his head in his hands. He was on the verge of tears when Leiber put his hand on his shoulder.

"That's quite enough, Günter. I'll take it from here."

Father Günter Kempff raised his eyes with a look of longing that resembled fear.

"It will all be okay, I promise you that," Leiber assured.

Kempff peered into Leiber's eyes and then turned to Rodi. Rodi also placed his hand on Kempff's shoulder to reassure his friend.

"I'll be back to you shortly, Michael," advised Leiber. "Take this brave man with you and have a bottle of wine on me." He handed some lire to Rodi who took the money. "Actually, you should have a couple of bottles, you'll feel better afterwards."

Rodi motioned to Kempff and the two left the room. Father Robert Leiber sat at his desk and contemplated his next move. Considering the circumstances, this new problem could easily prove to be his most complicated task undertaken in his present position as private secretary to Pope Pius XII.

Monday, April 13, 1944
San Gregorio Convent,
Padri Camaldolesi,
Piazza di San Gregorio al Celio, 1
Rome, Italy

Countess Donna Virginia Bourbon del Monte Agnelli could not believe that she was trapped in her present situation. Months earlier, a pair of fascist policemen had come to the Villa del Bosco Parrasio, her incredible 18th Century mansion on Janiculum Hill. The lawmen charged her with minor offenses and transported her to her current confinement, the San Gregario Convent. The convent was actually a prison for high caliber ladies of breeding and rank who demonstrated dangerous political intentions in the minds of the Fascists.

Several factors led to her arrest. First, she was the former wife of Edoardo Agnelli who had died four years earlier in a seaplane crash in Genoa. Agnelli was the heir to the expansive Fiat automobile fortune and one of Italy's richest men. Secondly, Virginia (as she was known to her friends) had an American mother and preferred speaking in English, to the chagrin of the Italian Fascists. She had lavishly entertained throughout the years. Her guests included princes, church leaders, nobility and many leaders of government including numerous prominent Fascist leaders. Her lack of contentment at Mussolini's ouster was the actual basis for her arrest and imprisonment.

Virginia Agnelli had unsuccessfully tried a number of times to gain her release. Fascist military officials and a number of diplomatic friends failed to gain her liberation. She was even on familiar terms with the present pope but she dared not ask his help on this matter due to the Catholic Church's ongoing clashes with the current Fascist Government. She realized that she was nearing the end of her options when she suddenly remembered the sophisticated German officer who had attended a number of her parties.

Colonel Dollmann, why didn't I think of him before? He probably has more power and better connections than any Italian at this time. He always seemed attracted to me. He was always teasing me about my English ties...He even told me in a kidding way that

I shouldn't be speaking in English...Maybe he wasn't kidding all that much...I will write him immediately and see if he will help me get out of this horrid place.

She reached for a piece of paper and began writing. She already knew the address, Via Tasso 145. It was an address familiar to many Romans for the past two years for the numerous abuses to Italian nationals perpetrated by the feared SS.

Tuesday, April 4, 1944
Office of Father Robert Leiber, S.J.,
Secretariat of State,
Palazzo del Governatorato,
The Vatican,
Rome, Italy

The initial stages of a strategy had begun to develop in the mind of Father Robert Leiber, S.J., which might possibly solve the dichotomy of intention that existed in his mind. He was committed to protecting the Seal of Confession of the German priest Father Günter Kempff and at the same time he was focused on assisting in a scheme that might save both the Vatican and pope from outside impairment.

He had already approached Pope Pius XII about the situation and was not pleased when his Church's leader seemed opposed to receiving a high-ranking German officer. The pope told Leiber that he had already inferred such to German Ambassador Weizsäcker a few weeks ago and that he intended to hold that view.

Leiber knew this presented a major problem. Any meeting that would be arranged through the German diplomat would have to be considered semi-official, at least from the German perspective. Leiber had learned long ago not to trust the Germans in diplomatic matters and the fact that the Nazis had broken their word on numerous occasions made him fearful of using any diplomatic channels for this current predicament.

There must be another way, he reflected. A phrase from his favorite American author Mark Twain came to mind. "There must be another way to skin a cat." *I must look beyond the obvious to find an answer. It is probably right in front of me and I just can't see it. His mind drifted back to the events of the past few days and fixated on the attack at the Via Rasella. He recalled the account that Father Michael Rodi had provided and suddenly a single thought emerged. Didn't we receive a short note from the Vatican that applauded Michael Rodi's efforts at the Via Rasella? I'm sure we did...I believe it might still be in this pile on my desk...* He searched through a large pile of papers and extracted one on the official stationery of the German

SS. He looked at the signatory and spelled it out in his mind. D O L L M A N N, *Oberstrumbannfuhrer Dollmann...he will do nicely...I must summon Father Rodi immediately; there is no time to lose.*

⌒

Wednesday, April 5, 1944
Offices of the SS,
Via Tasso, 155
Rome, Italy

He had just returned from a short walk to the nearby Archbasilica di San Giovanni Lateran on the Piazza di San Giovanni. The ornate building was among his favorite places to spend time and was close to his office.

This is what has always fascinated me about royalty, considered SS Oberst鬼sturmbannführer Eugen Dollmann as he examined the letter he just opened from Virginia Agnelli. *When they are in serious trouble they are not hesitant to go to whatever ends necessary to get out of that trouble. This wonderful woman is appealing to someone like me to get out of prison. I am flattered she thought of me. She knows everyone, from cardinals to powerful political figures. I'm sure she has done nothing wrong beyond hurting the feelings of some high-minded Fascists. She says she has been in prison for some time and I'm sure that's true. Come to think of it, I haven't attended any of her parties for a while now.*

I have no problem arranging for her release. Since we control Italy at this point, no one would dare refuse me. I will see to it the first chance I get, possibly this afternoon.

His attention was diverted as the phone on his desk rang. He picked up the received.

"Dollmann, here."

"Colonel Dollmann, This is Father Robert Leiber, the pope's private secretary. His Holiness just received your kind letter about one of our priests, Father Michael Rodi. He directed me to try to meet with you about this as soon as possible."

"But, I don't see why a meeting is necessary. My letter was very specific," Dollmann answered dubiously.

"I intend to bring Father Rodi with me, Colonel Dollmann. You would have a chance to meet with him directly."

Dollmann considered the prospect. *That was one brave priest and his actions for the fatherland were beyond virtue. I probably would enjoy meeting with him if only for a*

188

short while. It would take my mind off these other awful events that are still heavily hanging on my conscience.

"Do you want to meet here at my headquarters?" asked Dollmann.

"No, that would not be possible. We are priests after all. I had in mind something more pleasant. Are you familiar with a small outdoor café on Via Emanuele Filiberto named Emilio's?"

"Why, yes, of course. It's only a few blocks from my office."

"Can we meet there about six thirty this evening?"

"That would be convenient for me."

"And, Colonel. Can I please ask you to come in civilian clothes? It wouldn't do for two priests to be seen in the company of a high-ranking SS officer enjoying a bottle of wine."

"I understand, Father. By the way, what is your name? I seem to have forgotten it."

"Father Robert Leiber."

"Thank you. I will meet you later this evening."

A pleasant diversion for me, Dollmann reflected. *And a nice bottle of wine to start my evening. What harm could there be in seeing the pope's private secretary and a priest who is something of a hero to Germany?*

⁓

Emilio's Cafe
Via Emanuele Filiberto, 110
Rome, Italy

The two priests arrived promptly at 6:30 and took a table near the street. Leiber was pleased that a number of strollers were present that would reduce any attention to the table. The wine had just arrived and been poured when the suited figure arrived.

"You must be Father Leiber," Dollmann pronounced in passable Italian. "I see you are quite prompt. You must be a German priest."

Leiber rose, smiled and gestured toward Rodi who had also risen. He extended his hand and spoke in German. "I would prefer we speak German if you don't mind.

189

This is Father Michael Rodi, an American Jesuit who works for the Vatican. He also speaks excellent German."

Dollmann observed the younger man and extended his hand. "We meet again young priest. The first time we met you were quite busy."

Rodi ignored the comment and extended his hand.

"Please have a seat," Leiber motioned. "The wine has just arrived. I ordered a pleasant *verdicchio* for us to enjoy."

"I know the wine. If it's chilled correctly, it is a fine wine on a spring evening."

Leiber shook his head and took a taste. *Nice, cooled to the right temperature.* He took another swallow and placed his glass on the table.

Dollmann and Rodi did likewise and waited.

Finally, Leiber sat back in his chair and addressed the German officer.

"Colonel, I know you are wondering about our meeting. Events have transpired that might have a bearing on ending the war."

Dollmann froze. *Oh, God. He is going to bring up the massacre of the Italians.*

Leiber hesitated, carefully choosing his words. "Certain information had been verified by the Vatican at the highest levels. If this information were made public, it would be entirely possible a large number of people in the world would turn against Germany.

How did they find out about the executions so quickly? We were very secretive about the actual executions and there were no witnesses except the members of the SS. Dollmann suddenly realized his forehead had begun to sweat. He proceeded to drink another sip of the chilled wine.

Leiber continued. "When your Ambassador Weizsäcker first approached the Vatican with the news of Hitler's plan to invade us and kidnap the pope, we were unsure of the validity of his information. We believed that he thought the information genuine, but we were not able to verify it at the time."

Dollmann relaxed. *He is talking about the kidnap plan, not the massacre. I might just be in luck with all this.*

"Additional intelligence has surfaced that substantiates the ambassador's initial communication. We now believe such a heinous plot is entirely possible."

190

Dollmann considered the situation. *This is not entirely bad. General Wolff has already indicated to me that he would like to meet with the pontiff if it could be arranged. Maybe I can convince the Vatican, and perhaps the pope himself, to see General Wolff. Such a happening might even forestall any possibility of an invasion.*

Leiber spoke again. "There is an added problem, Colonel Dollmann. Anything we do must be done with utmost secrecy. It would not do for the Vatican to tolerate even casual get-togethers with members of the SS. I trust you understand."

Dollmann nodded his agreement. *This will take some doing. The pope will have to be persuaded to meet with Wolff. But how do I do that? I know no close intimates of the pope. I will have to think hard about this before I act. I might only get one chance.*

The German officer finished his wine and rose to leave.

"Thank you for the wine," he said. "You have given me something to think about."

"One additional thing, Colonel. Our idea of secrecy is paramount to anything happening about this matter. I brought Father Rodi here to meet you for a reason. I would hope that he will figure in any plan you develop. He is a relatively minor priest in the service of the Vatican and will draw no attention as he performs his duties. I consider him an asset and hope you will be able to use him in the future."

Rodi looked at the German officer who looked back in return. "I will see what I can do," Dollmann replied. "I will also contact Father Rodi in the event I come up with something useful."

"He can be reached through my office," Leiber instructed. "After all, according to your letter, he is a hero to the German military."

Dollmann smiled as he shook each priest's hand. "I understand fully."

Dollmann replaced his chair and turned to leave. Both priests followed him until he disappeared into the crowd in the distance.

Chapter Seventeen

"Anyone can deal with victory.
Only the mighty can bear defeat."

— *Adolf Hitler*

Wednesday, April 5, 1944
Hitler's operations room,
Wolfsschanze,
Rastenburg,
East Prussia, Germany

The reports that continued to arrive at the Wolf's Lair were uplifting to Adolf Hitler. Luftwaffe Field Marshal Albert Kesselring's details of his successes in holding the Anzio beachhead some 35 miles south of Rome from the intruding American 5th Army was the first good news the Fuhrer had received from his military in weeks and buoyed his spirits. Since mid-February, the German commander's Army Group C had fought a series of defensive battles to protect the three German defensive lines that had been organized. The Barbara, Berhhardt and Gustav Lines were designed to make Allied flanking of Wehrmacht forces quite difficult ---and were demonstrating just that. Kesselring's strategy was proving to be a major thorn for the 5th Army and its associated forces.

Hitler was finally able to concentrate on matters other than German defeats along the Eastern front and in other areas.

The utter capitulation of Italian forces and the fact that a number of his former Italian allies were now fighting against Germany caused him great concern. So did the fate of his friend Benito Mussolini who was currently under German protection in Northern Italy.

I wonder how Il Duce is handling his current activities. He seemed pleased with our rescue but he wasn't overjoyed with the prospect of the new government being located so far north. He wanted us to go into Rome and oust everyone who had opposed him.

193

That was simply impossible; it would have taken too many men and resources. He is safe where he is as long as he stays under Germany's protection.

Thursday, April 6, 1944
Offices of the SS,
Via Tasso, 155
Rome, Italy

SS Obersturmbannführer Eugen Dollmann sat at his desk in the Gestapo's offices on the Via Tasso. Even though it was a Thursday morning and nothing was scheduled, he felt it appropriate that he be present in his office. He had reshuffled the dispatches from various points in Italy and elsewhere. Still perplexed as to what action to take regarding the Vatican, his eyes eventually settled on the letter he had received from Donna Virginia Agnelli. He opened the letter and reread the contents.

Suddenly, a light bulb in his head went off, and he pounded his fist on the antiquated table that served as his desk. *Why didn't this occur to me before? This woman knows everyone in Rome and I have even seen her at the side of the pope. She probably knows him as well as anyone outside the Vatican and his immediate family. And, she is asking me to help get her out of prison. Why didn't she ask the pope to intercede? Surely he would have been happy to help.*

Getting her out of prison will be easy; I already made up my mind to do that earlier. The Italian Fascists never refuse a direct order of the Gestapo. When she is out, I will have a little chat with her. She would be in no position to refuse to help me with the pope.

Dollmann picked up a pen and began writing. In a matter of minutes, the order freeing Donna Virginia Agnelli was on its way to the authorities in the fascist government. He knew that she would be freed in a matter of hours.

Friday, April 7, 1944
Villa del Bosco Parrasio,
Via Garibaldi,
Rome, Italy

Countess Agnelli was relieved to be back in her palatial home on Janiculum Hill in the Trastevere District of Rome. She found everything in the villa neatly arranged and thoroughly cleaned. Her original staff remained in the home despite the fact they had not been paid in some time. She immediately paid her staff and included a sizeable bonus for each person.

Her first personal undertaking after she reached her home was to treat herself to a long bath in the marbled bathroom that accompanied the villa's master bedroom suite. She remained in the water for almost an hour until her skin started pruning. She exited the oversized tub and dried herself completely, now feeling comfortable for the first time in months.

Signora Agnelli was impressed at the swiftness displayed by SS Obersturmbannführer Eugen Dollmann. Upon receipt of Dollmann's order, the Fascist police in charge of the San Gregorio Convent made immediate arrangements for her release. When the police vehicle arrived to take her home, a series of abject apologies gushed forth from various police officers. She acknowledged the expressions of regret with grace and charm, and politely entered the car in the same outfit she had worn when she was first arrested.

Signora Agnelli rethought the events of the past months and immediately put those sordid happenings behind her.

No need to carry laments she thought. *That will do no good. And I wasn't treated all that badly by the Fascists. I must get on with my life. Next thing for me will be a decent meal with a nice bottle of wine. I wonder if there is any of the pinot grigio from Collio still around. As my memory serves, it was one really nice bottle of wine.* She entered the villa's wine cellar and located the bottle she was looking for. *This will do nicely.* The countess returned to the kitchen and gave instructions for a light meal. She then retired to her drawing room to await the food.

The meal had just arrived when her *maggiordomo* (butler) appeared with a piece of paper in his hand. He offered the piece to Agnelli and stepped back.

Agnelli read the note. She was surprised to see the signature at the bottom.

"Please bring him in to see me," she instructed the servant. "And inquire if he has eaten."

The *maggiordomo* acknowledged her instructions and departed.

I wonder what he wants. It must be important and I'm certainly in his debt. I'll just wait and see.

She had just finished a delicious piece of salsiccia (sausage) when the dapper German appeared in the drawing room. She rose and extended her hand. Dollmann kissed her hand and genuinely smiled at the attractive woman.

"I must thank you, Colonel Dollmann," she offered. "Without your help I would still be confined to that deplorable place."

"I was happy to assist, Countess. There must have been some sort of mistake in the first place. A person of your breeding..."

"The Fascists are out of control, Colonel. There are others still in the convent that should be released. I can give you their names..."

"All in good time, countess. All in good time."

"And what brings you to Bosco Parrasio, Colonel Dollmann? I know you are a busy man."

"Yes, Countess. It seems I am always busy these days." Dollmann paused, attempting to choose the correct verbiage.

"There is a small matter that I need to discuss with you, Countess Agnelli. I hope you don't mind the fact that I took it upon myself to come here without any notice."

"You can ask me anything you want, Colonel Dollmann. I will be forever in your debt."

"Thank you, Countess. You are most gracious. The matter involves you and your relationship with the Vatican."

"The Vatican? I don't understand. I know many people at the Vatican. Many are friends of mine and my husband's family."

"I had counted on that, Countess. I knew that you relished the friendship of the Vatican's hierarchy"

"Hierarchy?" Agnelli questioned somewhat puzzled.

"Yes, the very highest personage in the Vatican. Pope Pius XII himself."

"Well, you are correct. I have known the pope since he was Cardinal Secretary of State. In fact, I saw more of him then than I do now. As pope he hasn't been able to attend many of my affairs. That was unfortunate, as I genuinely enjoyed His Holiness."

196

"Excellent. That is what I had hoped for. I will need for you to go and see the pope, tomorrow if possible. No one should be aware of your visit or at least as soon as possible."

Why the secrecy? This must be important for both Germany and the Vatican. I now know why I was released from prison so quickly.

"Let me explain the circumstances to you countess. Once you have heard…"

Saturday, April 8, 1944
Mouther House of Order of Salvatorians,
Residence of Abbot General Father Pankratius Pfeiffer,
Piazza San Pietro adjoining papal apartments,
Rome, Italy

Undaunted when Countess Agnelli reported her first attempt at gaining an audience with the Pope proved fruitless, Dollmann decided on a different approach to take in making the meeting a reality. Along with Countess Agnelli, the pair was presently calling on Dollmann's old friend, Germany's liaison with the Vatican, Father Pankratius Pfeiffer, for his help.

Dollmann quickly explained the problem and Father Pfeiffer immediately understood the urgency of Dollmann's request.

"I know just who to call, Eugen. Cardinal Caccia-Dominioni can help us and he won't ask questions. He is the Cardinal Protodeacon of the Vatican and he even crowned Pius XII when he was elected. I will call and make an appointment to see him. If he is free, I will be able to see him later today. I feel he is the best person to help us with this delicate matter."

"I knew I could count on you Pankratius. You are a great asset to the fatherland."

"And also to the Vatican, Eugen. I must remind you of that."

Dollmann acknowledged the prelate's words and extended his hand. He now felt the meeting between General Wolff and the pope was a real possibility.

Sunday, April 9, 1944
Papal Apartments
The Vatican,
Rome, Italy

Cardinal Caccia-Dominioni had persuaded Pope Pius XII to grant an immediate audience with Countess Agnelli and Dollmann with the provision that Dollmann wear civilian clothes to the encounter.

The pair arrived on time and was shown to the pope's apartments where he met them in a small anteroom. He was not in favor of the audience, but agreed with the older Cardinal that the meeting could prove beneficial to the Holy Church.

Countess Agnelli kissed the papal ring and proclaimed, "Thank you, Your Holiness, for agreeing to see us about this matter. It is good to see you again."

"You are looking a bit pale, Countess. Are you well?"

"That's another story, Your Highness. Let's just say I have been in an inhospitable environment."

Dollmann held his breath. Surely she won't tell the Pope what happened to her.

"What may I do for you, Countess?"

"My German friend, Colonel Dollmann has a matter to discuss with you, Your Highness. He feels it might easily have an effect on the war and the Holy Church."

Pius XII looked directly at Dollmann and spoke. "Colonel, you realize this is all off the record. In my position, I cannot have visitors from the German SS at the Vatican."

Dollmann shook his head and replied, "I am aware of the circumstances, Your Highness. I feel what I am about to tell you will circumvent the civilities involved."

The pope showed no reaction and moved his hand for Dollmann to continue.

"I have been made aware of certain circumstances that might allow for a termination of this war and other certain matters that would affect you and the Holy Church."

"Does this include your Fuhrer's order to invade the Vatican and kidnap me?" Pius probed.

Dollmann was taken aback by the pope's frankness but managed to respond. "Yes, Your Highness. I am happy to say it does."

"And are you here officially or unofficially?"

"Most unofficially, Your Highness. I would be shot if the wrong people knew I was even here."

Pius considered the matter. "I just don't know if Germany is to be trusted."

"The SS Commander of Italy, General Wolff wants to meet with you, Your Highness. He is the person Hitler has ordered to head the invasion of the Vatican. He has stalled the order because he believes it would do no good for Germany to take such an action. He is putting his career and life on the line just to be able to talk to you. I believe him to be a fair and just man."

Again, the pope considered Dollmann's appeal. He finally responded. "Even though such an action places our home in serious peril, I believe in hearing out someone who has everything to lose on the matter. You may go and tell your General Wolff that I will receive him in the immediate future. I cannot say what my reply to him might entail, but I will listen cautiously to what he has to say."

Countess Agnelli sighed and smiled at the pope. "Thank you, Your Highness."

"Thank you for coming to me, Countess. I hope your mission proves worthwhile for both Germany and the Holy Catholic Church."

He turned to Dollmann and stated, "You are a brave man, Colonel. I hope your effort is not in vain."

Dollmann nodded his agreement. He turned to Countess Agnelli to begin their exit. The Countess reached for the pope's ring and kissed it softly. Dollmann observed the countess and nodded affirmatively to the pope. Pius offered his ring hand to the German officer who had bowed his head. This time Dollmann also kissed the pope's symbol of authority.

Monday, April 10, 1944
Just outside Porta Sant'Anna,
The Vatican,
Rome, Italy

Father Michael S. Rodi, S.J. had been summoned to Father Robert Leiber's office earlier that morning and given instructions to meet German General Karl Wolff just outside the columned Vatican gate named after Saint Anna dei Plafrenieri. He had been given a picture of the general who would appear in civilian clothes for his meeting with the pope. General Wolff had also been informed that Father Rodi would conduct him through the Vatican gate and escort him to the papal audience. A special pass had been prepared that Rodi now fingered in his coat pocket.

Why am I so nervous about all this? It's only the most important job I might be given in my service to the Lord. Why should that make me edgy? After all, he's only the most important Nazi officer in Italy. I must remember what he looks like. He shouldn't be hard to recognize, he was quite distinguished in the picture I was shown.

He took a few steps and eyed several of the Swiss Guards who stood by with their shouldered Pál Király-designed SIG MKPO submachine guns that could fire 900 rounds a minute. A single guard also stood with his 9-foot steel halberd that has seen use since the time of Michelangelo as a symbol of the Vatican's storied antiquity. The guards returned his stare and provided welcome grins for the young priest. They had been ordered to watch him closely and render him aid if necessary.

He glanced at his watch and observed that it was almost one p.m., the time scheduled for Wolff's arrival. Rodi surveyed the passing walkers and eventually settled on a tall, middle aged man wearing a fedora. The man seemed to be looking for someone or something.

As the man approached, Rodi was able to make out the sharp features of SS General Karl Wolff. He gestured to the man who looked around and finally extended his arm.

"I am Karl Wolff and I ask you to please excuse these horrible clothes I am wearing. I had no civilian clothes with me and I was forced to borrow these from Colonel Dollmann. As you can see, they are at least two sizes too small."

Rodi smiled as he shook the general's hand.

"At least your hat fits, general."

"Yes, fortunately," Wolff returned the smile.

"I am Father Michael Rodi and I am to take you to meet with His Holiness."

"Colonel Dollmann has told me of your work in helping our soldiers who were attacked. We are in your debt, Father Rodi."

"It's nothing that any priest would have done in such a situation. I was glad to be able to help."

"And you are a member of the Jesuits? Wolff inquired.

Rodi met the unexpected question with a resounding "Yes, I most certainly am."

"You might be interested to know that our Fuhrer admires your society a great deal. We would talk about many things when I accompanied him on his daily walks. We talked about the Jesuits and their wonderful organization. The Fuhrer even used much of the Jesuit structure when he developed the SS. Were you aware of that?"

Rodi thought quickly. *Is he trying to bait me into something or is he just making conversation? I had better answer this wisely.*

"No, Colonel. I have never heard anything like that."

"Did you also know that Hitler was Catholic? I was taught in Catholic schools, but I was never baptized or anything."

"I know about Hitler, Colonel. I am pleased you had a good education."

Wolff grinned and spoke. "My teachers were very strict. They used their asts on me more than once."

"Asts? Rodi questioned. It was an unfamiliar German word to the priest.

"A long stick, more likely a branch from a tree. We were whipped with it."

Rodi nodded knowingly. "Same for us. There's nothing like good discipline when you are young."

"Yes, you are correct."

Rodi continued. "We should get going. I have your pass here if you are ready to go. And, before I forget to tell you, please address the pope as Your Highness when speaking with him."

"By all means," Wolff replied. "I'll follow you." The German officer again looked around to see if anyone was watching.

Rodi approached the Swiss Guards at the Saint Ann's Gate and showed the pass. The guard glanced briefly at the note looked closely at Wolff and signaled the pair forward. The historic enigmatic meeting between the sitting head of the Catholic Church and one of Nazi Germany's top generals was no more than minutes away.

———

Sistine Chapel,
The Vatican,
Rome, Italy

The pope had ordered the Sistine Chapel closed for his meeting with General Wolff. He also thought the setting brought a sense of ecumenical meaning to the meeting. It was one of his favorite places inside the Vatican and was used for special appointments such as the one today. After arriving at the chapel, Wolff was shown an ornate, high-backed chair and sat facing the pope whose chair had an even higher back.

Pius XII spoke first. "I have heard some disparaging rumors about the actions at Via Tasso 145," he said in excellent German. "I ask that you do something about the measures your men employ in their duties. Sometimes human boundaries can be easily abused." The pope paused, and continued. "There is also the matter of the son of a friend of mine named Giuliano Vassalli who is being held there. I would also ask that he be released."

"I'll speak to Colonel Kappler about this person as soon as possible, Your Holiness. You have my word."

"Good, General Wolff. Now, can we talk about ending this war as quickly as possible?"

"I'm afraid I am not the person who will end this war, Your Highness. My superiors are in a better position than I to accomplish such an end. I trust you understand my position."

"Certainly, general. I just wanted you to know that it would be preferable to the Vatican that some sort of agreement could be reached between the Allied Governments and Germany that could thwart the advance of the Soviet armies. The Communists are direct enemies of the Holy See and have openly stated their desire to remove our church from the face of the earth. I see them as a much more antagonistic enemy of the future."

"I agree they are a menace, Your Holiness. That's why we are fighting them at this very moment."

"Together with the Allies, you would have a much better chance." Pius offered.

"You make a valid point. I will bring the matter to my superiors. Would you be able to orchestrate such an accomplishment, Your Holiness? I believe it would take someone such as yourself to bring this about."

"I am prepared to do whatever is necessary to save our Holy Church. Whatever."

Wolff was totally captivated by the pontiff's words and demeanor. He listened attentively as the pope continued.

"General Wolff, we have heard other rumors about Germany's plan to evacuate most of the men in Rome and send them to the north. Such a plan would be baseless and would cause great pain and suffering on the part of many Roman families. I would urge you to halt this needless order that would affect so many people."

I'm already against such a plan, Wolff grasped. *We don't have the manpower to evacuate even a percentage of Roman men. This will be easy for me.*

"Your Highness, I can assure you that this order will not be carried out. I have already studied the consequences and have let Berlin know of my findings. I am confident such evacuations will not take place."

The pope was impressed with Wolff's candor. *I am finally in the presence of a German officer whose dignity and grace come before his duty. I actually believe he is telling the truth. I also feel I can trust him in other issues. This is a blessed day for Rome and the Holy Church.*

The pope replied, "I am happy to hear that. I have been worried that such a plan would take place. I couldn't be responsible for my people's reactions to such a plan."

Wolff shook his head in agreement.

Pius XII then brought up the subject of the plan to invade the Vatican and kidnap him. "What if your Fuhrer overrides your wishes and decides to invade us? I will tell you now, whatever happens, I will not leave Rome voluntarily. My place is here and I will fight to the end for the Christian commandments of humanity and peace."

"I will do everything in my power to avoid fighting and bloodshed in Rome. I wish for Rome to be an open city and its historical places and beautiful surroundings be untouched by the ravages of battle. You have my word on that," responded Wolff with authority.

The Pontiff breathed a sigh of relief. *This is the best news I have had in many months. I must thank Our Lord for allowing me to meet with this man.*

A thought crossed his mind and he continued, "How many injustices, how many crimes, how many offenses against the Christian spirit of love for his fellow men, how many misunderstandings could have been avoided if you had come to me first of all?"

Again Wolff acknowledged the pope's deeply felt admonition by shaking his head in the affirmative.

As the audience came to an end, Pope Pius XII rose and asked his visitor, "You have had a hard road to travel, General Wolff. Will you allow me to give you my blessing as you tread this perilous road---you and the members of your family?"

Wolff was totally stunned by the pope's offer and allowed the blessing. The pope prayed for the German officer and finished the benediction.

For some reason, a mechanical reflex inside his mind surfaced and Wolff clicked his heels together and rendered the Nazi salute. The pope smiled broadmindedly and the session was over.

Father Michael Rodi was standing near the Sistine Chapel's entrance along with Father Pankratius Pfeiffer who had wandered over to the entranceway in time to see Wolff's salute.

The two men looked at each other and Father Pfeiffer uttered, "At least he didn't say Heil Hitler." Rodi broke into a big smile and shook his head in concurrence.

General Wolff emerged totally galvanized from the meeting. He saw Rodi and approached him.

"I understand why everyone honors your pope," Wolff said politely. "He is someone who is trying to save the entire world. I am honored to have met him."

Rodi accepted the appreciation and led the man back to the gate. They shook hands again as they parted.

"Go with God," Rodi declared.

Wolff looked back and again acknowledged the blessing.

Chapter Eighteen

"My spirit will rise from the grave
and the world will see I was right."

— *Adolf Hitler*

Wednesday, April 25, 1945
Prefettura di Milano,
Corso Monforte,
Milano, Italy

Almost three weeks had passed since Benito Mussolini made the decision to move his offices and residence to the *Prefettura di Milano*. At the time, there was no actual *prefetto* or divisional head of that part of Northern Italy. Mussolini continued to validate the now-irrelevant expressions of his puppet government while the Allies continued their northern movement through Italy.

Mussolini's mistress, Clara Petacci, had accompanied the Duce to Milano. Petacci, the 33-year- old raven-haired beauty had been the Duce's mistress since the age of nineteen. For the past two years, she had been the closest person to the Italian leader and shared his many intrigues with great devotion. She had arrived in Milano a few days earlier. The two were currently involved in a spirited exchange inside Mussolini's office, the same room that was the office of the last prefect.

"Ben," Clara implored. "You must do something to save yourself. I have heard the reports about the progress of your enemies and I have noticed there are fewer Germans around here to protect us. The radio has played an announcement that calls for everyone to rise up and throw us out. I heard it myself not an hour ago. Some of your leaders here with you are worried about your safety. They asked me to intercede with you."

Mussolini smiled and replied, "These troops are under Hitler's specific order to stay and guard me, and the Fuhrer phoned me to tell me that. We are still safe here and our government needs to be intact to function."

"To what end, Ben?" Petacci replied. "There is little of the Salò Republic left. Only you and a few of your Fascist friends who are still here can be counted. I am afraid for both of us. I will not leave you under any circumstances, and you know it." She touched his hand in an act of genuine caring.

Mussolini thought for a few moments. "Perhaps you are right, Claretta. I have heard the rumors and I fear the dispatches I receive are no longer reliable. A great many of my followers have either fled Italy or gone underground for their own safety."

"I am right. We should leave this place immediately. We can take my car and go to Switzerland. We will be safe there."

Il Duce's thoughts wavered for a moment. *The Alfa Romeo. The 6C Sport Berlinetta, the finest car ever produced in Italy. When I gave it to Claretta she was so happy. The car was beautiful and she was even more beautiful inside it. Maybe it was Divine Providence that made her drive it here to meet me. She is right. The trip to Switzerland would not be that difficult... I could run the Salò Republic from there...But, there are other considerations...My loyal friends here must also leave with us...and the Germans would have to protect us on the way...Her car is much too recognizable... we could easily be identified if we were by ourselves...I must consider all these things before I act...I must talk to the Germans at once...*

Thursday, April 12, 1945
Living room,
Little White House,
401 Little White House Road,
Warm Springs, Georgia

For the past twenty-one years, President of the United States Franklin Delano Roosevelt had traveled to the resort town south of Atlanta to avail himself of the nurturing waters and beneficial pace of life in the small Georgia town.

Along with the President at the cottage he had built in 1932 was Lucy Mercer Rutherford, a former social secretary of his wife Eleanor with whom he had begun an extra-marital affair in 1916. The President had rekindled the affair a little more than a year earlier. His cousin and confidant, Margaret 'Daisy" Suckley, was also in the room along with his faithful Scottie, Fala, that Suckley had given to the President.

It was a clear and warm day and the President had agreed to a painting session with artist Elizabeth Shoumatoff, a close friend of Lucy Mercer Rutherford. About fifteen minutes remained in the session when suddenly Roosevelt complained of a severe pain in the back of his neck and suddenly collapsed.

Navy doctor Commander Howard Bruen was immediately summoned and correctly diagnosed a cerebral hemorrhage for the thirty-second President. A shot of adrenaline was administered but the President was already gone.

Roosevelt's wife, Eleanor, was still in Washington, having just finished a speech at the Thrift Club near Dupont Circle and was listening to a piano recital. She was called to the White House by the president's secretary, Stephen Early. Upon entering the White House she went immediately to her sitting room when she was finally told of her husband's death. She then cabled her four sons who were all on active duty military service. The cable read in part,

DARLINGS: The President slept away this afternoon. He did his job to the end as he would want you to do. Bless you all and all our love.

Mother

After changing into a black dress in the company of her daughter Anna, she met with Vice President Harry Truman who had not yet been told the news.

Calmly she said in a low voice, "Harry, the President is dead."

Truman replied with genuine feeling, "Is there anything *we* can do for you?"

The First Lady then responded back, "Is there anything *we* can do for you? For you are the one in trouble now."

Two hours after the official announcement, Harry Truman was sworn in as the thirty-third president of the United States by the Chief Justice of the United States, Harian F. Stone, in a one-minute ceremony at the White House.

Five days later, British Prime Minister paid his respects to his close friend with a eulogy in Britain's House of Commons. In part, the Prime Minister said:

"I conceived an admiration for him as a statesman, a man of affairs, and a war leader. I felt the utmost confidence in his upright, inspiring character and outlook and a personal regard-affection I must say-for him beyond my power to express today. His love of his own country, his respect for its constitution, his power of gauging the tides and currents of its mobile public opinion, were always evident, but, added to these, were the beatings of that generous heart which was always stirred to anger and to action by spectacles of aggression and oppression by the strong against the weak. It is, indeed, a loss, a bitter loss to humanity that those heart-beats are stilled forever. President Roosevelt's physical affliction lay heavily upon him. It was a marvel that he bore up against it through all the many years of tumult and storm. Not one man in ten millions, stricken and crippled as he was, would have attempted to plunge into a life of physical and mental exertion and of hard, ceaseless political controversy. Not one in ten millions would have tried, not one in a generation would have succeeded, not only in entering this sphere, not only in acting vehemently in it, but in becoming indisputable master of the scene. In this extraordinary effort of the spirit over the flesh, the will-power over physical infirmity, he was inspired and sustained by that noble woman; his devoted wife, whose high ideals marched with his own, and to whom the deep and respectful sympathy of the House of Commons flows out today in all fullness. There is no doubt that the President foresaw the great dangers closing in upon the pre-war world with far more prescience than most well-informed people on either side of the Atlantic, and that he urged forward with all his power such precautionary military preparations as peace-time opinion in the United States could be brought to accept. There never was a moment's doubt, as the quarrel opened, upon which side his sympathies lay."

Saturday April 15, 1945
Joseph Stalin's Summer Dacha,
Sochi, Russia

The idea of a late spring visit to the beautiful summer home he had built in 1937 appealed to Soviet leader Joseph Stalin. The seaside location of the dacha amid a thick grove of cedar trees offered the Communist chief a welcome relief from the rigors of running his country that was currently involved in a world war.

Alexander Nikolaevich Poskrebyshev knocked once and entered Stalin's study on this beautiful early Saturday afternoon with a piece of paper in his hand. Poskrebyshev's actual title was Director of Administration of the General Secretary, a most important post during wartime. He was also Stalin's personal secretary. Anything that Stalin received first passed through the hands of the bald, 54-year-old with protruding eyes.

As Poskrebyshev approached, Stalin saw that his face was strained and gloomy.

"Why so glum Alexander Nikolaevich? You look as if you have lost your best friend," Stalin questioned.

Poskrebyshev handed the paper to his leader and stepped back. "Read it for yourself. I think it might make you a bit gloomy also," he declared.

Stalin took his time and finally lowered his eyes. "You are right, Alexander Nikolaevich. Roosevelt's death is something to make the entire world gloomy."

"You were fond of him, were you not?"

"Fond, I'm not sure. But *respect* him, I most certainly did. He was a most extraordinary man."

"If I am correct, he was the first leader to push for the United States to recognize our Soviet Union, even before the disaster of Pearl Harbor," Poskrebyshev added. "He was also the person who supported American aid to Russia when the war first started."

Stalin nodded his agreement and continued. "During our meetings, he never stopped talking. I believe that annoyed Churchill, but the Englishman never said anything about it. Somehow, it seemed quite humorous at the time.

Even when he became sicker, he still showed a great deal of energy in our dealings. I fear I will miss him in the future."

"What about the future, Iosif Vissarionovich? How will Roosevelt's death affect our alliance and outlook? Will everything be as it was?"

Stalin contemplated his answer. "I'm not really sure about that. The vice-president, Mr. Truman, is something of a mystery. I really don't know that much about him."

"If I am correct, he is the one who declared just after the Nazi's invaded our motherland that the United States should go with whoever is winning the war, either Germany or Russia," offered Poskrebyshev.

"Yes, I recall that. It seemed a strange statement at the time and seems even more bizarre in light of what has just happened."

Stalin considered the possibilities in his mind. *I really know little about Harry Truman. I don't even think he has been vice-president for three months. Roosevelt never even mentioned him when we met; I wonder how much of a hand he has had in making important decisions. .. I must find out more about him immediately, and be prepared for the worst... Too bad this had to happen with the war going so well, Roosevelt would have enjoyed seeing it through to its conclusion... We will probably have to have another meeting and I will have to be prepared...I wonder if Truman will be a pushover. That could come in handy if the war ends soon. We could take advantage of a weak leader under such circumstances...*

I do not think we can get to Rome before the Allies, the Eastern Front is just too difficult to overcome quickly...It would be better to concentrate on reaching Berlin first and guaranteeing our future in that city...My generals believe that the final defense of the city by the Germans is being finished around the Seelow Heights and our attack on the city is imminent...I believe that Eisenhower is not interested in entering Berlin first and that will be to our benefit...with any luck, we will control Berlin and therefore a great portion of Eastern Europe...

He turned his head to find that his secretary had already departed the study.

From Poskrebyshev's prospective, it would be unwise to disturb the Soviet leader when he was absorbed in one of his somber contemplations. Others had tried before and some had paid the price.

Friday, April 27, 1945
Along Lake Gorda,
Lombardy Region, Italy

It had taken the better part of two days for the convoy that escorted Benito Mussolini and Clara Petacci to finally get started. The Germans were hesitant to depart without specific orders from Berlin and general confusion reigned among the elements of the German Wehrmacht that still controlled the activities of the lackey state the Republic of Salò (ISR) had become.

Finally, the acting Plenipotentiary for Germany was contacted and gave his consent. The figure was none other than Rudolf Rahn, the former German ambassador to Rome. A German convoy was formed and included a number of trucks, anti-aircraft batteries and several cars that included Clara Petacci's sparkling Alfa Romeo Sport Berlinetta. There were nominal guards for the small procession that eased its way along Northern Italy's crowded roads.

After leaving Milano, a route had been selected that seemed the most direct to Switzerland. The course chosen wound through Brescia and then turned northerly at Descenzano del Garda.

Upon reaching the western shore of Lake Gorda, the vehicles would either turn West at Menaggio and then through Cardano or continue North to Dongo. Their map showed that Dongo was actually closer to Switzerland's border than the other choice.

There were numerous military vehicles and equipment on the road that made the progress slow. Mussolini let Clara Petacci drive since he was in no mood to navigate anything, much less a busy, crowded road.

Clara looked over at him. His face was pale and his features drawn. He had not spoken for more than an hour and seemed insentient. She pulled on his arm in an attempt to rouse her lover from his prolonged torpor.

She spoke lovingly in an even tone. "Ben, it is important that you remain alert to our surroundings. You know this area better than I and you might be able to spot anything out of the ordinary. Do you understand what I am saying?"

Mussolini muttered something unintelligible and Petacci repeated, "What did you say? I couldn't understand you."

The dictator finally mustered some strength and replied, "We are leaving like common criminals. I just cannot believe my precious Italy has fallen so far. There is nothing left, nothing. I have nothing to live for."

"You have me, my Ben. I will never leave you."

"Ah, Claretta, I fear you are the only one who cares. And you are right. I do have you, for what that's worth."

Clara sighed at his words, but did not answer the Duce. She continued driving as the convoy finally was able to speed up a bit.

When she realized that the procession had continued north, she informed the Duce of their progress. "We are on our way to Dongo, Ben. It won't be that long now. We are getting closer to Switzerland with each mile."

Mussolini looked around but said nothing. He stared ahead as if in deep thought.

The now speeding convoy passed through the town of Musso and Clara noted a sign that pointed north

DONGO

"There's a sign for Dongo, Ben. We will be turning soon."

Benito Mussolini acknowledged the remark with a nod, but remained silent.

As they neared Dongo, the convoy suddenly lost speed. Clara peered into the distance but there were too many German vehicles in front for her to see anything. She contemplated in her mind. *There must be something in the road, perhaps another slower military convoy. This trip is taking longer than we expected. It will be good to get to Switzerland so we can relax. I wonder what toll all this is taking on my Ben. He seems so lost. Oh well, he'll snap out of it when we are safe. He always has in the past, even when things looked their bleakest.*

She came out of her reflection as the trucks in front of her came to a complete halt.

What is it now? Why are we stopping out in the middle of nowhere?

Her attention was directed to several armed men who made their way through the caravan. The men looked inside each of the trucks and proceeded to make some of the inhabitants step to the ground with their hands up.

"Partisans!" she almost yelled at Mussolini. "They are searching the trucks, Ben. What are we to do?"

Mussolini looked ahead and then behind.

"There is an artillery piece behind us, Claretta. It has a canvass covering. I might be able to hide in there if they don't see me. They wouldn't check there, would they?"

"Do what you think best, Ben."

He opened the door and made his way out of the car. He closed it roughly but the sound of the convoy's engines hid the sound. The Duce made his way back to the big gun that was mounted on a four wheel platform. The 8.8cm FlaK 36 anti-tank artillery piece was covered with a series of tarps attached to the platform with eyelet brackets. Mussolini tried to remove a section of the tarp and finally succeeded in prying the material loose. He situated his small frame inside the tarp and attempted

212

to retie the tarp. His effort failed as the sound of voices approached. He decided to forego another attempt to tie the cover down.

The first of the partisans approached the Alfa Romeo and began talking to Clara Petacci. She informed him that she was on her way to Switzerland and became a part of the caravan due to the heavy road traffic. She produced her identity papers and handed them to the partisan. The man glanced at the papers, looked closely at her, but said nothing. He moved to the rear of the car and peered at the license.

"You have Roman plates," he pronounced. "What are you doing here? "

Before she could answer another Partisan appeared at the car. Urbano Lazzaro was the political commissar of the 52nd Garabaldi Partisan Brigade, a part of the *Comitato di Liberazione Nazionale Alta Italia* (CLNAI). A roadblock had been set up by members of the group who had fired warning shots to stop the first elements of the German column.

He took Clara's papers from his comrade and inspected the contents. *Something is not right here... This attractive Roman woman driving alone in this fancy car...I can't place it exactly, but somehow there is more to this than meets the eye.*

Lazzaro called forward and several other CLNAI partisans appeared with rifles. He spoke to them and they began a thorough search of the car. A number of fine leather suitcases were found that further peaked Lazzaro's curiosity.

"Search the vehicles to the front and rear of the car," he ordered. "And be careful not to miss anything."

One of the partisans went forward and began examining the truck. He found a number of people cowering inside. He pointed his rifle and the group began disembarking. Lazzaro inspected the group but said nothing.

Finally he asked in Italian, "*Sei tedesco?*" (Are you German?)

The group answered the question by shaking their heads affirmatively.

"*Poi dire qualcosa in tedesco*" (Then say something in German) Lazzaro prodded.

"*Wir sind alle Deutschen*"(We are all Germans) a weak voice from the group replied.

"Your bad German comes with a heavy Italian accent, my friend. Can anyone else say anything in German? "

The group remained silent. Lazzaro spoke again without emotion. "I suspected as much. You will all get back into the truck. Your fate awaits you."

He turned around and confronted the other partisan who had gone to check the artillery gun. The man waived him closer and pointed at the tarp that was array. Lazzaro peered into the opening and was startled to see a small pair of brown shoes. He nodded to the partisan who raised his rifle.

Lazzaro shook his head and began raising the canvas. As the canvas raised up, the pitiful figure of Benito Mussolini stood erect, holding on to the barrel of the gun. He slowly turned and faced Lazzaro, who broke into a wide grin.

"Well, well, Duce. You seem to have gotten lost or something. You may now consider yourself a prisoner of the CLNAI."

Mussolini said nothing. His face was impassive and somewhat lethargic.

Lazzaro helped the Duce down from the low platform and returned to the car. When Clara saw that Mussolini was under guard, she shrieked, "Ben, my Ben! Please do not hurt him, he is an unwell man."

Clara recognized most of the people inside the truck. Most were ISR leaders and their families. She also noticed the despair prevalent on most of the now-captives' faces. At length, the convoy made its way into Dongo.

Saturday, April 28, 1945
Village of Giulino de Mezzagra,
Province of Como, Italy

Walter Audisio was a senior member of the General Command of the CLNAI who had been selected to handle the execution of Benito Mussolini. His *nom de guerre* for the mission was Colonel Valerio.

Early on the morning of April 28, 1945, he left Milano along with Aldo Lampredi, another partisan, and headed toward Dongo to take official possession of Mussolini. By the time he arrived, he was informed that Mussolini and Clara Petacci had been moved to a nearby farmhouse.

Audisio met with the local partisan commander and arranged for the Duce to be handed over to him. Next, he went to the farmhouse with a group of partisans who then followed them a short distance to the small commune of Giulino de Mezzegra.

When they reached the gated entrance to the Villa Belmonte, a majestic manor house, the vehicles stopped and both Mussolini and Petacci were told to get out. They were made to stand in front of the villa's stone wall.

Audisio then read aloud the sentence of death that had been handed down by the Central Command.

Neither Benito Mussolini nor Clara Petacci said a word. They stared ahead with vacant gazes on their faces, seemingly prepared to meet their maker.

Audisio raised his Beretta Model 38A submachine gun and aimed it at the pair. The gun clicked once and malfunctioned. Audisio tried to make the weapon work but was unsuccessful. He turned to another partisan, Michele Moretti, and asked for the gun he held. Moretti handed the French MAS-38 to his comrade and stepped away. The 7.65mm submachine gun was raised and a volley of shots rang out in the otherwise peaceful spring afternoon.

The bodies were examined and pronounced dead. The incredible lives of Italy's fascist dictator and his loyal mistress lay swaddled in a pool of their now comingled bloods.

Sunday, April 30, 1945
Führerbunker,
Wilhelmstraße, 77
Berlin, Germany

Adolf Hitler had taken up residence in the Führerbunker on January 16th at the advice of his inner circle to seek protection from the Allied air raids that were devastating the City of Berlin. The Führerbunker was a subterranean bunker complex that was formerly an air raid shelter that had been upgraded and finished in October of 1944.

Eight days earlier, Germany's Fuhrer had suffered a total nervous collapse when he was informed that the orders he had issued the previous day for SS General Felix Steiner's Army Detachment to move to the rescue of Berlin, had not been obeyed. Hitler's tirade against his commanders culminated in his initial declaration that "the war has been lost." He also announced that he intended to stay in Berlin "until the end," and that he also intended to shoot himself.

Shortly after midnight of the 29th, Hitler decided it was time to marry his 16-year-long companion Eva Braun. Hitler had declined to marry Braun before on the basis he would lose status with the German people if he married and also that he was already 'married' to Germany.

A minor official from the German Propaganda Ministry, Walther Wagner, was summoned and performed the ceremony in the Führerbunker's map room in the early hours of April 29th. Braun signed the marriage document as Eva Hitler after crossing out the capital B she had already started. Joseph Goebbels, minister of propaganda, and Martin Bormann, head of the Nazi Chancellery, signed the license as witnesses. A modest wedding breakfast celebrated the unusual event.

Hitler then moved to another room with his secretary, Traudl Junge, to dictate his last will and also a political testament. In the will, he named Martin Bormann as executor and also acknowledged his marriage to Braun. He concluded the will with the phrase,

"I myself and my wife--- in order to escape the disgrace of deposition or capitulation---choose death. It is our wish to be burnt immediately on the spot where I have carried out the greatest part of my daily work in the course of twelve years' service to my people."

In his testament, the Fuhrer expelled both Reichsmarschall Hermann Göring and Interior Minister Heinrich Himmler from the Nazi Party due to their offensive actions with the phrase,

"Quite apart from their disloyalty to my person have done immeasurable harm to the country and the whole nation by secret negotiations with the enemy, which they conducted without my knowledge and against my wishes, and by illegally attempting to seize power in the State for themselves."

Earlier that day, news was received that Benito Mussolini and Clara Petacci had been executed by Italian Partisans and that their bodies had been subjected to revile and the pair had been strung up by their heels by the raucous crowd. This news made the German leader resolve that neither he nor his wife would suffer the indignities that his friend and Axis ally had endured.

At 4 a.m. in the morning, the couple finally retired to their bedroom to sleep.

The following day, now the 30th of April, Hitler met with General Helmuth Weidling, commander of the Berlin Defense Area and was informed that the Russians were only about 1600 feet from the bunker and that his force's ammunition would run out around midnight. Hitler took the news indifferently and dismissed the general.

He summoned one of his personal doctors, SS Obersturmbannführer Dr. Werner

Haase, and discussed the most reliable means of suicide. Haase proposed the "pistol and poison method" that combined a dose of cyanide with a gunshot to the temple.

Hitler was paranoid of the SS's cyanide capsules and ordered that Haase test the capsules on his favorite German Shepherd, Blondi, and one of her pups who were with him at the Führerbunker. Haase later reported that both animals were dead.

Shortly after one o'clock, Hitler finally gave permission to General Weidling for his men to attempt a breakout later that night.

Around two in the afternoon, Hitler sat down to a lunch with his secretaries, Traudl Junge and Gerda Christian, along with his personal cook and dietitian Constanze Manziarly. The four had a simple meal.

He then summoned Eva and the couple extended their farewells to other members of the Führerbunker that included Bormann, Goebbels and his family, the secretaries, and several other military officers.

At 2:30, the couple entered Hitler's private study. One hour later, a single shot rang out.

After waiting for a few minutes, Bormann and Hitler's chief valet, SS Obersturmbannführer Heinz Linge, opened the door to the study and found both bodies. Hitler had confided in Linge a month earlier of his suicide plans and placed him in charge of burning the bodies.

The two bodies were wrapped in the blood-stained rug from the study and carried upstairs, through the bunker's emergency exit to the garden immediately behind the Chancellery, and doused with petrol. Linge attempted to lite the petrol and was unsuccessful. Linge returned to the bunker and reappeared with a thick roll of paper that he handed to Bormann. Bormann lit the paper and then ignited the now torch on the blankets. A small group had gathered, came to attention and performed the Nazi salute. The corpses were allowed to burn until around 6:30, a period of about two hours and thirty minutes. The remains were then buried in a shallow bomb crater by SS Hauptsturmführer Ewald Lindloff and SS Hauptsturmführer Hans Reisser.

Adolf Hitler's Third Reich would officially surrender a week later on May 7, 1944. The *Drittes Reich* was 988 years short of its Nazi leader's declaration that it would last for a thousand years.

Afterword

The turbulent times immediately preceding the Second World War and during the actual agonizing conflict are among the most documented in all of history. Countless scholars and writers have sought the answers to every conceivable thesis and happening, and many disagreements have arisen as to exactly what occurred in certain situations.

It has been my intention in *Kidnap the Pope* to present a reasonable scenario based upon as many salient facts that I was able to uncover in my research about Adolf Hitler's attempt to invade the Vatican and capture Pope Pius XII. During this research, I became keenly aware of the extreme difficulties for anyone performing pontifical duties, especially during a world war.

I have attempted to relate the story from both German and Vatican standpoints. Due to the nature of the latter, some historical fact is still shrouded behind the Vatican's strict veil of secrecy. The German side is also tarnished, with several accounts originating from Nazi officials seeking to enhance their chances with their conquering enemies.

But history is a most sacred gift and should not be distorted in any manner. I have never believed in altering history, even remotely, for it is the reader who suffers under such untrustworthy circumstances.

I believe that the events surrounding *Kidnap the Pope* actually occurred and fortunately came to a benign end. Our world is blessed that it did so.

Jack DuArte
Lexington, KY

Heroes, Heroines and Adversaries

THE VATICAN

Eugenio Maria Guiseppe Giovanni Pacelli (Pius XII) — chose diplomacy as the hallmark of his time as pope. After the war he violently opposed Communism and issued a decree in 1949 that authorized the Holy Office to excommunicate Catholics who joined or even collaborated with the "godless" communists.

The Israeli diplomat and scholar Pinchas Lapide concluded his careful review of Pius XII's wartime activities with the following words: "The Catholic Church, under the pontificate of Pius XII, was instrumental in saving the lives of as many as 860,000 Jews from certain death at Nazi hands." His health failing, Pius XII died at his summer home Castel Gandolfo on October 9th, 1958.

Father Robert Leiber, S.J. — was Private Secretary to Pope Pius XII even though he suffered from acute asthma for many years. He turned down an appointment from Pope John XXIII in 1958 due to his health. He died in Rome in 1967 at age 79. To his death, he stood by Pope Pius XII as a staunch defender of Jews and Jewish rights.

Angelo Guiseppe Roncalli (John XXIII) — was appointed papal nuncio to Charles de Galle's newly liberated France in 1944, a move that Roncalli first believed to be a clerical error. His geniality and hard work united the splintered country. Pius XII made him a cardinal in January, 1953. Upon the death of Pius XII in 1958, his fellow cardinals elected him the new pope. He took the name John XXIII and became one of the most beloved pontiffs in modern Catholic Church history. He died in 1963 as one of the most esteemed persons in the entire world.

Monsignor Hugh O'Flaherty — was credited with helping more than 6,500 escape the Nazi occupation of Rome. Given numerous awards after the war, O'Flaherty was decorated by five countries. He suffered a stroke in 1960 and moved to Cahersiveen, County Kerry, Ireland, to live with his sister. He died on October 30, 1963 and is buried in the small Irish town.

Abbot General Father Pankratius Pfeiffer — led the Salvatorian Society for thirty years and was considered as one of the unsung eroes of WWII. A true ideologist, he believed in oral and written exchange of thought. His life was cut short by a street accident on May 12, 1945, just four days after VE Day ended Germany's participation in the war.

Cardinal Camillo Caccia-Dominioni — Milan-born Caccia-Dominioni was a protégé of Pius XI and was present when that pope died. He died in Rome of a heart attack on November 12, 1946 and is buried in the crypt of the Basilica of Saints Ambrogio and Carlo.

GERMAN

Adolf Hitler / Eva Braun — Sometime after midnight on 29 April, 1944, Hitler married Eva Braun in a civil ceremony in the Führerbunker. A modest wedding breakfast followed, after which Hitler summoned his secretary to another room and dictated his will and testament. Later that afternoon, Hitler was informed of the Mussolini execution, which probably increased his determination to avoid capture.

When intense street combat the following morning placed Soviet troops within a block or two of the Reich Chancellery, Hitler and Braun committed suicide; Braun bit into a cyanide capsule and Hitler shot himself after also biting into a capsule. Their bodies were carried up the stairs and through the bunker's emergency exit to the bombed-out garden behind the Reich Chancellery, where they were placed in a bomb crater, doused with petrol and set on fire.

Sigrid von Lappus — Hitler's young mistress was set up in a fabulous apartment in Berlin where the two met frequently during 1939- 40. She became pregnant in late February 1940 and died in childbirth on September 23. The child, a girl, died a few days later.

SS-Obergruppenführer and General of the Waffen-SS Karl Friedrich Otto Wolff — ultimately became the top German officer in Italy. He surrendered to the Allies six days before Germany's actual surrender. He was tried several times and served several years in prison for his actions during the war. When released due to ill health, he retired in Austria. He died on July 17, 1984 in a hospital in Rosenheim, Germany and was buried in the cemetery at Prien am Chiemsee a week later. He steadfastly held to his accounts of Hitler's plot to kidnap Pope Pius XII until his death.

Minister Joachim von Ribbentrop — was ostracized by Hitler prior to the end of war and had little power. He was captured in Belgium and stood trial in Nuremberg. Found guilty of multiple war crimes, von Ribbentrop was the first convicted political prisoner to be hanged on October 6, 1946. He was cremated after death and his ashes scattered in an undisclosed location. He remained loyal to Hitler until his hanging date.

Prince Philip of Hesse — Fell out with the Nazi's in 1943 and was arrested by Hitler who suspected his family (he was the son in law of Italy's King Victor Emanuel) of complicity in Mussolini's ouster. Eventually sent to Dachau concentration camp, he survived and was arrested by US troops in Niederdorf in the Italian Dolomites. He died in his favorite city, Rome, in 1980.

Generaleutenant Rainer Stahel — was assigned to Poland after Rome and then later to Romania where he led various city defenses for the German Army. He was captured on September 20, 1944 by the Soviets who imprisoned him in their deadly Gulag system. He died at 63 of a heart attack at Voikovo just after he was informed of a possible transfer to Germany.

Dr. Theodor Morell — After his capture by American forces on May 18, 1945, one of his interrogators reported that he was "disgusted" with the doctor's personal hygiene and his extensive obesity. For some reason he was never charged with any crimes despite his closeness with Hitler. He died of poor health in Tegemsee Hospital on Lake Tegemsee in Southern Bavaria on May 26, 1948.

Hildegarde Beetz — Count Galeazzo Ciano's friend and confidant, survived the war and returned to Germany. She divorced her husband and married Carl-Heinz Purwin. Under the name Hilde Purwin, she had a brilliant career as a journalist. She died at 89 on March 29, 2010.

SS-Obersturmbannführer Eugen Dollmann — After Germany's surrender, Dollmann escaped from an Allied POW camp and was hidden in a mental institution by Cardinal Idelfonso Schuster, Archbishop of Milan. Later in life, he participated in the making of Fellini's La Dolce Vita. After living in Monaco for three decades, he died, broke and alone, in Munich at age 84 on May 17, 1985.

SS-Obersturmbannführer Herbert Kappler — approached the Vatican about refuge after Allied forces entered Rome but was refused. He was tried by an Italian Military Tribune in 1947 and sentenced to life imprisonment at the Gaeta Military Prison. He converted to Catholicism mostly because of his relationship with Mgr. Hugh O'Flaherty who visited him often while Kappler was in prison. Kappler escaped to West Germany and died at his home in Soltau on February 9, 1978 of cancer.

Field Marshal Albert Kesselring — was considered one of Germany' greatest generals but his record was marred by massacres committed in Italy. Tried and found guilty after the war, his sentence was commuted to life imprisonment. He was released in 1952 after a political and media campaign. He died on July 16, 1960 in Bad Nauheim, Hessen, West Germany at age 74.

Consul Eitel Friedrich Möllhausen — Turkish-born, Möllhausen was fluent in four languages. Entered German Foreign service as a translator and rose rapidly to become, at 30, Germany's youngest diplomatic head in Rome. He tried repeatedly to help Rome's Jews and played an important role in thwarting Hitler's plan to kidnap the pope. He published two memoirs after the war, but little is known of his life thereafter.

Generalleutnant Kurt Mälzer — German commander of Rome was the highest ranking individual directly associated with the Ardeatine massacre. A classmate of Abbot General Father Pankratius Pfeiffer, he was put on trial after the war and sentenced to death that was later commuted to a prison term. He died in prison on March 23, 1952 at the age of 57.

SS Hauptsturmführer Erich Priebke — Along with Kappler, Priebke sought Vatican assistance after the war. Priebke escaped from a British prison camp in 1946, and fled first to Germany and then to Rome. He then used false papers supplied by the Vatican ratline to immigrate to Argentina. He was eventually unmasked on camera in 1994 during a television interview by ABC television reporter Sam Donaldson. Priebke was brought back to Italy for trial, and sentenced to house arrest in the home of his lawyer, Paolo Giachini. He died on 11 October 2013 from natural causes at age 100.

SS Sturmbannfuhrer Hellmuth Dobbrick — Commander of Bozen Regiment refused order to avenge his men who had fallen at Via Rasella. He was immediately placed under house arrest by Generaleutenant Kurt Mälzer under charges of insubordination. All charges were dropped due to the rapid Allied advance through Italy. His fate at the end of the war is unknown. Surviving members of the Bozen regiment were absorbed into other German combat units or discharged as the defeat of Germany grew closer.

Martin Bormann — pie-faced head of Nazi Party Chancellery was second in command to Hitler by war's end. Stories on his demise vary but it is believed he was killed by a soviet shell while attempting to escape in a tank along with Hitler's Chauffeur, Erich Kempka. Another account has him whisked away by British Intelligence and resettled in Great Britain. He supposedly was the key in retrieving the vast quantities of gold stolen by the Nazis to be restored to the bullion's rightful owners.

SS-Obersturmbannführer Doctor Werner Haase — was captured by the Soviets on May 2nd 1945, and made a prisoner of war. He suffered from tuberculosis and died as a prisoner at the Butyrka Prison hospital on November 30, 1950 at age 50. Butyrka Prison is also the place where Hitler's favorite nephew, Heinz Hitler, died after a number of days of torture in 1942.

SS-Obersturmbannführer Heinz Linge — the former bricklayer was one of the last to leave the Führerbunker early in the morning following Hitler's death. He was captured near See-Strasse by the Soviets who discovered his identity and sent him to the infamous Lubjanka Prison in Moscow. After spending 10 years there, he was released in 1955 and died in Bremen in 1980 at the age of 66.

SS-Hauptsturmführer Ewald Lindloff — was part of the German break out from the Führerbunker and was killed while crossing the Weidendammer Bridge, one of the few bridges across the Spree that had not been destroyed. He was 36 at the time of his death.

SS-Hauptsturmführer Hans Reisser — Reisser was another who attempted the break out. Nothing is known of him after the attempt.

Traudl Junge — arrested in June 1945 at the age of 25, she was imprisoned by both American and Soviet forces. After the war she worked as a secretary in West Germany, living in relative obscurity and claiming she never knew about Nazi atrocities during the war. She died at 82, on February 10, 2002, of cancer in Munich.

Gerda Christian — was given a cyanide ampoule by Hitler that she never used. Was part of a break out group that was captured by the Soviets. She lived in Dusseldorf and worked for the Hotel Eden in central Dusseldorf after the war. She died there in 1997 of cancer at the age of 83.

ITALIAN

Il Duce Benito Mussolini — After their executions, Mussolini and his mistress, Clara Petacci, were taken back to Milano and dumped unceremoniously in the Piazzale Loreto, a suburban square close to the main railway station. After a great deal of raving by the hostile crowd, their corpses were hung upside down on meat hooks and subjected to additional abuse. It was an unfitting death for someone many consider one of the more intellectual political figures of the era.

Count Galeazzo Ciano — Italian Foreign Minister and son-in-law of Mussolini. Ciano had been Foreign Minister since 1936 but during the war he lost respect for Mussolini and resigned from his post of his own volition in February 1943. Ciano, however, remained a member of the Fascist Grand Council and, in July 1943, voted to remove Mussolini. In August of the same year he was tricked into being captured by the Germans and later executed with the approval of his father-in-law.

Countess Etta Mussolini Ciano — escaped to Switzerland with her children two days before her husband was shot to death on January 11, 1944. From her interment in a Swiss convent, she was finally able to get Galeazzo Ciano's diaries published by Doubleday & Co. in 1945. After returning to Italy, she was sentenced to two years of detention on the Island of Lipari. She died in Rome on April 9, 1995 at the age of 84.

Field Marshal Pietro Badoglio — Served as Chief of Staff of the Italian Army from the beginning of the war until December 1940, when he resigned after the failure to conquer Greece. Badoglio subsequently he plotted against Mussolini and after the dictator's downfall in July 1943, became the first Prime Minister of the new non-Fascist government. He died in 1956.

Italian Minister Dino Grandi — fled Italy a month after directing Mussolini's downfall. Sentenced to death in absentia by the alternate Fascist government, the Italian Social Republic, he eventually escaped to Spain. He then lived in Portugal, Argentina and Brazil. He returned to Italy in the 1960's and died in Bologna on May 21, 1988, just two weeks short of his 93rd birthday.

Field Marshall Giovanni Messe — considered Italy's ablest military leader, he led the Italian forces in Russia and later the Italo-German Tank Army in Tunisia. In 1953, the still popular royalist was democratically elected to the Italian Senate. He died on December 18, 1968 at the age of 85.

Rosario Bentivegna — leader of the GAP attack at Via Rasella continued his guerilla activities in both Italy and Yugoslovia for the Communists. After the war, he married Carla Capponi and resumed his medical studies, graduating as a pathologist in 1947. He divorced Carla Capponi in 1974 but the two remained friends. He became disenchanted with the PCI (Italian Communist Party) in 1985 and eventually joined the Democratic Party in 2007. Bentivegna died in Rome on April 2, 2012 just short of his 90th birthday. His ashes were scattered along with those of Capponi in the River Tiber in 2014.

Carla Capponi — Roman-born, Capponi was law student when WW2 began. Fearless and cunning, she participated in numerous guerilla actions and killed a number of Germans while a member of the GAP. In 1953, she was elected a deputy in the PCI and was a member of the Judiciary Committee. She wrote a book covering the activities of the GAP in Rome entitled *With the Heart of a Woman*. She died in Rome on November 23, 2000 at age 79, two weeks short of her 80th birthday.

Carlo Salinari — Commander of GAP Central was captured and tortued on May 14, 1944. Sentenced to death, he was spared through efforts by the Vatican. Post war scholar and author, he died in Rome in 1977 at age 57.

Urbano Lazzaro — was not present at Mussolini's execution but investigated the circumstances and authored a book on the subject after the war. Moved his family to Brazil but returned to Vercelli, Italy where he died, on January 3, 2006, at age 81.

Walter Audisio — Mussolini's executioner remained active in the Italian Communist Party after the war. In 1963, he was elected into the Italian Senate. He later worked for the Italian oil company, Eni. He died in Rome on October 11, 1973 of a heart attack.

AMERICAN, BRITISH

President Franklin Delano Roosevelt — The thirty-second president of the United States returned to the US after the historic Yalta Conference with Churchill and Stalin. A chain smoker, his health began failing as early as 1940. Confined to a wheelchair by polio since 1921, Roosevelt was an incredibly popular Democratic president. He was in his fourth term as president when he visited the Little White House at Warm Springs, Georgia on April 12, 1945. That afternoon he succumbed to a massive cerebral hemorrhage. The New York Times dutifully declared, "Men will thank God on their knees a hundred years from now that Franklin D. Roosevelt was in the White House."

Prime Minister Sir Winston Churchill — Considered the face of Britain's WWII's war efforts, Churchill was also named "Greatest Briton" in 2002. He successfully administered a second term as prime minister in 1951 and retired in 1955. He remained a member of Parliament until 1964. When he died at age 90, Queen Elizabeth II granted him a state funeral which culminated with the largest assemblies of world statesmen in history. He was buried at his request in his family's plot at St. Martin's Church, Bladon, near Woodstock, not far from his birthplace at Blenheim Palace.

Prime Minister Neville Chamberlain — resigned as his top post in Britain on May 10, 1940. Replaced by Winston Churchill and served in Churchill's War Cabinet until ill health forced him to resign. He died of cancer at age 71 in Heckfield, Hampshire, a day short of six months after leaving office.

RUSSIAN

Premier Joseph Stalin — his health deteriorated by the end of the war and his heavy smoking caused atherosclerosis. On March 5, 1953, at age 74, he died from the effects of cerebral hemorrhage suffered on March 1st at his Dacha in Kuntsevo, some 11 miles west of Moscow. His body was viewed by 1.5 million people and laid to rest on March 9th in Lenin's Mausoleum. Eight years later, the body was moved and buried in the Kremlin Wall Necropolis as part of Russian de-Stalinization.

Minister Vyacheslav Mikhailovich Molotov — described as shy and quiet, Molotov lost Stalin's favor in 1949. After Stalin's death, Molotov was again named Foreign Minister. When Khrushchev assumed power, Molotov was ousted from office and the Communist Party. In 1984, he was allowed to rejoin the party. He died on November 8, 1994 at the ripe old age of 96 and was buried at the Novodevichy Cemetery in Moscow.

General Alexander Poskrebyshev — The phenomenal Soviet organizer remained active in Communist Party affairs after the war and was elected to the Politburo in 1952. He had three wives during his lifetime and died in Moscow on January 3, 1965, at age 73

Also by Jack DuArte

The Resistance (Revised)   *SINGAPORE* (Revised)   *Spitfire*

MALTA   *The White Mouse*

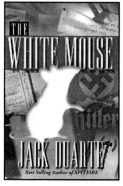

Preview all five at:
www.jackduarte.com

Kidnap the Pope is the sixth installment of Jack DuArte's best-selling World War II series that includes *The Resistance, Singapore, Spitfire, Malta and The White Mouse.*

DuArte is a decorated Vietnam Veteran who resides in Lexington, KY with his wife Susan, their chocolate Lab Carley, Havanese Cisco and miniature horse Darleigh.

He can be reached at jackduarte41@gmail.com.

CPSIA information can be obtained
at www.ICGtesting.com
Printed in the USA
FFOW02n0313310116
20950FF